Praise for...

End of Summer

A deeply moving and passionate book, Michael Potts' *End of Summer* is a poignant literary novel about childhood and memory. This is contemporary Southern fiction at its best. In textured language and with heartfelt attention to detail, Potts' nuanced portrayal of rural life in southern Appalachia and a young boy's initial encounter with death reminds us that life at the economic margins can be culturally and spiritually rich, and that even as absences and losses sometimes damage us, these can also strengthen and redeem.

- Michael Colonnese, Ph.D.
Author of *Sex and Death, I Suppose*
and *Temporary Agency*

In Michael Potts' novel, *End of Summer*, an idyllic rural childhood is the setting that reveals deep psychological insights. Innocent obsessions of childhood are juxtaposed against the Tennessee childhood, allowing for a rich tapestry of drama. The child is indeed father to the man in this gripping and lyrical read.

- Charlotte Rains Dixon
Director emeritus, the Writer's Loft at
Middle Tennessee State University

Quietly compelling, *End of Summer* skips, meanders, rushes headlong, then stops, plops down and spends time examining the smallest detail...just like a nine year old boy in the backwoods of rural Tennessee. Michael Potts writes Southern literary fiction, the kind Flannery O'Conner called *Christ-haunted*. Extraordinary!

- Mike Parker
Author of *The Scavengers*

End of
SUMMER

Brenda,
 I hope you enjoy
the book. "Grandpa Conley"
who comes in toward the
end was based on Ernest
Pitts.

Michael Pitts
June 19, 2019

End of
Summer

Michael Potts

WordCrafts

End of Summer is a work of fiction. All References to persons, places or events are fictitious or used fictitiously.

End of Summer
Copyright © 2011
Michael Potts

Cover concept and design by David Warren

Published by WordCrafts Press
Tullahoma, TN 37388
www.wordcrafts.net

Ad maiorem Dei gloriam.

In Memory of Jeffrey Potts
December 25, 1961-December 25, 1961

CHAPTER 1

"It all started with the rabbit," I said out loud, stepping out of my Chevy S-10, ice-covered grass crunching under my boots. The barren hayfield where I had hunted with Granddaddy thirty years before looked the same - God, how time runs away like life. The cold gray sky threatened snow. I plodded ice-slicked earth, exploring the place I once called home. I lived here eighteen years, from which only college in Nashville forced me to leave. Thoughts invaded my mind, day-terrors I tried to squelch. Closing my eyes, I held my gloved hands against my ears, but the memories did not stop. They forced themselves inside, thoughts of my ninth year. Until that time, I lived in oblivion, a ghost stuck in Purgatory. Before that year, Death had made multiple visits, stretching his bony fingers to shake the hands of family members.

My fraternal twin, Michael, died two hours after birth, drowning from fluid in his lungs. When I was two, my Mom and Dad were killed in a head-on collision with a tractor-trailer. I was reared by Granddaddy and Granny, who had lived with my folks in the same rented home. I remembered neither my parents' lives nor their deaths. I suppose that's a blessing and a curse. My grandparents had provided details my young mind could understand, but I pushed them away. I did not want them.

Back in that field after thirty years, I stood poised at the edge of an abyss. The darkness was middle age yielding itself into an even darker old age. Then death. Utter blackness at the hand of a curved sickle.

I remembered the previous six months of counseling with my therapist, Dr. Goodman. I never liked the idea of going to a counselor, but my wife, Lisa, insisted. I knew she loved me, but I hated going to the sessions. They were necessary because I obsessed constantly about death. My library at home held over three thousand books; five hundred concerned with death and dying.

In my home office, my computer rested on a small brown wooden desk, shiny with varnish. I sat in a cheap but comfortable black office chair I bought at Wal-Mart. Around the desk were two bookcases, a two-drawer filing cabinet, a TV stand with an old Sears black-and-white TV and a Radio Shack component stereo system. This space was my cubby. My man-hole. My hideout from the world where I could read, write or surf the Internet.

My mind wandered back to that night at Barnes and Noble, when I discovered Sherwin Nuland's *How We Die*. I could not believe my eyes: finally, there was a book that would detail how disease and injury cause death. I bought the book before Lisa and I went to see the re-release of Star Wars at the Omni Theater. I carried the book inside and started to read before the previews. When they began I continued to read, and I did not stop when the movie started. I looked through Nuland's detailed descriptions of how various diseases and injuries kill people, holding the book on my lap, straining to see the words by the light of the imploding Death Star on the flickering screen. Lisa touched my shoulder, and I turned to find her looking at me with such anguish and concern that I decided it would be best to continue reading the next morning.

I slept in most mornings during summer break. Not that next morning. As soon as Lisa left for work at 7:30, I rushed from bed, dressed, ate a quick breakfast of oatmeal, yogurt and an orange, brushed my teeth, then took the book to my office, sat down, and began to read. I hung on every detail of dying hearts, cancer-eaten bodies and blood spurting from burst vessels. I sat riveted to the seat, even though my neck and back hurt, shifting only when the pain grew unbearable. By noon, I was hungry and thirsty, but I kept reading. I was upset with myself that I did not remember to bring one of my Diet Pepsi's but I could not peel myself away from reading long enough to go to the refrigerator. Before Lisa got home at 5:30, I had read the entire book and was lying on the couch, my neck and back throbbing like a perverse heartbeat. When Lisa walked in the door, she opened her mouth, paused, and then asked, "What in God's name did you do to yourself today?"

"I read the book I bought last night."

"Honey, you need to stop worrying about death so much. Can't you just enjoy being alive?"

"If you rub my neck and back, I'll enjoy being alive now."

She did. Normally that meant blessed relief - and on a good day, dessert in bed. But that evening, I knew Lisa was worried. So was I. My obsessions had grown worse over the past year. A few months before, I had ordered a human jawbone online.

"Why a jawbone?" Lisa asked as we sat on the porch. I was sipping a shot of George Dickel Whisky, while she had a glass of chardonnay.

"Because we can't afford a whole skull," I said, taking another sip.

"That bothers me. I know you collect animal skulls, and that's okay with me. But a human skull, part of a real person who once lived? Isn't that going too far?"

I couldn't answer. I wondered myself. The best I could come up with was, "You know, in the Middle Ages scholars had skulls in their work area to remind them 'In the midst of life we are in death'."

"Couldn't a plastic skull send the same message?" Lisa asked. "You might need to talk to somebody about this."

"I'll think about it."

Lisa told me once that she had warned visitors about the cow skull on the top of the bookcase in the guest bedroom. I also kept a cat skull I found in the woods near home. I washed and bleached it, then sprayed it with clear coat paint. I displayed that on my office desk at Southeastern North Carolina University. I didn't mind helping students when they needed it but disliked trivial visits to my office. That cat skull kept most students away. On test days, I brought the jawbone, which I named "Sue" after a former lover who jilted me, to class and told the students, "This is the last student who cheated on my test." I wondered if the students would start calling me *Dr. Death*, but was glad that never happened.

Speaking of doctors, I was also fascinated with hearts. In addition to the five-hundred books about death, I owned over one-hundred books on the heart: cardiology texts, *The Mayo Clinic Heart Book*, and *Cardiac Arrest and Resuscitation*. With money I made from reviewing a textbook, I ordered a plasticized sheep heart from a biological supply house. I kept a stethoscope in my desk drawer and listened to my own heart at least once a day.

But the heart was always more than a mere interest; over the years it had become a fetish. From the time I was twelve and puberty hit, I desired to listen to a female heartbeat. If I saw an attractive woman walking by, I would notice the usual items boys notice, but one of my first thoughts was *How does her heartbeat sound?* As long as I can remember, I have been shy and socially awkward and dated only two women before I met Lisa. I never told the others about my fetish. I was afraid they would think I was a freak. With Lisa, I waited a month after our marriage to confess.

We were sitting on her blue couch, my head on her lap. We were getting ready to go to a nice dinner at Red Lobster, and I knew Lisa was in a good mood. We sat down on the couch and I kissed her. After the passionate kisses I moved my head down to her chest, hearing her racing heartbeat. Suddenly the thought entered my mind that I needed to let her know about my fetish. My desire for her combined with my fear, and my heart raced to the point that my body started to shake with the force of my heartbeats. Lisa sensed that I was tense and put her hand on my chest. "Your heart's racing, honey. You okay?"

"I'm fine."

"Something must be bothering you. You've always worried about every bad thing you've done, like the time you lied to your third-grade teacher about being in a fight. You still feel guilty about that! So what terrible thing do you think you've done now?"

"It's something weird."

"Why don't you just tell me what's bothering you, and then we'll go out to dinner. You remember? Dinner at Red Lobster? If we leave any later, we'll have to wait in line an hour."

"I like listening.... I like to hear your heartbeat. That's why I put my head on your chest so much."

"Is that all? Here, I'll help you."

She pulled my head between her breasts, and I rested there, basking in the fast, regular rhythm, feeling myself become more aroused than I already was.

"What's the big deal about wanting to listen to my heart? It's kinda romantic in a way."

I shifted my head so that I could look into Lisa's green-blue eyes. "It turns me on. More than breasts, more than anything, the sound of a woman's heart turns me on. It's like, like I'm hearing your life, the life of the woman I love."

She cuddled my head in silence for a few moments. I thought I had blown it. My body shook, and my mind filled with images of divorce lawyers. I shut my eyes, opened them again, finding tears glistening in Lisa's eyes.

Finally, she spoke. "Listen Jeffrey. The heartbeat thing - it's you. You're different, that's true. But it makes you who you are. And that's fine with me."

She pulled me up and kissed my lips long and hard. I figured that our Red Lobster dinner could wait.

After that evening, Lisa played along with my obsession with the heart and allowed me to listen to hers with the stethoscope. She even held her breath when I asked her to. I liked to hear the changes in her heartbeat. This part of my obsession she accepted. However, she told me the other parts - the parts relating to death - troubled her deeply. The jawbone, for instance; and how I had become obsessed with how diseases caused a person's heart to stop. How did cancer stop the heart? How did a head wound stop it? I read articles online and kept a library of medical journal articles on cardiac arrest and resuscitation.

By that time, I was also beginning to feel out of control. Finally, I told Lisa, "I think I'm going to see my doctor so he can refer me to a counselor."

"I'm glad," she said. "I want you to be happy, and this stuff gets in the way. It wouldn't bother me as much if it didn't bother you so much."

"I'm afraid to tell him everything."

"If he - or she - is good, you'll tell. And I'll be right here when you get home if you want to talk about it."

"Okay, I'm going to call Dr. Davis now." Dr. Davis was our long time family physician, and he knew the best people around in any health care specialty.

On the day of my appointment, Dr. Davis recommended Dr. Joe Goodman, a psychologist. Within two weeks, I sat on a soft couch in Dr. Goodman's office. Dr. Goodman listened as I described my interest in death and in the heart. But I also told him other things - how, for instance, as a child I preferred to talk to adults. How my family and friends called me "the little professor" because I used adult words and inflections in my voice. How I had few friends my own age. How I had walked on my toes.

I had been in counseling six months before Dr. Goodman offered a diagnosis. Dr. Goodman picked up a copy of the *Diagnostic and Statistical Manual of the American Psychological Association*, a manual of standard descriptions of psychological disorders. He opened the DSM to a page and showed it to me. He asked, "Does this sound like you?" I sighed and said, "Yes." All the symptoms were there that fit my behavior. I finally knew why I was different, why I felt as if I lived on another planet.

The diagnosis was Asperger's Syndrome. Some psychologists consider it a mild form of autism. It explained my use of adult language as a child, my social awkwardness, my obsession with particular subjects. Since many autistic children walk on their toes and are uncoordinated, it explained that part of me as well.

I accepted the diagnosis, the result of months of digging. I was relieved. I now knew why I had such big thoughts as a child, thoughts that haunted most adults only when they either dealt with the death of a loved one or suffered a mid-life crisis. It explained the complexity of my mind when I was nine, the memories that broke through the wall I had erected around myself since then and were now chewing at my mind.

The memories that began with a rabbit.

How could I have forgotten that rabbit?

At the time, it caused a minor crisis in my life.

Granddaddy loved to hunt rabbit and quail. He would take his 20-gauge shotgun out to the field to wait. When he failed to bag a rabbit or quail there, he crossed the fence to the adjoining woods. I enjoyed joining him on these hunting trips, but I didn't feel safe carrying a real gun. One day I tried firing Granddaddy's gun at a can set up on a fence post. Not only did I miss the can, but the gun kicked back and bruised my shoulder - I yelped like a dog in pain. It took me four days before I could touch the right side of my shoulder. Eventually the bruise and pain faded, but not the memory of the gun's kick - so Granddaddy decided to buy me a pop gun - loud, but harmless.

Every fall I joined Granddaddy when he hunted quail. When we flushed a flock of quail, the rush of their wings sounded like shirts on a clothesline snapped by the wind. When Granddaddy located the bird, targeted and pointed his shotgun, I would point my gun in the same direction. If I was lucky, we fired at the same time. If Granddaddy fired fast enough to down one bird, sometimes he could get off a second shot and hit another quail. When the shot was on target, the quail's wings would flap for a few seconds and stop. Then the bird would fall like a rock to the ground. I was proud when I got off a shot at the same time as Granddaddy. I almost believed I had helped kill the bird.

We did not own a retriever dog, but I had a pet dog, Fuzzy, my white frisky Spitz. He couldn't join us on hunting trips - Granddaddy always tethered him. The problem was that Fuzzy would flush and warn the quail with his noisy barks, and they would all get away. Instead of dogs, Granddaddy and I were the retrievers. We searched in the tall, brown grass until we found the fallen quail. Granddaddy pocketed it. He usually bagged two or three birds per hunt. On a good day, he would get five. Then we returned to the back yard, where Granddaddy would pull the feathers off the birds and clean them for dinner.

New Year's Day was a clear and cold Monday in the year 1968. Frost formed crystals on the windows outside my room, and I marveled at the intricate patterns. The aroma of breakfast cooking diverted my attention from the window. I remembered this was the day Granddaddy and I would hunt rabbits for the first time. I wondered if they were as hard to hit as quail.

After breakfast, I watched the Tournament of Roses Parade on TV before it was time to go. Granny took my warm, brown coat, the one with a hood, out of the closet and helped me put it on. She also gave me gloves. I put on my boots, lined inside with fur to keep my feet warm in twenty-degree weather. The high was supposed to be twenty-five, cold for middle Tennessee. "You boys be careful out there," Granny said. "And Jeffrey, don't ever run in front of a gun. Do what your Granddaddy says."

"I'll be careful." I ran out the door into a sharp breeze that felt as if armed with darts of frost - but the sun shone bright for an early winter day. Granddaddy found Fuzzy and hooked a chain to his collar to keep him confined. Fuzzy howled and cried. I told Fuzzy, "Don't worry. I'll be back soon." That didn't stop his crying, but I left, following Granddaddy to the fence, and we walked into the field.

Frost lingered despite the sun, and our feet crunched the tall, dead grass. We walked side by side, moving toward the nearest thicket. The remains of acorns littered the ground. Surrounding some oak trees were limestone rocks, most of them flat and even with the ground. Others were free standing, up to five feet long and three feet wide. They were half my height then, looking like ancient monuments abandoned by the Cherokee. Around the rocks grew weeds. Some were thorny bushes with vines hanging from them like porcupine quills. There was wild holly with sharp-pointed leaves, the green color a contrast to the gray deadness around them. There were more benign bushes as well as dormant and dead vines I could not identify. Some grass clumps stood nearly as high as my head.

We approached with stealth. Granddaddy whispered, "See that long stick on the ground to your right? Pick it up and start pokin' round those bushes. We might scare up a rabbit."

As I started poking the brush, Granddaddy stomped loudly around the borders of the brush. All at once, a rabbit jumped, running toward the other side of the thicket. A puff of gray and white tail started to disappear around the circle of brush. Just before it moved out of sight, two loud shots rang out from Granddaddy's 20-gauge. The rabbit flipped over, dropped dead. We walked to the rabbit, and Granddaddy picked it up by its feet. A patch of shot had dug a red hole in the rabbit's side, just below the neck. I figured some of the shot hit the heart, causing instant death.

"Great shot, Granddaddy!"

"That'll make some good eatin' tonight. Let's find us another one."

I figured the rabbits in the nearest thickets would have heard the shot and run away, or else wouldn't come out of their hiding places. So we passed those thickets by, walking to the other end of the field. There was one more brush thicket to go, a place where Granddaddy loved to picnic in the summer. A path through the brush led to a long, flat limestone rock ending near the border of a walnut and oak. Two smaller Osage orange trees stood next to them. Their green fruits littered the ground in the summer. All made good shade, but now these branches were bare except for a few stray brown leaves stuck to the very top. My boots crunched the walnuts as we approached the thicket, but Granddaddy turned around, put his finger to his mouth, and said, "Shhhh."

I had kept the stick, but before I started to poke, a rabbit popped out like a cork from my pop gun. It ran into the open field toward the woods. Granddaddy raised his shotgun, aimed, and fired. The shot hit the rabbit, but it failed to fall right away. I stood transfixed as the rabbit ran about twenty yards, then collapsed. When we reached it, it lay on its side, still as the limestone outcroppings nearby. There was a small patch of shot on the rabbit's side, but on the lower end, around the abdomen. The death of the first rabbit didn't bother me. But this rabbit was different.

It did not die right away. It ran after being shot. I struggled to understand how the rabbit could keep going, only later to drop dead. I would have thought that the rabbit would either drop right after being shot, like the first one, or slow down before falling to the ground. Then a thought tugged on my mind and would not let go. Why did the rabbit's heart stop beating when no shot had hit the heart? Even though it died fast, seconds after being shot, how could a few pellets that had missed the heart cause such a strong thing to stop? How was the shot in the rabbit's belly connected to the beating of its heart? Were people's hearts the same way?

Two years before, when my great uncle Albert died of a heart attack, I asked Granddaddy "What's a heart attack?" Granddaddy answered that it was when the heart got tired and could not go on any more. After that I thought everyone, rabbit or human, must die of a heart attack because they did not die unless their hearts stopped. But how could the rabbit's heart get tired because of only a few pellets of shot?

I remembered Granny telling me how my mama and daddy died in a car wreck. Mama was just twenty, Daddy twenty-five. Their hearts were strong. How had the car accident caused their hearts to stop beating? Granny told me they did not have a mark on them when they were in the funeral home. Did the accident tear up their hearts?

I tried not to think, but a voice kept shouting inside my head, "Why did the rabbit's heart stop?" I blurted out, "Granddaddy, why did that rabbit's heart stop so fast?"

"Dad gum, boy, you ask the durndest things! Rabbit got torn up inside by shot. Heart ain't gonna beat when other stuff's torn up."

Granddaddy looked irritated by my question, so I decided to investigate the matter himself. I still did not understand how being torn up in another part of the body could stop the heart. But if I were to examine the rabbit's heart, I might discover why it stopped.

I decided to change the subject. "I figure those rabbits will make some good eating."

"Now you're makin' sense. Yeah, we'll have Granny cut up some carrots and onions and make rabbit stew. Couple o' those rabbits will be plenty for the three of us."

"I can't wait for dinner." Dinner was the midday meal to country folks like Granddaddy and me.

"Don't think she can get them cooked for dinner. I got to clean the dad gum things. You'll have soup for dinner, and I'll let you have some of my sardines. We'll have rabbit for supper." Supper was the late meal of the day.

"It sure is cold, Granddaddy." I rubbed my gloves together.

"Too cold. Only good thing is that the meat will taste better. But I sure hate this weather. Won't even get up to forty. I freeze every mornin' takin' the ashes out and gettin' coal off the pile. Now you go inside when we get back. Sit by the wood stove and warm those hands and feet. I'll be in after I clean these rabbits."

I welcomed the plume of gray-black smoke rising above the brown bricks of the chimney. I looked forward to seeing flames flicker through rectangular holes on the upper door of the wood stove. I loved to watch the warm orange color and the shifting light and shadow it forged on the floor.

We made it to the house. Granddaddy went inside to fetch a knife and a pan of water. Then he walked outside to the garage and found some spare wire. I went inside to get warm and stood on my toes to reach the door window to watch. Granddaddy stooped under the pear tree between the garage and gliders and wired one of the rabbit's back feet to a branch. He took the knife, cut underneath the fur at the rabbit's feet, grasped the rabbit's coat, and pulled off the fur and skin. When he reached the head, he cut it off - skin, fur and all - with the knife. Then he slit the rabbit down the middle, removed the viscera, which plopped to the ground. After that, he dropped the rabbit in the water. He repeated the process with the other rabbit.

My toes got tired, so I left the window and thawed out by the wood stove. Granny made hot chocolate, which I downed. The first swallows burned my tongue, but I was so cold I didn't care. I had seen Granddaddy clean birds and fish before and figured he would take the rabbits in for Granny to prepare before he buried the rabbit parts. When Granddaddy came inside with the rabbits, I said, "I want to play outside until supper."

"You'll freeze out there," Granny said. Granddaddy agreed, but said he figured they might as well let me play. I asked to be excused before I put on my coat and made a quick trip to the kitchen. I opened the drawer where Granny kept the sharp knives and snatched a small knife. I hid it in my jeans, hoping I would not cut myself. Then I walked to the back door, where Granny helped me into another coat, found a scarf to wrap around my neck, a pullover cap and a fresh pair of gloves.

Once outside, I ran under the pear tree and examined the piles of viscera. I thought it best to take only one heart. That way Granddaddy would be less likely to notice. I had to find the heart that was not hit by shot. I searched for the red form, thinking of the pictures I had seen in my science books from school. I found one heart, but it was filled with pellet holes. So I went to the other pile and saw the heart, without holes, shining in the sun. I picked it up, ran to the front yard into bushes surrounding a lone pine tree. The bushes made an outdoor room where I could hide and examine the heart in detail.

It looked perfect, healthy and larger than the first heart. I tried to squeeze it with my fingers, hoping for some visceral stir. It stayed still. The heart was hard as a rock. I put it between the bases of my palms and tried again, squeezing and squeezing, but nothing happened. The heart had failed. It had failed the rabbit, and it had failed me.

I took the knife and cut the heart in half. It was a lucky cut. The heart's interior reminded me of the pictures I had seen in books. I probed each chamber, strings of strong tissue, thick walls of muscle. It must have been powerful. But I failed to find what caused it to stop beating. Frustrated, I threw the heart to the ground. I felt bad and cried for a long time. My stomach became queasy, and I lay down on a cold pine needle bed until the tears stopped flowing. Then I took the heart, ran to the remains of the garden, found a place where no one could see me, and buried it. My own heart raced, and I thought of how strong it felt. But I remembered the deceased rabbit and wondered when my own heart would stop, letting me down, making me as dead as my parents, as dead as the rabbit.

All these years later, standing in that same field in the bitterness of January, I wondered how I could have pushed the memory of the rabbit aside so long, a memory that clarified one source of my fascination with the heart. I walked along the back of the field and stopped near The Thicket. I studied the outcropping of trees and vines protruding into the field from the woods. Overcome with emotion from the memory of the rabbit, I dropped to my knees, feeling the cold seep through my jeans.

CHAPTER 2

I stood up, took a deep breath, and felt better. Pleasant memories of my ninth year visited, and I relished remembering a journey Granddaddy and I took to The Thicket.

I had looked forward to a trip to The Thicket for a week. While I could walk there alone any time I wanted, Granddaddy told me the previous week that on Saturday we would go there together and have a picnic. We could bring sandwiches and Cokes. I knew it would be a good day - in one of my favorite places, with Granddaddy. We could talk and play on the swing vines.

The week before the picnic passed as slowly as Christmas Eve. Finally, the day arrived. It was a cool, June morning, two weeks after the end of school. Light slid through cracks in the blinds onto my bed. I opened my eyes, yawned, saw shimmering bright stripes dancing on the yellow spread. I raised my head for a few seconds, then lay back, rubbing my eyes. When I opened them again, I stared at the wood ceiling with its dark cross-beams and remembered Granddaddy telling me that much of the house was built from old railroad ties. As if that thought were a signal, a train whistle blew, the sound traveling from the tracks beyond Randallsville Highway.

Another sound, of bacon sizzling on the stove, its aroma wafting through the door, caught my interest. I slipped out of bed and changed from my pajamas into blue jeans and a tee shirt. I walked out my bedroom door, the wood floor creaking with every step, past the black wood stove that reminded me of the robot on the TV show, *Lost in Space*. I stepped into the kitchen, sat at my usual breakfast seat on the end nearest the door.

"Well, see you finally got up," Granddaddy said, sitting on the other end of the white speckled table, fooling with a knob on the radio.

"Want some breakfast?" Granny asked. She stood by the stove, wearing a light blue dress that covered her hefty body. Over the dress was a yellow apron with large pockets. Her hair, half-gray, half-red, glistened in the morning sun.

"I'd like three bacon and tomato biscuits!" I said, eager to eat so I could go outside and play with Fuzzy before the picnic.

Granny smiled and placed the bacon on a paper towel, then used another paper towel to soak out the grease. She put the three pieces along with some homemade biscuits on a plate, added the first garden tomatoes of the season, then poured me a glass of milk.

I thanked Granny and gobbled the food. It tasted good, but I was in a hurry. Granddaddy turned on the radio to the local morning news, which was finishing with the daily obituaries:

"Funeral services for Mr. Asa Jones, sixty-five, of Route 4, Randallsville will be held at the Crandall Funeral Home in Randallsville on Wednesday at 2:30. Burial will follow at Greenlawn Memorial Gardens. He is survived by....."

I listened to the obituary and felt a spark of fear. Granddaddy was almost sixty-seven. How much longer would Granddaddy have to live?

I breathed a sigh of relief when the obituaries were over and *Shop and Swap* began. It was a radio show where people sold anything from old plows to nearly new furniture. Granddaddy and Granny listened to the show every day, but if they'd ever bought anything, I never knew about it.

When the show ended, Granddaddy said, "Jeffrey, I need you to help me pull potato bugs off the potato plants."

"I want to play with Fuzzy."

"Okay, but I'll need you when I get out there."

I knew it would take about a half-hour for Granddaddy to get ready. He had been up since six chopping the garden, and he liked to wash up after breakfast before going outside again. I ran around the bar, past the sink and the ringer washer to the back door. Unhooking the screen door, I let it slam shut, eliciting a shout from Granny. "Don't let that door slam!"

"Sorry!" I said and ran outside, down two thick concrete steps to greet Fuzzy.

I put my hands on my knees and braced myself. "Here, Fuzzy!" As soon as he saw me, he ran at full stride, knocking me to the ground and licking me so much that I was afraid I would drown in dog saliva. I laughed, pushed Fuzzy away, and got up. Fuzzy wasn't finished, though - he ran and knocked me down again, an act followed by another licking fit. I rolled around to get away from his sloppy wet tongue. I found Fuzzy's baseball, which was in the process of being chewed into pieces. I pushed the ball with my palm, and Fuzzy ran after it. That bought enough time for me to get up. Fuzzy fetched the ball, and I played with him for another fifteen minutes until Granddaddy came outside. He also let the screen door slam, which resulted in the usual shout from Granny.

Granddaddy walked toward Fuzzy. Usually Fuzzy ran free, but Granddaddy was sensitive about threats to his garden. "Okay, Fuzzy, I'm gonna put you on a leash for a while," I said. "Granddaddy don't want you diggin' round his potatoes."

Fuzzy squeaked but did not run. I soon latched him to a chain. The other end of the chain was wrapped around a cedar trunk on the fence line separating a field from the back yard. I hated to leave Fuzzy - he was a dependable friend, and I had very few human friends. Even at school, most of the kids weren't my real friends. I preferred the company of adults. Granddaddy was my closest companion.

The garden was humongous, covering four adjoining rectangular plots. The two biggest plots bordering the field lay on the other side of a rusty wire fence. There Granddaddy set out cantaloupes and watermelons. In front of them was the small plot sewn in cucumbers. Potatoes were in another large rectangle separated from Bramble Road by a fence. Next to that were lima beans, black-eyed and Crowder peas, corn and tomatoes.

I stepped onto the hard clay with Granddaddy at the start of the first row of potatoes. We began to pull red-spotted potato bugs off the plants, their bodies sticky and damp. We threw the bugs to the ground and stomped them flat. Now and then, we found another kind of potato bug, striped white and black. We had to be quick to flick it down and kill it before it flew away.

I thought of this as play rather than work. Granddaddy and I would have a contest to discover who killed the most potato bugs. Although Granddaddy always won, I did not mind. When we reached the end of the fourth and final row, I was proud that I killed seventy-five, although Granddaddy killed nearly a hundred. Granddaddy took off his straw hat and used a handkerchief to wipe sweat from his brow.

"Let's go inside and wash up, get somethin' to drink, and then we can go to The Thicket," he said. I was glad because the thicket was my favorite place, a perfect place, my Eden. I had heard the story of Adam and Eve in Sunday School. I had felt sad to learn that God had expelled them to the east, sending an angel with a flaming sword to keep them out forever. I had no idea how eating fruit could be so wrong and sometimes wondered if Eden still existed on earth, perhaps in some remote spot, maybe in the woods beyond the field. Sometimes I thought that The Thicket was as close to Eden as I would get. When I was there I hoped never to go back home.

The Thicket was what Granddaddy always called "the place." It was located at the far corner of the fifty-acre field where Granddaddy raised cotton before he retired. Unlike the other thickets that dotted the field, it was not an island of brush. It was more like a peninsula, part of the deeper woods that extended inside the fence that divided forest from field. In The Thicket were tall hardwoods, such as pin oaks and sugar maples, with Eastern Red Cedars nestled between them. Thick vines hung from trees. At the edge of the fence bordering Mr. Blake's farm was an old pear tree that had been damaged in a storm. The trunk was bent down, and the top branches broken off. The surviving trunk had re-grown into a hard knot that looked like the ones I sometimes tied in my shoes, the knots I could not unravel. New branches had sprung from the trunk's side, and I liked to sit there and watch Mr. Blake's cows.

Later that day, we would walk from field to thicket, but in the meantime, we were hot and tired from our work in the potato patch. We turned back toward the log house. The logs had been covered with wood siding years before, and Mr. Benson had hired people to paint it white. Smoke from an old pot-bellied stove in which Granddaddy burned coal in winter stained parts of the siding gray. Green shingles covered the roof. Granddaddy always said coal was "cheaper than cord wood." I loved that old thing.

When we walked into the kitchen, Granny had iced tea ready. We grabbed the glasses and moved to a couch in the living room. Granny sat in an unpainted wooden rocking chair across from us.

"Have a good time?" Granny asked. She was a quiet woman, and I never heard of anyone having much of a conversation with her. I knew her mother had died when she was twelve-years-old and that she helped her father, Great-Grandpa Johnson, rear her two younger sisters. Because of her responsibilities, she was unable to continue in school. Neither she, nor Granddaddy for that matter, could read or write.

Granny was a year younger than Granddaddy. They did not get along well. I hated hearing them fight and when they got too loud, I would cover my ears. Granddaddy would say cruel things, using bad words, and threaten to leave forever. I feared he might leave and never come back, especially when he packed his suitcase. But, so far he always put the clothes back in the drawers of his dresser and into his closet.

When I was five, I heard them quarrel until Granny cried and did not stop crying for at least an hour. Angry, I threw mud balls at Granddaddy when he was working in the garden. Granddaddy yelled and went after me with a switch. He did not catch me, but after that he never tried to hit me again.

I understood that Granddaddy wasn't perfect, and I tried to get along with both my grandparents. I wanted to know Granny better, but I was just as shy as she was. She brought me bacon at breakfast, made dinner and supper, made sure I went to bed on time. That was about it.

I told Granny about the potato bugs we killed. She said she was proud of me. Then she and Granddaddy started to fuss about Granddaddy's cousins Myrna and Myra and how he spent too much time at their house. "Are you trying to get away from me?" she asked, her face flushed. I was afraid of another quarrel and put my hands over my ears again, but Granddaddy said, "We'll talk about this later. I'm taking the boy to The Thicket," and he rushed out the door as I followed. This time, I did not let the door slam.

I ran and unhooked Fuzzy, who was barking. We walked to the large steel gate leading to the field. A rusty chain hooked it to a nail. Granddaddy unlatched it and, after we went through, he hooked it back.

As we entered the field, we passed an old bathtub filled with water for the cows. After Mr. Benson died, Mrs. Benson leased the field to a farmer who kept ten beef cows and a bull. To the left of the tub was a salt lick. I was fascinated by those smooth curves where cows licked the salt. We walked though green grass and avoided cow piles. We also watched for the bull, but he was with the cows on the far side of the field by Bramble Road.

After we passed the fence line bordering the back yard, we entered a wide expanse. I looked to my left and noticed the line of trees and bushes by a fence. I picked out the pecan tree where I walked with my grandparents to gather pecans last fall, filling two buckets. I remembered that just beyond my line of sight was a patch of daffodils, which I called buttercups, I sometimes walked there by myself in March, kneeling to sample the aroma of a new spring.

As we drew closer to The Thicket, we saw a flattened area of grass that water covered after every heavy rain. On cold winter days when the water had frozen into a thin film of white ice, crystals formed intricate patterns on the surface. Granddaddy and I put on our boots, went out to the field, and crunched frost-covered grass until we reached the ice-pond. There we stood and gazed at a rainbow of red, orange, yellow and blue light splitting into colors as it reflected off the ice. A thin film of slick, shiny water covered the ice, and I was tempted to stand on it to see if I would fall through. I knew Granddaddy would stop me. Although the water was less than a foot deep, he was not going to take a chance with me, his only grandchild. "Anyway, you might catch cold if you got wet," he said.

Now it was summer, and the water had evaporated, Granddaddy and I walked into the indentation. Deep cracks covered the clay that had dried beneath the new grass. We reached the border of The Thicket. As we crossed the threshold of the first trees, I felt a sense of accomplishment. We had arrived.

The leaves of the trees were the darkest green they would be before the heat and dry weather of July and August drained their colors pale. They gave welcome shade, for a while the morning was cool, June days in middle Tennessee warmed as fast as hands held in front of a coal-burning stove. Granddaddy said, "Let's find a good spot to sit." We looked around for a space between the trees and found a flat spot with a bed of leaves.

"Got somethin' for you," Granddaddy said, and I noticed for the first time that Granddaddy had snatched a couple of Cokes from the fridge - right under Granny's nose. He took a bottle opener from his pocket, opened both Cokes, and handed me one of the glass bottles.

"Thanks, Granddaddy," I said and drank the whole Coke in a few gulps. The middle of the thicket was dark, but cool and comfortable, and I lay down with my eyes closed while Granddaddy finished his Coke. Fuzzy came and licked my face.

I hoped then that summer would last forever, that I would never grow up, that Granddaddy wouldn't get any older, or if he did, he would live until I was at least twenty-one. I figured that since I had to grow up, I might be able to handle Granddaddy dying if I was an official adult. When I said my prayers at night, I asked

God, "Please let Granddaddy live at least 'til I'm grown."
I hoped that God would understand how close
Granddaddy and I were and keep us together as long as
He could.

I refused to dwell on those thoughts and focused
on the flashes of light and shadow I saw as I opened my
eyes and looked up at the sky. Branches swayed in a
fresh breeze, as the green canopy hiding the sky shifted
between opening and closing. The odor of old leaves
mixed with distant honeysuckle made me long for
something I could not name.

Granddaddy liked to play word games, and I
found them funny. As I sat up, Granddaddy said, "Jeff,
the left, stick-stock step," and I laughed. I asked, "Can we
go to the vine-swing?" and Granddaddy said, "Yeah, if I
can find the durn thing," and off we went. Fuzzy walked
around, sniffing every leaf on the ground.

The "vine-swing" was one of the larger vines in
The Thicket, thick enough to support my weight. It hung
between two trees, about two and a half feet off the
ground. I enjoyed swinging on it in the past and hoped it
was still there. Fortunately, The Thicket was not big,
and it was not long before Granddaddy called out, "Here
it is!" near the knotted pine tree close to the fence. I sat
in the middle of the vine and swung with glee, thrilled to
fly free in the air. I could see across Mr. Blake's fence
into his field. Brown beef cattle with their white faces
and bellies bounced up and down with every upstroke
of the swing. The Blake's small white farmhouse stood
like a shining beacon of stability beyond the field. Time
ticked like the wait for Christmas but without the pain
of anticipation. It was as if the joy of play and feeling of
rest beneath the warm sun were combined in one

timeless moment.

The swinging had to end, more from tiredness of muscles than from weariness of desire. I jumped off the vine, climbed onto the bent trunk of the knotted pear tree, and sat down. I asked Granddaddy to tell me a story. I loved Granddaddy's stories, even though he repeated them. But today Granddaddy told me a new story.

"I once knew a man who sleepwalked. One night, his wife didn't see him stand up and walk out the door. He hooked his horse to a buggy, got in the driver's seat and started ridin.' He must have rode five or ten miles down an old dirt road before he woke up. He had no idea where he was. He'd lit the lantern when he was sleepin,' which was a good thing since the moon wasn't out that night, so he took it off the buggy and looked around. Eventually his old beagle hound, who'd run after him from home, found him, and the poor man figured he made the whole trip in his sleep. Put the beagle in his seat, turned around, drove home. Scared his wife half to death when he opened the door. Don't think he ever did anything like that again."

"Can people really walk in their sleep?"

"Funny things folks do sometimes."

I thought for a moment about the man making his way without seeing, but could not quite figure it out. I only knew that I was getting hungry again, and while I hated to leave the thicket, I understood it was time to go. Granddaddy picked up the Coke bottles and said, "We'd better get back before your granny starts hollerin' 'cause we're late to dinner."

So we left, man and boy and dog, and passed by the place where we sat on dry leaves, passed the last trees in The Thicket and into the field. The grass appeared as if it had been struck by sun-fire, lit by golden light, too bright, too precious, to bear. I held my right hand over my eyes, my eyes adjusted, and all three of us walked toward the gate.

As Granddaddy opened the old gate, he stopped, unsteady on his feet. For a moment it looked as if he would fall, and I was suddenly afraid, but then Granddaddy said, "It's just indigestion. Get it all the time. Felt like I'd have to burp or somethin.' I'm fine - let's go inside and get some iced tea."

Three decades since that trip to The Thicket, and I wondered why I'd believed what Granddaddy had said - that his problem was only indigestion. Was it the naïve trust of a small boy? Or was it denial? Perhaps I'd known even then that Granddaddy wasn't well.

I stood up, turned, and looked away from The Thicket toward Randallsville Highway. I took a deep breath and sighed, feeling my heart swell and swell until I wondered if I would pass out.

CHAPTER 3

The day I saw Fuzzy's dead body began with the sun's first rays seeping through bed covers to warm my own body. I lay there for a minute, listening to the sound of the mockingbird whose home seemed to be the roof of the house, before I noticed that something was missing. I was used to Fuzzy's barking, fast and furious every morning, always impatient for food in his dish and my greeting him with a hug. I thought that maybe Fuzzy was outside playing in the field. I got dressed quickly and went to the kitchen. Granddaddy looked worried.

"Don't know where that Fuzzy's run off to."

"Maybe he's out carousin' somewhere," Granny said.

"Well, I'll go look for him after breakfast. You can come along if you want, Jeffrey. Don't worry too much. He's probably just out courtin' some girl dog."

"I'm not worried. God wouldn't let anything happen to Fuzzy."

Granddaddy put his biscuit down, looking stern. "Don't you go tellin' God what he can and can't do. That ain't up to us."

"I'm sorry," I said.

"Now look what you done, you hurt the boy's feelings," Granny said, turning red and facing Granddaddy.

"Woman, lay off me. Always have to criticize everything I say."

He turned back to me. "It's just that we can't judge God. Like I said, Fuzzy's probably courtin.' Found himself a pretty lady in the woods. Probably some beagle hound. Hope she's not a poodle."

I laughed, though I did not understand how Fuzzy could have a dog girlfriend. I imagined Fuzzy putting his paw around a girl beagle's shoulder.

The phone rang, and Granny answered. After talking for a few minutes she returned to the kitchen table. It was Aunt Susie, Granny's younger sister, who was planning to come down from Nashville with Uncle Rick.

Granddaddy said, "It'll take an hour for them to get here, but they'll help us look for Fuzzy."

I was disappointed at having to wait, but with more folks around, there was a better chance of finding Fuzzy. As I left the table, Granny was wiping it with a dishcloth, and I went outside to sit on the glider on the front porch. Granddaddy stayed inside to talk with Granny.

I was glad to be by myself for a few minutes. I remembered when Granddaddy and Granny came home from the pound where they'd found Fuzzy almost a year ago. They drove into the back yard in their faded blue

Ford pickup. Granny opened the passenger side door holding a blanket. From the blanket sprouted a puppy, yelping and wagging its tail.

"Look what we got for you," Granddaddy said as he got out of the truck. "A little puppy dog! Look at that cute little thing!"

Fuzzy ran to me and bounced into my arms with a high-pitched yelp. He wriggled and licked my face. We rolled around in the dirt, Fuzzy's white fur turning brown, matching my stained shirt.

Granddaddy asked, "Why don't you play with him? Here's a ball." He threw an old rubber ball. Fuzzy leapt two feet into the air, caught the ball and raced back to Granddaddy, sliding on the ground into Granddaddy's legs like a runner trying to beat a throw to second base. "Maybe I'll buy you a baseball," Granddaddy said, pointing his finger at Fuzzy. "You learn to swing a bat, you'll make me a rich man."

Granddaddy wrestled the ball from the growling puppy's mouth, pitched it to me, and I threw it high into the air, an orange dot against the blue sky. It fell and bounced into Fuzzy's teeth. He ran to me, but I could not dislodge the ball from the vise-grip of Fuzzy's jaws.

"Fine, Fuzzy," I said. "Go play by yourself!" Fuzzy dropped the ball. I picked it up, threw it again. After several repetitions, we sat down under the shade of a large lilac. Granny brought iced tea for me and water for Fuzzy.

"You two rest a while," Granddaddy said. "Then we'll see if we can teach that dog to live in the house."

Over the next few days, Granddaddy and Granny kept Fuzzy inside most of the time, using newspaper for the puppy's bathroom needs. They tried to house train him, but failed. No matter what they did - rubbing Fuzzy's nose in his poop, spanking him when he did not wait to go outside - nothing worked. It seemed as if Fuzzy was missing that part of his dog brain capable of learning to house train. They finally gave up and decided that Fuzzy would be an outdoor dog. Most country folks did not mind their dogs running free, and most of the time Fuzzy could roam and play without being hooked to his chain.

Unlike Granddaddy's previous dogs, which were used in hunting to fetch rabbits or birds, Fuzzy was a pet. He was my dog, which meant that I had to take care of him. Most of the time I remembered my duties, since I wanted to see Fuzzy as much as I could. Every morning I fed the dog scraps from supper the day before and filled his bowl with water from the garden hose.

The only time I was late with my chores was when I did not want to leave a TV show. One show I enjoyed watching during the day was *What's New?* - a science show on public television. One day, the show's subject was dinosaurs. Granny told me, "Go outside and feed that durn dog! He's out there barkin' because he's hungry."

"I want to finish my dinosaur show."

"Do it now. It won't take two minutes to feed and water that dog."

"The show's almost over! Let me finish and I promise I'll feed Fuzzy then."

"Don't sass me, boy! Your granddaddy gave you the dog. You've got to learn you can't do what you want when you want. You got an animal out there to take care of. Don't make me get after you with a switch!"

I decided to do the reasonable thing and feed

Fuzzy. I took the scraps that Granny stored in an old milk carton and emptied them on old newspaper next to the dog's water bowl. Then I filled the empty bowl. Fuzzy stopped barking and ran straight to the food and drink. When he finished, he started to bark again. I figured I bought Granny about a five minute break from dog-noise. When I returned to the TV show, I found that it was over.

Feeding Fuzzy and pouring water in his dish were small prices to pay for friendship. Soon Fuzzy was as much a part of my landscape as those hills haunting the skyline twenty miles to the west. It did not matter that Fuzzy chased cars or tried to eat the spiked boots off the man who came by to fix the telephone line - Fuzzy would beat the odds and survive his bad behavior. Fuzzy was so full of energy and life that I sometimes thought that dog could flee from Death itself. Maybe my parents weren't able to outrun Death, but Fuzzy would.

The honk of a horn startled me. Uncle Rick and Aunt Susie had arrived. I ran to hug them - Aunt's Susie's short, stocky body first, then tall, lean Uncle Rick. Rick was originally from Wisconsin, "a damn Yankee," but nobody held that against him. He went inside the house to greet Granny, but Aunt Susie stayed outside. Then Uncle Rick came out with Granddaddy, who said, "I'll guess we'll go lookin' for that dog now."

"I'm sure he didn't go far," said Uncle Rick, as they checked the bushes bordering the garden. There was no sign of Fuzzy there, so Granddaddy opened the gate, and they began searching the field.

Uncle Rick suggested they walk toward Randallsville Highway to check that area first. I started to yell, "Fuzzy! Come here, Fuzzy!" but there was no answer. We walked past a patch of daffodils, their long green shoots still rising from the ground, but it was way past the time for blooming. Granddaddy and Uncle Rick searched from bush to bush, pushing away stray brush so they could find a good line of sight on both sides of the fence.

As we approached the old pecan tree, Uncle Rick said, "I think I see something." Granddaddy and I followed him down the fence line to the place where he had stopped. I could not see anything, but Granddaddy hung his head. Uncle Rick found a low spot in the barbed wire, held it down with his right hand, and crossed without touching it. He asked for the old blanket Granddaddy had been carrying just in case, lay it over what he found there, wrapped it up, and handed it to Granddaddy on the other side to lay on the ground. Uncle Rick told me to turn away. Then he pulled apart the blanket's edges. I heard Granddaddy say, "Yeah, that's Fuzzy all right."

I wanted to look, but Granddaddy pushed me away, saying, "Not good for you to see this," but not before I caught a glimpse of a white snout. The mouth was open, and white teeth shone in the sun. The gums were red and exposed. The dog did not look real. He looked like a Hollywood monster. Maybe he was not real. Maybe he was not Fuzzy. It had to be a mistake. It had to be some other dog. It might not even be a dog.

I kept these thoughts to myself as Uncle Rick described the scene he saw on the other side of the fence. "There was a black skid mark from truck tires running from the highway toward the ditch. The truck had hit a mailbox, shattering the wood post. The dog was lying beside the post. It looked like the truck driver tried to run over the dog on purpose."

"Don't think so," Granddaddy said. "Durn dog probably chased the truck, turned one way. Driver thought he'd turn the other way. When he hit the mailbox post, he figured he'd get out of there, especially if this happened in the middle of night. No, Fuzzy did his own self in. Chasin' cars finally caught up with him."

They stood there a few moments. Then Uncle Rick placed his right hand on my shoulder and said, "You know, I had a dog when I was a kid, and one morning she ran in front of a neighbor's car. She whined for a long while before she passed. Afterwards, I didn't feel like doing much. But you know, one day I started to do things I liked to do - reading adventure stories, playing football with my buddies down the street. Things got better. But I never forgot Frisky. Talking about her now, I get sad."

Uncle Rick bent and lifted one corner of the blanket, frowned, and straightened up again. "Young man, my advice is to go ahead and cry if you feel like it. Sit around a day or two and do nothing. Don't make it too long, though. Take a bike ride with your grandpa, swing on that tree swing in the front yard. You'll start feeling better, I promise."

I said, "I can't believe Fuzzy's dead."

"I know. I felt that way about Frisky. Take your time. Let it sink in."

Granddaddy looked at his watch and said, "Well, guess we'd better go on and bury him. Jeffrey, you go on home. You don't need to watch your dog put in the ground."

I considered protesting, but figured it would be

no use. I walked back along the fence row to find a hole I had discovered beneath the fence. I made my way between bushes to my favorite spot and sat down. My body was numb, my stomach heavy, as if filled with a sack of coal from the pile in the back yard. Fuzzy would come back. I knew it. Fuzzy wasn't dead. He would crawl under the hole in the fence and find me.

Then I remembered the stories my grandparents had told me about my parents, as one death recalled others. My parents were once part of my life, but I never could remember them. I felt bad if my classmates at school asked about my parents. On rare occasions, like this one, I wondered what might have been. My life had felt so full at my grandparents' that I couldn't have imagined anything emptying that fullness.

Fuzzy had been a part of that. If he were gone for good, there would be a hole in my world that could never be bridged. "Fuzzy," I whispered. "Fuzzy," I said louder. My voice grew louder every time I said the name, but for some reason I found I could not shout. "Fuzzy, come home to me. I know you're there, somewhere in that field. I'll look for you later."

I heard a dog's bark, felt a surge of hope in my heart as the barking grew louder. Then it faded into the distance, and I knew it was probably Mr. Bruce's bulldog from across the highway.

Many times during the thirty years since Fuzzy died, he found a way back into my thoughts. Fuzzy turned up in my dreams or appeared in my mind at a boring faculty meeting - an image of a white frisky ball of energy followed by another image - the bloody grinning monster lying on the ground.

Even though thirty years had passed, as I walked in my grandparents' hayfield, I wondered if I could find the exact place where Fuzzy lay buried. I wandered around the field and heard some dogs barking nearby, from the new houses built down Bramble Road. For a few seconds, I thought I heard Fuzzy's bark but then considered the absurdity of a thirty-year-old dog. I walked away from the fence, to a spot where I had a good view of The Thicket. I sat down on a cold, flat, limestone rock, watching crystals on the surface sparkle from sunlight. I looked back toward The Thicket, saw cedars and evergreen bushes interspersed between the gray, leafless trees of winter. I stood there listening to my own heartbeats in my ears and wondered if Fuzzy could hear them from his soiled grave.

CHAPTER 4

I was eating the turnip greens I hated when I figured out how to handle Fuzzy's death. I took a bite of greens, then a quick bite of roast beef or meatloaf, anything to make the taste bearable. In the same way I followed Uncle Rick's advice. I could bear death's bitter flavor if it were mixed with other flavors - reading the science books I found in the public library, swinging on the tree swing, or playing with Granddaddy.

The hardest days were those after Fuzzy's burial. I dreamed of playing fetch with Fuzzy. Then I woke up, feeling bad that I had forgotten to feed the dog the evening before - and then I remembered that Fuzzy was dead and felt even worse.

Summer was a slow and lazy time, and Granddaddy and Granny let me do what I wanted. The combination of heat and Southern humidity made me drowsy. My bedroom was too hot to lie in my bed, and the coolest surface in the house was the living room floor. That is where the fan was. An Emerson electric fan, square, with metal blades painted white. There I took off my tee shirt, lay down in front of the fan and enjoyed the coolness of the wooden floor as it crept up and down my body. First I would lie on my stomach. Once my body had heated that spot on the floor I moved a couple of feet to a cool place and rolled over on my back, turned my head toward the fan, and watched the hypnotic whirr of the blades.

There, I dreamed of that picnic in The Thicket - every detail reproduced right up to the shape of the individual leaves on the ground. It seemed a dream of the heaven I did not want to leave - but I felt the cold of Death tugging me out, the smell of Fuzzy's rotting body tainting the memory. I struggled to stay but sensed myself being pulled away - then my eyes opened to feel the artificial wind hitting my face. I was wide awake, the memory fading fast, and after a trip to the kitchen for iced tea, I ran outside to the swing Granddaddy had hung from a maple in the back yard. The tree provided shade and in the fall, orange and red leaves carpeted the earth. I made a pile of leaves and jumped into it, sitting in the middle with only my head sticking out.

Today I wanted to swing, and I did, pushing off back and forth across the dirt driveway. I listened and watched for cars turning in, though that was rare. I swung higher, the breeze brushing my face, sparkling sunlight dancing with shadow among the young leaves. I got dizzy if I swung too long, so I hopped off the swing, crossed the drive, and walked alongside a row of bushes. Out of some of the bushes pushed strands of wild rose, honeysuckle and day lilies. On the ground were passion fruit. Granny called them "wild apricots."

They produced green pods that turned pale, dried and wrinkled in the fall. I would pick them, open them, eat the sweet jelly around the seeds inside.

I found a hole in the bushes, crawled under it, and walked upright through the secret passageway. I followed it to "my place," a small spot of grass, where I sat, sniffing the day lilies and wild rose around me. I tried to think about how good my life was, how happy I was with Granddaddy and Granny, how blessed it was that I had people who loved me after my parents died. Sure, it was sad that Fuzzy was lost, but maybe someday he would come back. I lost the sinking feeling I had right after my dream. I would always have my grandparents, I would always have The Thicket, I would always have "my place" to think. Nothing else mattered - even schools could change and it would still be okay. In the fall, I would even move up to fourth grade and attend a new school, Gilead Elementary. But *here* would remain the same.

When I went back inside the house, Granny asked, "Goodness child, where you been?"

"I was playing outside in the bushes."

"You'll get yourself into poison ivy - be itchin' all over."

"Ah, let the boy play," Granddaddy said. "He's got 'nough sense to stay out of the poison ivy - I showed him how it looks."

"Well, you'll be sorry when that boy forgets how it looks and needs his itchin' arms soaked in Blue Stone. I'm telling you, it's gonna happen."

"Hateful woman! Will you get off my back!"

Granny backed down because I was there. Supper was ready and I was hungry.

It only was 4:00, but supper was always early at the Wilson place. I enjoyed the meatloaf, lima beans, corn on the cob and rolls left over from dinner. After supper I sat outside with Granddaddy on one of the gliders on the porch. Granddaddy told me about his younger days in Limestone Springs, an old resort town now covered by Perry Lake.

"I'd take the train to Limestone Springs. It had three blacksmith shops to make horseshoes and to fix the buggies, a bowling alley and a dance hall. Used to be a girl I'd square dance with, little Annie, when I was sixteen. I loved that girl so much. But, she liked Mr. Puckett better and married him. I was sad and mad and wasn't anything I could do 'bout it. For years she'd send me and your Granny a Christmas card." Granddaddy scratched his nose, then continued.

"I used to go all over the place on trains; they had good passenger trains back then. I went to Manchester, Winchester, Chattanooga and up to Bowling Green. I wanted to see the sights. Quit school when I was sixteen. Never did my homework, never learned how to read. Boy, did Daddy whip me, but I was stubborn. Didn't want to work either. Got odd jobs now and then and spent the money on train tickets or going to the picture shows. You should have seen Charlie Chaplin, that funny man. Had him a mustache. Used to walk around with a cane, do all sorts of funny things. Sneak up behind folks and hit them with it or pull girl's dresses up. I like funny men - Jack Benny, Red Skelton, he's on TV tonight. We'll watch that." Granddaddy looked straight ahead, as if trying to remember more.

I let him ramble on. I loved to listen to Granddaddy talk about the past. When he talked about

Limestone Springs, he did not talk about other things, like hell. I did not like Granddaddy to talk about hell and prayed he wouldn't do that today. I would try to keep him reminiscing. I asked him, "How long did people use horses and buggies?"

"Only rich folks had cars back then. I remember old lawyer Stone driving 'round his Model T, one of the first I saw 'round here. He lived in a big house, like a mansion, over off Carter Lane. But poor dirt farmers like my daddy and me, we had to wait. My first car was a Model T, but I didn't get one 'til the thirties. I remember an old farmer riding on a wagon down Randallsville Highway in 1948."

To me, that seemed a long time ago.

"People were mostly poor back then, not like now. Folks used to rent shacks, farmed land they rented from some farmer that owned land. Farmed some myself after I stopped working at Schmidt's, where they made beer. Finally, we stayed with my Aunt Fanny and barely got enough to eat, between farmin' and cuttin' wood to sell."

I swung my legs back and forth. Granddaddy had already talked for over an hour. The sun was lower in the sky and the temperature had dropped a little. We moved to the concrete steps and sat there. It started to get dark, and the lightning bugs began to appear, flashing their yellow tail-lamps. There was a sound of a vehicle pulling into the driveway.

"Who in the world could that be this time of evenin'?" Granny asked

Around the corner crept an ancient tractor. Its faded paint was once dark red, but weather and time had done its work. Patches of rust blotched the surface.

Its paleness was accentuated by the twilight. The engine sputtered to a stop right by the back door.

On the metal seat sat a white-haired man, his face so wrinkled it made a prune look smooth. He had a lit cigarette in his mouth. Granddaddy stood and approached the man, offering his hand. The man's veins popped out when he grasped Granddaddy's hand.

"Mr. Denny! Good to see you!" Granddaddy said.

"Figured I'd stop by and see how things are goin.' How's that garden of yours?" Mr. Denny spoke in a low voice between wheezes and coughs. Perhaps it was his loudest voice. Mr. Denny's lips did not move when he spoke.

"Garden's doin' fine. Been tryin' to get that durn Johnson grass out every mornin' but it seems to grow back every night. It's like more grows the more you chop it."

Mr. Denny wheezed and laughed at the same time and said, "Know what you mean. Hell, my garden's always full of weeds by the fall. Can't find a damn thing there. Oh, sorry, didn't notice your grandson. How you doin,' son?"

"Fine," I said. I didn't mind the bad words; a boy named Kenneth used to say them all the time in my third grade class.

"That's good, son. You have a fine lookin' grandson, Bud."

"Bud" was what most people called Granddaddy. His given name was David Wilson, and Granny's was Anna; but I couldn't remember their names half the time. To me, their names were "Granddaddy" and "Granny."

"Yep," Granddaddy replied to Mr. Denny. "Smart,

too. Does real good in school."

"Well, good for you, young man! I never learned how to read and it held me back. I have a feelin' you'll do just fine."

"Thanks, Sir," I said.

Mr. Denny said, "Polite, too. Not like most young folks these days. Never seen the likes of it. 1968 and the whole durn world's goin' to hell. Makes you think the Lord be comin'.'"

The two men talked as twilight began to merge into night, and the branches of the Kiefer pear by the gliders turned from brown to black. After Mr. Denny drove off, the sound of his tractor fading as he approached Bramble Road, Granddaddy said, "Oh, shoot! We're about to miss Red Skelton."

Every Tuesday night at 7:30, Granddaddy would turn the TV to Channel 5 to watch Red Skelton. We ran to the black and white TV, turned it on, and waited for the tiny dot in the center to grow. It was slow in warming up and Granddaddy looked as if he would start cussing, but the picture finally opened up and show was on. It was Granddaddy's favorite part: *Silent Time*. No dialogue, just pantomime. Red Skelton playing Freddie the Freeloader. I enjoyed listening to the familiar theme music as Freddy made one of his trips to the trash can to hunt for food.

After the show, it was time for bath and bed, though I wanted to sit outside on the steps for a while. Although Granny said it was past my bedtime, she gave in when Granddaddy said, "Will you just let Jeffrey stay outside a while? Ain't gonna do that boy any harm."

Granny relented and granted my request to stay up - "but only until 9:30."

After my bath, I joined Granddaddy outside on the cool steps and listened to the crickets chirp. We were facing the gliders and the row of bushes behind them. The outside light on the corner to our right drew most of the bugs away. Moths gathered around the light as well, and I could hear their flapping wings. The lightning bugs were still out, though flying higher than before, above the tops of tall trees. Now and then, a frog croaked, and I wondered where it was in the bushes and whether I could find and catch it.

There was no wind, but I was getting cool. I nudged next to Granddaddy, who put his arm around me. "Looks like it's getting time for you to get to bed, boy." And I said "Yeah, I'm getting sleepy."

"Well, let's go then," and we walked past the open screen door into the house. Granddaddy hooked it, then closed the large, wood door, varnished dark brown, and locked it. I poured a glass of water in the kitchen, walked to my room, put on my pajamas, and after a stop at the bathroom, turned out the light and found my way to bed, almost hitting a bedpost in the dark. I crept under the covers, pulling them tightly against my face. Almost the whole day I had walked in happiness, and I had no reason to believe that would ever change. The feel of the mattress, the sheet and spread, the pillow, was perfect. I started to pray, thanking God for Granddaddy and Granny. I also prayed I would be a good boy, make them proud. My eyes slammed shut almost as soon as I said "A-men." I fell asleep, dreaming of catching lightening bugs in the back yard.

CHAPTER 5

I stopped to take a break, my feet freezing inside the thin tan-colored leather loafers I sometimes wore to faculty meetings so I could slip them off under the table. Middle age had caught up with me. At nine, I could circle the entire hay field three times in my Keds without getting tired. But now, I leaned on a fence post, careful to avoid the barbed wire. I looked toward the south, toward Randallsville, where my favorite aunt, Aunt Jenny, still lived on Hooper's Lane. She owned a small house covered with white vinyl siding. I planned to see her later. Uncle Lawton had died twenty-five years ago. Emphysema.

I always looked forward to their visits on the weekends. I liked Uncle Lawton, too, found him interesting. Uncle Lawton was "cool." He had a balding head with one long hank of dark hair that, combed sideways, partly covered a bald spot. He wore dark sunglasses and had a mysterious smile. Although I sometimes imagined that Uncle Lawton was a spy on the side, I knew my uncle also ran a gas station on the outskirts of Randallsville. It was a tiny wood building with two gas pumps.

Aunt Jenny arrived every Saturday morning to clean the house. I was glad to see her and gave her a hug when she got out of her light blue '62 Ford Falcon. I talk to her after she finished vacuuming, and sometimes she gave me her old Reader's Digests, which I read cover to cover. I hoped she would bring some today so I could forget about Fuzzy's death for a little while. If necessary, I would skip over any stories about dogs.

When I ran outside to greet my aunt, she hugged me long and hard, pulling my head against her chest. When I heard her heartbeat I started to sob. "I'm sorry about Fuzzy," she said. "I know you loved him. Maybe you can get a new dog."

"I don't want any more dogs. Fuzzy's just run away. That dead dog Uncle Rick found didn't even look like him."

Aunt Jenny looked like she was unsure of what to say. There was a long pause. I heard her heart beat a little faster, and she released the hug, placed her hands on my shoulders, and looked into my eyes. "Jeffrey," she said, "Fuzzy's not coming back. He's dead. I wish he were coming back, too, but he's not. When someone's dead, they don't come back to see you. Ever. But God took Fuzzy to heaven to be with Him. He's jumping around and playing with other dogs, and he's waiting for you. One day, a long time from now, you'll see him again. And you'll see your mama and daddy, too - and I know they'll be glad to see you. By now, I'm sure they've both met Fuzzy and know how good you were to him."

"How long will it be before I get to see Fuzzy?"

"Hopefully a real long time. But that makes it even better. Fuzzy will be happier than ever when you get to heaven. You'll be happier than ever, too. But you have to be patient. Fuzzy wants you to have fun, to be a boy, to grow up. I bet he's looking down at you now, feeling a little sad, but happy knowing he's in heaven and that one day he'll see you again."

"What if he didn't go to heaven. I once heard a man yell out of a car window at Fuzzy when he was chasing the car. He said, "Damn dog must want to die and go to hell!""

"Oh, no, that man was wrong to say that. People say things they don't mean when they get upset. He was likely afraid he would hit Fuzzy with the car and hurt him. He was mad about that. That's why he said those bad words. He didn't really think Fuzzy would go to hell. Fuzzy loved you and played with you. He didn't know that it was a bad thing to chase cars. He was just a dog. Animals can't tell right from wrong. All dogs go to heaven, all cats, all animals. It's only people that don't all go."

Granny stuck her head out the screen door and said, "Hi, Jenny. Didn't see you come. I should have known 'cause my nose was itchin.' That means company. You two been talkin' 'bout Fuzzy, I reckon. Poor thing."

"I miss him too, Mama. I think Jeffrey misses him most."

"Yeah, he loved that dog. Played ball with him all the time, ran out there in the field with him. Well, come on in, get some tea before you start. Big ole' house, too durned hard to clean."

I went inside too and drank a glass of iced tea in the kitchen before running outside again. I knew the first thing Aunt Jenny would do after finishing her tea was to roll out the vacuum cleaner. I hated the sound of a vacuum cleaner. Hearing the high-pitched whine would send me into a frenzy and out the door. I opened the gate and ran across the field to the far side bordering the woods.

I walked along the side of the fence toward The Thicket, but didn't get far until I saw an area of disturbed clay. I knew right away it was a dog's grave. My feet gave way, and when I fell, my chin nearly hit a small limestone rock used as a grave marker. I wanted to ignore the grave, to run as fast as I could from it. Although my aunt's words were comforting, accepting them meant accepting Fuzzy's death. Yet here was the grave. Wrong dog, I thought. I tried to stop thinking, closed my eyes, crawled off into the tall grass, cutting my hand on some thorns from a vine sticking out. I cried out, wept, stood up, and walked quickly toward the thicket. That would be a place that could heal me, where I could remember the good and forget the bad.

I arrived just in time - I felt like my heart was being ripped apart, that only here could it be pieced back together. As soon as I crossed over into the cool shade, I lay down on the leafy ground and closed my eyes. When I opened them again, I knew I had somehow fallen asleep, but when I looked at my watch, it showed that only twenty minutes had passed since I left the house. That was good. Aunt Jenny would still be vacuuming.

I walked to the swing-vine and sat on it, looking out at green grass and cows and blue sky. The day slowly shifted gears from *horrible* to *tolerable*. Soon it might even shift to *good*. I remembered the time I spent here with Granddaddy. I hoped he and I would come here again soon.

Then I heard Granny's voice calling, "Jeffrey! Come home!" The Thicket had calmed my mind, and I walked back to the house in a better mood. As soon as I made it inside the screen door, Granny said, "Your aunt Jenny's got somethin' for you. She's on the couch in the living room."

I was afraid it might be a puppy. But I didn't want another puppy - not so soon after Fuzzy. I walked toward the couch and my aunt picked a bundle off the coffee table and said, "Something for you to read." It was a new pile of Reader's Digests. "Thank you," I said, meaning it.

"Would you like to help me dust?" Aunt Jenny asked.

"Sure." I didn't mind doing housework. I helped her take photos and ceramic dogs, which bothered me a little, off the mantle behind the wood stove. I placed them on the floor, wiped off the photos and dogs with a paper towel, and then took a cloth and wiped my side of the mantle. I liked how the dark brown color of varnish reappeared as the cloth removed a layer of dust. We moved to the coffee table, to the old piano that was always out of tune, and on through the house.

Aunt Jenny still had more cleaning to do, so I picked one of the Reader's Digests out of the bundle my aunt had given me. I thumbed through it, reading articles that caught my interest first. I always had trouble understanding humor, so I skipped "Laughter - The Best Medicine" for now. But I loved anything to do with science, especially the section called "News from the World of Medicine," or any article about a historical topic. For a while everything was okay again. As soon as I finished one article, I immersed myself in the next one.

Today, my eyes tired before I was halfway through the first issue. I wanted to keep reading - at least until I could ask Aunt Jenny whether she would take me to Uncle Lawton's gas station. My eyes burned, and spots of light flashed in front of them, keeping me from reading. I shut my eyes, but the afterimage kept flashing. For a brief moment I thought the image looked like a white dog. Then the images of Fuzzy and the rabbit I had tried to keep locked out burst through into a daydream. Just as I was about to cry, I felt someone touch my shoulder. It was Aunt Jenny. "Would you like to see Uncle Lawton at the gas station?"

"Sure," I said. Blessed relief.

We climbed into the Ford Falcon and traveled down the curved gravel drive, through dry mud puddles that Mr. Benson didn't fill often enough with rocks, past the sugar maples and onto the Randallsville Highway. Aunt Jenny drove past a shattered mailbox post on the right. A lump grew in my throat as I looked away to the other side of the road. There Mr. Parker's place sat, a white, three-story brick house over a hundred years old. He owned a country store on the Ridgeway Highway where Granddaddy and I often bought cokes after school. Mr. Parker said that the house was used as a hospital by Confederate soldiers in the Civil War and that blood stains remained on the floor that wouldn't scrub out.

Blood, I thought. That's it! The rabbit lost all its blood, all at once - like the time Granddaddy's car ran out of gas on the way to Nashville. The car stopped. It had a good motor, but the motor couldn't run without fuel. The rabbit had a strong heart, but it ran out of blood all at once. The heart had nothing to pump. It had to stop. That was how my parents had died. Maybe that's how Fuzzy... Thoughts rushed like rapids through my skull, and I struggled to contain them. I tried to focus on the scenery.

We turned right on Farris Road, where there were fewer houses. Fields of wheat and hay alternated with cedar woods to make a patchwork country quilt. I imagined each field dipping into the woods, peninsulas in a vast forest sea, each a world of its own. I wanted to explore them, one by one.

We turned into Mason Lane, filled with hills and sharp curves that made me sick to my stomach. I held my head by the open window to feel the breeze. It did not help. Just before it was too late, we reached Fayette Road, a smooth, straight highway that had been recently repaved. I focused on the yellow lines in the middle, and as the car closed on them, they hypnotized me. Then I saw the gas station. Aunt Jenny pulled into the gravel parking lot and stopped under a red maple tree. She left the windows open to beat the afternoon heat.

Uncle Lawton stood at the screen door and waved us in. He kissed Aunt Jenny and patted me on the head. "Hello, Son. Sorry about your dog. Here, let me get you a Coke." He pulled two glass bottles out of an old-fashioned red freezer with a large white Coca-Cola logo in cursive across the top. I thanked my uncle and enjoyed the feeling of cold Coke in a dry mouth.

I enjoyed exploring the store - especially the glass case with penny candy. I loved the tiny Tootsie

Rolls, but I did not feel like eating candy after being sick in the car. I examined the wood shelves on the back wall stocked with cans of motor oil, brake fluid and other supplies. I loved the smell of the gas station, a musty odor of old wood mixed with oil and gas. Another odor - that of cigars - hung in the air. Uncle Lawton loved to smoke cigars—not the thick ones - but small ones that looked like fat brown cigarettes. I felt cocooned and comfortable in the tiny building, as if nestled in a blanket. I wandered to the window fan and enjoyed the cool air blowing through my hair. I placed my face close to the fan, seeing only a green blur from the grass outside through the fast metal blades.

I found the back door and walked outside to a fenced lot. There stood two oak trees and a pear tree filled with new pears that would ripen in August. I wanted to come back there and harvest some of them in a bucket. I could eat them when they were hard and crisp, with the tangy taste I liked. Granddaddy and Granny, though, waited until the pears were soft and very sweet.

I sat under the shade of one of the oaks, plucking blades of grass and picking up acorns, rubbing them between thumb and forefinger to polish them. I pocketed some to take home. They reminded me of varnished wood. I collected many kinds of acorns, lining them across a bookshelf in my bedroom - twenty in the past year. I picked them carefully, weeding out those with holes or flaws. I made sure their caps were still intact. Their surface had to be perfect - smooth, and without scratch marks. Sometimes I snuck into the kitchen cabinet, took the can of Pledge, and sprayed a little on a paper towel to wipe the acorns down. They showed their brown color like the fireplace mantle after Aunt Jenny had finished wiping it.

I heard Aunt Jenny calling. "Jeffrey, time to go home!"

"Coming!" I was disappointed. I wished to stay longer. For a while, I had escaped unpleasant memories. I wanted to keep hiding. I walked through the door, looking back one more time at the items in the store. "See you tomorrow at church, Uncle Lawton."

"Sure thing, Jeffrey." Every Sunday, Aunt Jenny and Uncle Lawton took Granddaddy, Granny and me to church.

From the front seat of the car, Aunt Jenny asked, "Did you have a good time outside? I see you picked some acorns."

"Yes, ma'am, I did. Can we go back when the pears are ripe?"

"How many pears can you eat? You can pick them right off the tree at home. Granny said that last week you ate so many you had a belly ache and stayed in bed all afternoon."

"I won't eat too many. I promise. I like them when they make a noise when I bite into them. They taste better then."

"All right. I'll ask Mr. Bright to let us pick pears in August. But, you'd better leave some for him. Your uncle just rents this place from Mr. Bright."

"I will."

The ride back was smooth, and I did not feel sick at all. As we approached the driveway at home, I closed my eyes as we passed the ditch were Fuzzy was killed. When I opened them again, Aunt Jenny had turned in the drive. I had gathered some good memories today. It was like gathering pears: you pick the good ones and throw away the bad ones. Tomorrow I hoped to gather more good memories - at church and Sunday dinner.

CHAPTER 6

When I awoke Sunday morning, I checked the rectangular face of the Timex my grandparents had given me on my birthday. 7:30 a.m. At 9:30 Aunt Jenny and Uncle Lawton would come by to bring us to Sunday school and church. I knew I had to polish my dress shoes. They had been scuffed from my playing in the churchyard after evening services the previous week. This Sunday, as I ran to the bathroom, I skipped to the kitchen, wearing only my pajama bottoms. If I dressed up before breakfast, I might spill something.

I scarfed down my first sausage and tomato biscuit. Granddaddy was already wearing his white shirt and black pants. "What's the hurry? Seen a snake runnin' after you?"

"No, but I have to polish my shoes today!"

"Slow down. You got plenty of time."

I ate the second sausage biscuit with more finesse. I loved how the flavors of the first fresh garden tomatoes of the year mixed with the flavors of the sausage and biscuit. I looked out the window, its bright yellow curtains parted. Another sunny day, a great day for church and Sunday dinner. After church, I knew at least two great aunts and uncles would arrive, maybe more, to sit around the slick, shiny dinner table and eat the best pot roast dinner anyone could have. It would be ready and waiting in the oven when we returned.

After breakfast, I searched under the kitchen cabinet for the cleaning products to clean my shoes. In a plastic container, I found a round metal container of black shoe polish and a shoe brush. I sauntered back to my bedroom, fetched my black dress shoes from under the bed, and shook them out. Granny had told me that I should shake my shoes out every morning, since spiders might be inside, though I never found any.

I took shoes, polish and brush out the back door and sat on the rough concrete steps that felt cool in the morning. I heard the mockingbird that liked to sing from the top of the chimney, along with the songs of robins, thrashers, and less often, the "bob-white!" of quail. Dew glistened in the grass, and the air smelled fresh like the newborn day. I took a paper towel I pulled from the rack in the kitchen, opened the can of polish, and applied it to each shoe before scuffing, allowing time for them to dry. I savored the scent of shoe polish and how it mixed with honeysuckle and iris. I waited a few minutes, relishing the sights, sounds and scents of outdoors. Then I brushed each shoe, working front to back, enjoying how the dull black colors of the polished parts began to shine. Soon the shoes looked almost new, except for a few lines along the tops from wear.

I had the shoes almost a year now - dress shoes

from Sears, and before too long the time would arrive for the long trip to Sears in downtown Nashville. I loved going and trying on new shoes, but that would be a sad time for me as well, for I had grown attached to the old ones.

Now I was happy to have the shoes I had. I stepped inside, put away the supplies, and hurried to get dressed. In the bathroom, I brushed my teeth. When I returned to my bedroom, I checked the closet, found the dress shirt my grandparents bought at Sears. Aunt Jenny bought my light gray suit at Penny's, just off the square in Randallsville, where she also picked out the matching gray clip-on tie. I returned to the bathroom to brush my flat-top haircut - not that much brushing was needed.

I checked my watch. It was 8:30. I decided to watch TV until Aunt Jenny and Uncle Lawton arrived. I turned to Channel 2 to watch "The Three Stooges." My favorite episodes were the ones with Moe, Larry and Curly, and I would laugh at the way they would bop each other on the head and poke one another in the eye.

After the Stooges was church programming. I liked to go to church but did not like watching church on TV. So, I turned off the TV and filled out my Sunday School lesson. The lesson was about Good King Josiah who destroyed idol worship in Judah and followed the true God. I was fascinated by the stories about kings, so I liked this lesson. I read it in fifteen minutes and finished the exercises just as Aunt Jenny and Uncle Lawton pulled up in their car.

I walked outside the door with Granddaddy and Granny - Granny in her white dress decorated with flowers and Granddaddy with his black suit, tie and matching Fedora hat, and felt love to the point that my heart hurt. So long as I had them both, everything felt safe. True, I had lost Fuzzy, but today I felt, for the first time since Fuzzy had disappeared, that I would be all right.

In Aunt Jenny's car, I sat in the back seat between Granddaddy and Granny. Granddaddy turned and asked me, "Think the preacher's gonna have a good sermon today?"

"I hope so."

"Wonder what songs they'll sing today. Hope they sing *Sweet Bye and Bye.*"

That song was Granddaddy's favorite, and because of that, it was my favorite. I loved every song that Granddaddy loved: *What a Friend We Have in Jesus*; *Throw out the Lifeline*; *Softly and Tenderly Jesus is Calling.* I had my own favorites: *Hallelujah Praise Jehovah*, *Fairest Lord Jesus*, but the song I liked the best, next to *Sweet Bye and Bye*, was *There's a Great Day Coming*. The melody moved like a march, and I could imagine the dead marching to God's judgment. I hummed the hymn in my head, recalled the words:

There's a great day coming,
a great day coming,
there's a great day coming by and by,
when the saint and the sinner shall be parted
right and left -
are you ready for that day to come?

I had the numbers of Granddaddy's favorite songs memorized - this one was number 23 in the hymnal.

Then my mind snapped back to Granddaddy's question, and I answered, "I hope they sing *Sweet Bye and Bye* too."

I looked out the window. Church was eight miles away over winding country roads, and I was comforted by the familiar houses I saw Sunday mornings, Sunday evenings and Wednesday evenings on the trips to and from church. Granny pointed out the homes of various cousins I barely knew and rarely saw. There were old three story houses that fascinated me, and I wondered what secrets I could find in their rooms. Perhaps I would find rare books, or maps, or treasure. Some looked haunted, especially the house with peeling paint surrounded by old oaks and twisted cedars. A small family graveyard stood to one side, its tombstones leaning over, looking as if they would fall into the ground and sink down to the dead. In the fenced backyard lived cats of all colors: calico, white, black, orange, yellow. There must have been thirty of them. That Sunday I saw for the first time an ancient woman with faded dress feeding the cats, her shoulders stooped, her hair whiter than dry sand. I could not see her face.

"Who lives in that house?" I asked no one in particular.

Taking his ever-present cigar out of his mouth, Uncle Lawton answered, "Old Miss Robertson lives there. Old maid, never married. Nobody knows much about her other than her name. I heard she had two sisters who have been dead several years now. Boys and girls who live round there say she's a witch. One time some boys decided to steal some of her cats, and nobody ever saw those boys again."

"You don't know if that's true," Aunt Jenny said. "Stop spreading rumors. You know if those boys really came there and disappeared the sheriff would have come. It would have been in the paper. I never heard anything about that. I think she's just a lonely old woman."

"Well, Jeffrey, if you take my advice," Uncle Lawton said, "don't go around that house. Don't even pass by when you ride your bike. The old lady will get you!"

I started in my seat and Aunt Jenny gave Uncle Lawton a fierce look. "Do you have to scare the boy?" she asked. "Be careful. You'll give him bad dreams."

Out the back left window, I saw a log cabin. Granddaddy loved to talk about it, and this Sunday was no exception. "Old James Hicks built that cabin before I was born. I was born in 1901, so it goes back a ways. His son lives there now."

We turned right into a gravel drive and parking lot and parked under a huge sugar maple. Uncle Lawton was thankful that we arrived early enough to find a shady spot. As we walked toward the building, our feet crunched the gravel. I liked the sound. It reminded me of corn flakes before the milk had soaked them soft. The wood church building had fresh painted white siding. A small porch offered protection from rain and heat. Two benches lined the back of the porch. Five old men were sitting in the benches smoking.

"How are you doin', Brother and Sister Wilson, Brother and Sister Carter? How are you, young man?"

"We're doing fine. "I'm doing fine," everyone said. I had learned it was not good to be honest before services if I was not doing so well. One day I answered, "I feel sick today" and people either told me I should have stayed home or else ignored me. Now, I always said "Fine." After church, people talked about their lives. Time enough then for aches and pains.

The age of the church fascinated me. Over the overhanging porch was a small sign reading "AD 1888." Granddaddy used to tell stories about preachers he heard when he was a boy. Brother M.C. Pollman had such a loud voice Granddaddy could hear him from the other side of the log cabin. I could not imagine a voice that loud, because the log cabin was a good 500 feet away and across Andrews Road.

I would sometimes get in trouble at church for asking too many questions. Once I had checked out a library book about early man and showed the book to Uncle Lawton. There were pictures of some creature the book called the "Java Ape Man." For reasons unknown to me at the time, Uncle Lawton was angry. It was the only time he had been angry with me. "Don't check out junk like that! Next time Granddaddy takes you to the library, put it back. We came from God. Not monkeys! Don't let any book or any teacher tell you otherwise."

"Yes, sir," I replied, although I did not really understand what Uncle Lawton had said. I thought it was good to ask questions, but I found that some church people would get upset if I asked the wrong ones. Trouble was, I couldn't figure out in advance which questions were wrong and which ones were right.

On the porch at church, the planks creaked as the five of us walked from the porch to the carpet inside. The carpet was a deep red color that I felt was *churchy*. The men of the church agreed to buy an air conditioner in the spring, for which the congregation was grateful. It worked better than hand-held fans. I appreciated the cool air when it hit my face. I walked to the front of the church through a door leading to the Sunday school rooms. I entered a tiny classroom with barely enough room for a table and chairs for the students and teacher. The room contained a free-standing blackboard on which Brother Bill Martin, the teacher, wrote. It also had a two-foot square window, which let in some sunlight, but I felt confined.

The students in the class were in third, fourth and fifth grades. They included Billy and Dan Conwell, my third cousins. They were big boys, slightly heavyset, with black hair and mean looks. Granddaddy said they were meaner than snakes, and I agreed with him. I made sure to sit as far away from them as possible, next to the McRae twins. They were fraternal, a boy and a girl, Johnny and Maggie. They lived on a farm, and, like me, were active in 4-H. Unlike the Conwell boys, they would not flip my ears with their fingers when Brother Martin wasn't looking.

Brother Martin asked me to read the first paragraph from the Sunday School book. I was proud of my reading ability. I read through the paragraph, I thought, without a glitch - but I had pronounced the name of the good king "Josiah" as "Joshua." Brother Martin kindly corrected my pronunciation. I was still embarrassed. The Conwell boys were giggling and whispering, "Jeffrey can't read, just like his granddaddy." I turned around, but as usual, Brother Martin failed to catch the boys' meanness. "Jeffrey, don't turn around to talk to someone else when I'm talking. Pay attention to the lesson."

That brought more giggles from the Conwell boys. I wanted to hurt them. I never did, in part because they were bigger than me, and in part because I always tried to turn the other cheek like Jesus said. I was naturally meek and did not like to fight. It didn't much matter who started a fight at school. Both students would get in trouble. There were few things I hated more than getting in trouble.

After the lesson was over, I admired Johnny's dress shoes. They were brown, shiny, laceless. "Where did you get those shoes?" I asked.

"Oh, Santa Claus gave them to me for Christmas. You haven't seen 'em before? I wear 'em all the time."

Billy Conwell, who had been listening in, said, "There ain't no Santa Claus. You're so stupid. Both of you. It's your parents you know. They buy all the stuff and hide it from you. They eat the cookies that they leave out. How can you be dumb enough to believe all that crap!"

Johnny and I both raised our fists as if we wanted to fight. "There is too a Santa! You're lying," I said. Billy just laughed. Before Johnny and I could react, he turned away to go back into the auditorium and said, "You'll find out soon enough, stupid."

I wiped my eyes before walking into the auditorium. I didn't want anyone to know what had happened. I joined my grandparents, aunt and uncle on the far back pew next to a window. Resting on the pews were comfortable red cushions that matched the carpet. Before I was six, my relatives allowed me to lie down and sleep during the sermon. After that, they expected me to pay attention to the entire service, but I was not in the mood to focus on the service this Sunday. I looked out the window when Brother Whitson came up to the pulpit to make the announcements and list the names of the sick.

There was no stained glass in the windows, so I had a clear view of the maple trees and tall green grass outside. I imagined that I was a character in the Bible. I heard that the apostle Paul went on long journeys, so I pretended I was Paul, carrying a backpack with food, clothing and cooking supplies, wandering between trees on a path to some mysterious city.

I was interrupted by the voice of Brother Martin, the song leader. "Please open your songbooks and turn to number one hundred fifty-three. One hundred fifty-three." At first I was excited, because 154 was *Sweet Bye and Bye*. But then I heard the "three" at the end of the number, and I was disappointed. I liked *Blessed Assurance*, but I knew Granddaddy would be happier singing *Sweet Bye and Bye*. Although I never cared for how the congregation dragged out singing *Sweet Bye and Bye*, at least they sang it. Just then I felt my heart jump inside like an excited frog when Brother Martin said, "The song of invitation will be number twenty-three. Number twenty-three." *There's a Great Day Coming*. Maybe today would be that day.

I looked forward to hearing the sermon by Brother Noland. Brother Richard Noland had started preaching at Harrell's Corner two years ago. He was a part-time preacher with only a high-school education. During the week, he worked a small dairy farm about a mile from the church. A tall man with close-cropped brown hair, he was striking in the pulpit. His baritone voice was loud, but not overbearing. He rarely shouted.

I liked to hear Brother Noland's sermons best when they focused on Bible heroes. I always enjoyed the stories of Old Testament heroes, especially the battles between the good prophet Elijah and Ahab, the wicked king of Israel. I would shiver at the story of Naboth's vineyard. I did not know for sure what a vineyard was, but I saw it was something that the evil king desired. I imagined Ahab's wicked wife, Jezebel, nagging Ahab, then whispering in his ear, "Don't worry about that vineyard. Just let me take care of it." I felt fear when Brother Noland spoke of Naboth's arrest and of the liars hired by Jezebel to accuse him of cursing God and the king. In my mind I heard Naboth's cries as he was murdered. I was glad when God sent the prophet to tell Ahab he would die and dogs would lick his blood. However, Ahab repented and God told Ahab that bad things would happen to his family - but only after he died. I always wondered if maybe God was too merciful to Ahab.

This Sunday's sermon was not to be about an Old Testament hero after all. Brother Noland began in a tone of voice that made me shiver.

"If you died today, would you be ready to face God in eternity? One day, you will die - this is a certainty. Not one of us will leave life alive. When Judgment Day comes, will your name be written in the Lamb's Book of Life so you can enter into heavenly glory? Or will your name be missing? What a terrible thing it would be to fail to hear your name when they read from the Book of Life! To face eternity without God, to be without hope, to be lost in hell forever!"

I usually liked sermons about hell. I found them exciting - like horror movies. I wrapped my fingers around the edge of the pew as Brother Noland continued.

"How long is eternity? It's hard for our minds to follow. Imagine that the earth and sun are solid balls of steel. Imagine that an eagle flies constantly to and from the earth and sun. Each time it reaches the earth, it brushes a wing against the earth. Each time it reaches the sun, it does the same. Now the eagle's feathers aren't really hurt by all this, but they wear a little scratch of the steel away from the sun and earth every time! The time it would take for that eagle to wear away the earth and sun is nothing compared to eternity."

I listened - transfixed. Until now, my sense of time and space had been limited and circumscribed. About the longest time period I ever thought about had been summer vacation, and distance was either measured in tilled acres like Granddaddy's field, or in the time it took to get to school in Gilead or else to ride to Randallsville. The geographical limit of my world was the Sears store in downtown Nashville. Going there was a voyage of adventure.

I shivered in my seat, even though the seventy bodies in the building had made it warm despite the squeaky air conditioner. I felt constricted, as if I were smothering. The immensity of eternity was like a weight, the steel sun and earth crushing me. I felt my small size, my short life. The lives of others grew smaller, too, as did the things I thought were permanent: the house, the field, The Thicket, the earth itself. As these thoughts ran through my head like a rabbit, I tried to stop them. I focused on Brother Noland's eyes.

"Do you really want to spend eternity in hell, in a place prepared for the devil and his minions? Imagine the hottest heat you've felt on earth. Take a stove eye. Imagine you turn your stove on high, until the eye turns bright red. Then take one hand, hold the other hand with it against that stove eye. Feel the searing pain. Listen to your hand sizzle. Then turn it around to the other side, do the same. Repeat with the other hand. The agony you feel is a small pinprick compared to the pains of hell. The pain of your sizzling, swollen hand will stop one day. The pains of hell never end. Trillions of times hotter than the sun. Darkness all around. Demons taunting you. And eternal regret. You'll know you could have followed God, could have been baptized, could have become a faithful Christian, could have gone to heaven to be with God forever. But now you can't! Not now! You're lost, lost, lost for eternity."

Brother Noland never raised his voice. He sounded like the calm of the sea. Yet I found that made the message more frightening. I held my hands over my eyes, which I shut as if squinting to avoid the light of the sun. That made things worse - I felt pulled into darkness and saw a demon face with thick, leering lips sneering at me, its razor claws coming to cut my face before throwing me into eternal flames. I opened my eyes, focused on the schoolhouse lights hanging from the ceiling. Their warm yellow light calmed me. I was just a boy and had not yet reached the age of accountability, the age at which you had to be baptized. Most people figured that was about the age of twelve. When you reached that age, if you died without being baptized, you'd go to hell. No exceptions. But I was nine and should be safe for a while. If I died, I would go to heaven because I did not fully understand right and wrong. At least that's how Brother Martin had explained it in Sunday school class.

I thought about Granddaddy. He was lucky. He waited until he was sixty-five to be baptized. He did not die first and go to hell. I was grateful that Sunday when I witnessed Brother Noland lower Granddaddy into the water, then raise him up, dripping wet, out of the baptistery. Granddaddy was safe unless he sinned again. Even then he could ask God for forgiveness. I hoped that he asked God for forgiveness whenever he was mean to Granny. I could not bear the thought of Granddaddy burning in hell.

Brother Noland gave the invitation for sinners to come forth during the invitation song. "If there's anyone here is not a Christian, you should believe with all your heart that Jesus is the Son of God, repent of your sins, and confess them before men. Then you should be baptized into Christ for the remission of sins, and you will be a new child of God. If there's anyone who is a Christian who has fallen away, we invite you to come forward and confess your sins so we can pray for you. Whatever your need, won't you come forward as we stand and sing?"

We all stood, stretching our legs to the sound of opening song books. Brother Martin began singing the words, and I sang along. I loved the first verse about judgment - the second verse was about heaven:

> *There's a bright day coming,*
> *a bright day coming,*
> *there's a bright day coming by and by.*
> *But its brightness will only be for them who love the Lord:*
> *Are you ready for that day to come?*

It was the third verse that reminded me of the sermon's end and made me want to scream. I almost did. Words struck with the force of fear itself.

> *There's a sad day coming,*

a sad day coming,
there's a sad day coming by and by,
when the sinner shall hear his doom, "Depart, I
know thee not;
are you ready for that day to come?

I was about to leave my seat to come forward, but I caught myself, recalling that I was only nine and not old enough to sin.

Still, God's all-seeing eye seemed to be everywhere. I wanted to hide, to play outside for a while so I could avoid God's fiery glare. I felt as if God were waiting for me to sin before killing me. Then he could send me to hell. Maybe I would be one of the eternally damned.

What about my mama and daddy? Did they curse God just before the other car hit them? If they cursed, they did not have time to pray for forgiveness. And if they did not have time to pray for forgiveness, God would not forgive them. Unless God forgave every one of their sins, they would go to hell. I remembered that Brother Noland said in another sermon that it was wrong to assume that God would forgive someone in an accident who didn't have time to pray.

I read most of the Bible and knew what God did to sinners. God told the Children of Israel to stone a man to death who picked up rocks on the Sabbath Day. I figured that was kind of unfair. Not only would the man suffer when the rocks hit him; but, when he died he would go to hell.

Later, in the New Testament, Ananias and Sapphira had lied to God about the amount of money they gave the church, and God had killed them both. I figured they went to hell too.

It seemed so easy to get to hell and so hard to get into heaven. Didn't Jesus say that the way was narrow? What if Granddaddy died and went to hell? What would I do? I thought about that, and figured that if I saw Granddaddy falling into hell on Judgment Day I would do something bad right then and there and go to hell myself. I would not want to be in heaven for eternity without Granddaddy. Then I was scared God would be angry at me for thinking such a thought, and I wanted to go home and hide under the covers.

I felt better after the invitation song. No one had come forward today. Most of the time, nobody did. It was time for the Lord's Supper. That, at least, was a break. Several men from the congregation assembled in the back of the church, then walked to the front. They stood behind a long wood table loaded with metal trays. Some trays contained what I had always thought were Saltine crackers, although people called them "unleavened bread." The men would then distribute the trays row by row to the congregation. Church members would break off a piece of cracker and eat it. I did not understand what they were doing or why I was not permitted to partake. Only those who were baptized could eat the crackers. I figured that was good in a way, since my mouth was already dry.

The men returned to the front, replaced the small trays, and distributed the big trays filled with tiny cups of grape juice. A man would pray for "this cup, the fruit of the vine, which represents Christ's shed blood. May we partake of it in a manner well-pleasing in Thy sight." I wanted to take one of those cups and drink, but I knew I would be in bad trouble if I did.

After that, the men took two bamboo baskets and

passed them out. Aunt Jenny gave me a quarter to put in the basket. I would hold the quarter flat in front of my eyes, where it would shine like polished silver. I liked the "clink" it made when it fell into the basket full of dollar bills and change. I calculated how many tiny tootsie rolls a quarter would buy. Then I thought about Sunday dinner. My stomach growled.

It was finally time for the closing prayer. After the prayer, I quickly moved outside to shake Brother Noland's hand. I didn't have time to play with the other children on Sunday morning because the service ended after twelve noon, and Granny was not happy if the roast beef dinner in the oven burned.

I walked to the car and waited for my family members. I got inside and sat in the back seat. I was glad Uncle Lawton had parked the car in the shade. It was hot enough in the car without the sun cooking it. When everyone else was finally in the car, Uncle Lawton put on the air conditioner, and once we were on the road, he lit a small cigar. In the enclosed space I felt as if I were about to choke, but I knew it was no use to ask Uncle Lawton to stop smoking. Aunt Jenny said, "Jeffrey, why don't you crack your window just a little if that cigar smoke's bothering you?" I did, and it helped some.

We pulled into the gravel drive and parked under the Kiefer pear tree where a swarm of wasps had congregated to enjoy the fallen fruit. Stepping carefully to avoid the wasps, the whole family went inside as the screen door slammed shut.

CHAPTER 7

Decades after that childhood visit to church, I looked out over the patches of frost still dotting my grandparents' field. My arms hurt from leaning against the fence post so long. *Jesus wept*, I thought. The members of that church had been country folks, good people. But those teachings had damaged me, perhaps forever. It would be a long time before I thought of God as anything other than a sadist enjoying Himself as he watched people burning in hell for eternity. Looking back, I felt ashamed that I had once enjoyed hearing sermons about hell fire and brimstone.

    If church was hell, Sunday dinner after church was heaven, the best time of the week. I looked back to those delicious Sunday dinners I enjoyed as a child. They blurred into each other, a blur of warm spots on my heart that grew until my entire body felt warm, even in that cold field. I reached back and grasped one of those Sundays, perhaps a Sunday in that fateful summer of my ninth year. I sat on a clump of grass that had been dried by the sun. I remembered.

"Will you stop sliding on that floor in your good socks?" Aunt Debbie said. "Sorry," I replied, and left to change clothes in my bedroom. I did not mind dressing up for church, but I did mind staying in my Sunday best. I loved changing back to my ordinary clothes after church, my legs free in shorts, the coolness of the pullover shirt. After changing, I rushed to the kitchen table and found my favorite seat. Behind the table was an old mirror which had once stood above a space for a fireplace. I loved to sit by that mirror with my back to the wall and my legs hidden beneath the long white tablecloth.

As I sat down, I heard a familiar voice. "Hiya, Jeffrey."

"Hi Uncle Bob!" I said.

"Want to go outside and look for frogs after dinner?"

"Sure! And maybe we'll find some good bugs too. Maybe another praying mantis."

"I hope so. They look like sticks to me."

"Be great if we found a snake. You could go inside and scare your Aunt Jenny. I bet she likes to be scared."

I puckered my mouth, uncertain.

"I'll be standing right behind you," Uncle Bob said.

The others joined us at the table: Granddaddy and Granny, Uncle Lawton and Aunt Jenny, Uncle Rick and Aunt Susie, and Uncle Bob and Aunt Debbie. Aunt Debbie looked at Uncle Bob with a smirk and asked, "What mischief are you putting that boy up to?"

"Oh, no, no. We were just talking about picking some wildflowers after dinner."

Aunt Debbie said, "I'm glad the beans aren't ready to pick. You always eat them raw and they're not even washed!"

"Oh, they're safe; won't hurt the boy. I wouldn't give him the raw beans if I thought they might hurt him. Make him toot."

Aunt Debbie turned to the others and said, "He's hopeless, I tell you. Imagine! I've had to live with this man for twenty-seven years!"

The others laughed, and then grew quiet, for it was time for Granddaddy to say the blessing. "Lord, we thank Thee for this food and for all the many blessings of this life. Forgive us our sins. In Jesus' name. A-men."

"A-men," everyone intoned, and it was finally time to eat. Sunday dinner was a sacrament, a gift of grace, with the whole family gathered. Despite Brother Noland saying that you couldn't find eternity in his life, Sunday dinner felt eternal. If God ate dinner, I thought, He couldn't do better than this.

The food sat in a line along the bar. Roast beef, lima beans, mashed potatoes, fried okra, squash - it was all there. In the middle of the table sat an oversized bowl of salad and a big bottle of creamy-orange French dressing. Aunt Jenny helped prepare my plate. I loved putting Tabasco sauce on my roast beef. "You ought not put that hot stuff on your food!" Granny said. "You'll burn a hole in your stomach. My brother Joe did that - ate hot stuff all his life, grew hot banana peppers. Ate them on everything, even country ham sandwiches. Then he got an ulcer so bad they had to do an operation."

For once, Granddaddy agreed with Granny. "Yeah, I remember seein' him in the hospital. Whiter than a snow drift, and he didn't even have to get baptized. Doctor said he'd lost too much blood. Lucky he lived. Just use a little of that stuff, Jeffrey. Don't want you to end up like ole Joe."

"Don't worry." I said, but I was disappointed because I liked to use a lot. I figured that later, at suppertime, I could snatch some of the leftover roast beef, sneak into the refrigerator, and drown it in hot sauce. I would wash the plate in the kitchen sink when I was finished so no one would notice.

Iced tea was poured from a special crystal pitcher. I preferred sweet tea with lemon. The more lemon the better. I got in trouble for that, too. "Money don't grow on trees; stop using so much lemon juice," Granny would scold, so I cut down a little. But it seemed part of the natural order that sweet tea had lemon. Otherwise, the world itself would be off kilter.

I rarely remembered the dinner conversation. My focus was the food. The iced tea was strong, the way I liked it. My favorite dish was the salad - drowned in rich French dressing. It was tangy and sweet at the same time, and I loved how the tomato flavor mixed with cucumber and iceberg lettuce. I figured it was worth being called "fat boy" by classmates at school. Those other kids didn't know what they were missing.

Then there was dessert. Pecan pie, chocolate pie, Coca-Cola cake - I took a piece of each.

After dinner, the men went outside to sit in the

gliders and talk. The women stayed inside and talked
about lady things that I had no interest in. They talked
of relatives, who was doing what, who was marrying or
divorcing whom. I preferred to stay with the men or
play with Uncle Bob.

Uncle Bob never joined the other men right
away. He wandered around looking for a flower to put
in his shirt pocket. In March he found a daffodil. In April,
an iris blossom. The rest of spring and all summer, he
found whatever flower fit his mood. Today he picked an
orange day lily that almost fell from his pocket from the
weight and length of the stem. When Uncle Bob arrived
at the gliders, I sniffed the flower and said, "Let's look
for creepy-crawlies." So we searched the dark corners
of bushes, cracks in wood, flattened grass under rocks.
On a wild rose bush, we made a discovery.

It was a small green garden snake. Uncle Bob
said, "I'll show you how to hold it," and carefully picked
it up, holding its head so it wouldn't bite. I took it from
Uncle Bob. The snake wrapped around my fingers but
seemed content. Uncle Bob said, "Let's go inside. You
hide it behind your back, then show it to Aunt Jenny." So
we sneaked inside, closing the screen door gently
instead of allowing it to slam. We found Aunt Jenny
washing dishes in the kitchen sink. "Look what I found,"
I blurted out, and Aunt Jenny screamed as the snake
crawled onto the sleeve of her housedress. She didn't
stop screaming until Uncle Lawton pulled it off.

"Kill that ugly thing! Kill it," she said, looking as if
half her life had been scared away. Uncle Lawton
thought about it, then started to take the snake outside.
"Why aren't you killing it?" Aunt Jenny said.

"Well," said Uncle Lawton, "The snake will eat

nasty bugs and do more good than harm. I'll put it in the field where it won't be likely to come back." He tried to touch Aunt Jenny on the shoulder, but she pulled back.

I figured I was going to get a lickin' - hopefully with a belt instead of a switch. I hated being hit with switches, especially when I had to cut my own. When Granddaddy heard what happened he started laughing and couldn't stop. Granny was not amused. She told him, "If somebody doesn't spank that boy for scaring Jenny half to death, I will."

Aunt Jenny said, "Let me take care of it." She led me into my bedroom. "You know you did wrong, scaring me like that. I could have had a heart attack and died! You wouldn't want me to die, would you? Now bend over."

I did, and she smacked me one time with her hand. My shorts were still on, and it didn't hurt much, but I still cried from the embarrassment. I kept saying, "I'm sorry, I'm sorry." I didn't want to get Uncle Bob in trouble. But after Aunt Jenny left I looked out the door and saw Aunt Debbie pulling Uncle Bob by his right ear into my grandparents' bedroom. She spoke to him in a low tone of voice. I never knew a low voice could sound so loud. When Uncle Bob walked out of the room, he went out the door and sat with other men. I figured I should wait a few minutes before joining them when I heard Uncle Bob using dirty words. He seemed to be saying the dirty words about Aunt Debbie, though I wasn't sure.

After the conversation cooled off outside, I joined the men. They were talking about politics. As usual, Uncle Rick knew the answers to all the problems of the world. I was amazed at his knowledge. If he were

President, everything would be all right. I never really cared for politics, though. I sat under the shade of the pear tree and the small overhanging branches from two tulip poplars. If the wind was right, it was like sitting in a wind tunnel. As long as the wasps kept their distance, I could imagine myself in Eden, walking like Adam in the cool of the day.

While Uncle Rick and Uncle Lawton were talking politics, at times raising their voices, Uncle Bob spoke to me. "One day I'm going to take a lawn mower engine and some wheels and make you a go cart. If I can just figure out how to make a brake, I'd let you ride it around the yard. Don't go on the road though. There are too many cars, and it won't go fast enough. It's not like riding a bike."

"That would be great!"

"Well, I'm working on it. I have a little workshop in my garage where I like to tinker with engines."

I was not mechanical at all. In my third grade project when students painted chairs, I got in trouble because my paint dripped all over the place. Mrs. Wilson mocked me in front of the entire class. She acted like I had meant for the paint to drip.

I admired people who could tinker with mechanical things. I knew I would never do anything like that, but thought I could still be a scientist. Science was my favorite subject, and I figured you didn't have to build things as much as think about them.

Uncle Bob got up, and Granddaddy, who had been tinkering with tools in the garage, sat down. Suddenly he turned to me, looking worried, and I dreaded what was coming.

"You know, I'm worried about going to that hot

hell. Preacher talked about it today, you know. I heard another preacher say the fire would be seven times hotter than any fire on earth. I think about that all the time. I don't want to go there. Preacher says you have to do enough works to get to heaven. But how do you know when you've done enough works?"

A lump grew in my throat. It always formed during these conversations, but today the lump sank to my stomach and I felt sick. "I don't know," I replied.

Granddaddy continued. "I got baptized. Preacher said I had to be baptized to be saved. Old Tom Baker—he's nearly eighty-years old and hasn't got baptized. Goes to church every Sunday, but turns his head away every time they sing the invitation song. If he dies, he'll go to hell. Doesn't he know that?"

"I'm gonna be baptized."

"That'll be good. Just as soon as you reach the age of accountability. I know God washed away my sins when I was baptized, but I still sin. Every day I try to do the right thing. Go to church on Sunday morning, Sunday night, and Wednesday night. Lots of people just go Sunday morning. Preacher said they must not love worshippin' the Lord enough. I try to do people right, try to do your granny right. She's mean to me, but I try to do her right."

My face flushed with anger. I turned away, not wanting Granddaddy to see. Surely Granddaddy knew how mean he was to Granny, how he yelled and argued with her, made her cry. I never knew why Granddaddy treated her that way. And she took it, put up with him packing his suitcase or calling her a string of dirty words. I held back my temper, because I didn't want to fight with Granddaddy - and it wouldn't help Granny either.

Then I grew scared. Granddaddy was old. What if he died? Would Granddaddy go to hell? Sometimes he tried not to be mean to Granny. Was that enough? Most of the time Granddaddy didn't seem to think the way he treated Granny was wrong. But he was. He would be unable to repent of his sins against Granny before he died. He would go to hell for sure. I figured Granny would probably go to heaven, if only because of what she had suffered during her life. She had sinned, too, I knew, for everyone sinned who was of accountable age, according to the preacher. But she didn't sin in any obvious ways, and she had probably repented of her sins.

I was glad when Granddaddy stopped talking about hell and began talking about his ancestors. "Great-granddaddy was a full-blooded Irishman. Came to New York with four brothers. They got separated, and only two of them met again. Means my granddaddy was half-Irish."

"Wow! Why did they come here?"

"Starvin' to death. Potatoes went bad on them. That's all they had to eat. So they had to leave. My great-granddaddy worked hard, farmed. Was picking some corn in the field one day when he was in his fifties, dropped dead. Heart attack. My granddaddy didn't live too long either. Just 62 when he died."

"I hope you live to 100," I said."

"Well, I hope you do, too" Granddaddy said and smiled.

We went inside. It was suppertime. It was less formal than dinner. The great aunts and great uncles said their goodbyes and made their way back to

Nashville. Uncle Lawton and Aunt Jenny stayed because they would take Granddaddy, Granny and me to the 6:00 P.M. evening service at church. I felt sad as people left but knew that most or all of them would be back next Sunday.

CHAPTER 8

On the second Tuesday of every month, Granddaddy would open the gray metal mailbox by the road. It had the name "WILSON" scrawled on it with a marking pen in large, uneven letters, and he would find his and Granny's social security checks in the box. The mail came about 9:30, and immediately afterwards he and Granny prepared to travel to Randallsville to cash their checks and shop. For me, going downtown was a treat not to be missed. One day I was sick with a bad cold and was too dizzy to sit up. I asked Granddaddy and Granny, "Can I ride in the back of the truck?"

Granny said, "Okay, as long as you're careful." So I lay down in the back of the truck and shut my eyes.

Today I felt fine, and we got into Granddaddy's pickup. I sat between Granddaddy and Granny. Granddaddy had driven the truck so much the shocks were going bad. It shook like the old roller-coaster at Fair Park in Nashville. Unlike most vehicles in the South,

Granddaddy's truck did not have an air conditioner, but I enjoyed the breeze rushing in from the rolled-down windows, although Granny would complain about the air blowing her hair. Granddaddy said, "Boy's gonna burn up in here, sitting there in the middle. You want him to ride in the back of the truck again?" I hoped she'd say "yes," but Granny didn't like me riding in the back too often. She was afraid the truck would turn over if they had a wreck and that I would be thrown out. So she said, "No, just leave the windows down. I'll try to get my hair in shape when we get to town."

We traveled down the Randallsville Highway. After passing Mr. Parker's house, we drove over rolling hills, going slowly, maybe thirty miles an hour. Granddaddy said that it was safer to drive slow and as far below the speed limit as possible. Other drivers didn't agree, often blowing their horns as they passed, but there wasn't much traffic on the Randallsville Highway. Most people took the new road. The Ridgeway Turnpike was finished seven years before, but I liked the fact that Granddaddy took the older highway. Both Granddaddy and Grandpa Conley, my other granddaddy, had worked to build and repair the Randallsville Highway when they had worked for the WPA. I wasn't sure then what those initials stood for, but Granddaddy said he was glad to have a job during "the Depression."

On the highway, the Ford pickup crept along, past a three story house that was beginning to fall apart, its white paint peeling and chipping, exposing brown spots that grew day by day. We crossed the Drowning Creek bridge. The water was shallow, just a foot deep. Granddaddy stopped there from time to time to catch crawfish to use for fishing bait, but I didn't help catch them. I feared their pinchers. I asked Granddaddy how a creek so shallow could be called "Drowning Creek." "It's not shallow everywhere, and it's not shallow when it rains hard. Two little boys drowned in that creek. Washed away in a flood. Ever since then it's been called Drowning Creek."

I bowed my head, hoping I would never drown. I did not like stepping into deep water since I never learned how to swim. I panicked whenever I tried, so I gave up. I imagined drowning as the worst way to die - choking on water, unable to breathe, eyes bulging before I passed out.

On the top of a hill past the bridge to the right was a small white house owned by an old farmer. The name JONES was neatly printed on his mailbox. Sometimes when we passed by on the way back from Randallsville on winter nights, I would look inside the window of that house and see the shadow of an old woman rocking in a chair. I wondered whether I had seen a ghost or whether the woman really was rocking. There was a graveyard near the highway in front of the house where several worn gravestones stood. Some had fallen down. I wondered whether an old man could stay married if his wife were a ghost.

We passed a large graveyard, Greenlawn Cemetery, where my parents were buried. I felt a chill each time we passed, as if my parents' spirits were part of the breeze. I was glad to get past it.

We whisked through an underpass. On the other side to the left was a road I thought mysterious. I often wondered where roads led, and this one, parallel to the railroad track, intrigued me. I never could get

Granddaddy interested in going that way. One day, I figured, after I had learned to drive, I would find out what was there.

We came to the end of the Randallsville Highway, past CeeCee's Trailer Court. Granny said bad people lived there. "Trashy people." Then Granddaddy pulled the car onto the Ridgeway Highway, where cars were plentiful as hay stems in a farmer's field. Somehow, we made it across three lanes of the highway to the far left lane. Drivers blew their horns and shouted at Granddaddy. I figured those other drivers were bad people to be yelling at a safe, experienced driver like Granddaddy, who drove slowly just like he was supposed to.

Granddaddy stopped at the bank so he and Granny could cash their checks. After that, he drove down Main Street toward the public square. Granddaddy told stories of the way it used to be: wide, dirt streets with wagons filled with cotton to be sold, people staying up til' nine at night on Friday and Saturday. There were outdoor fruit stands, candy everywhere. It was like walking through a carnival.

Now all that had changed. Women pushed babies in carriages, old men talked and walked around, doing nothing in particular. A few younger men were out, but they were in the minority. Granddaddy could not find a parking space, so he decided to drive to Aunt Megan's store. She was Granny's mother's brother's wife. I couldn't keep up with what all that family stuff meant, but she was my Aunt Megan and that was good enough for me. Plus I liked her store.

It was a second-hand store not far from the square in a poor part of town. When I left the truck, I had to take care not to trip on the cracked sidewalks. We walked down three stone steps into the store. "Well hello there," said Aunt Megan, her smile revealing several missing teeth. Her hair, more black than gray, was tossed up in a bun. The shop had a shiny concrete floor filled with boxes of clothes. On faded wood tables sat dishes and other household goods.

In reply to Aunt Megan's greeting, Granny said "Howdy. We figured we'd stop here for a while since we were in town."

"Well, you're welcome any time. Have a look around."

They talked as they looked, catching up on people I'd never known were relatives. I decided to head upstairs, where the windows had steel bars. When I got there, the room smelled musty, like the inside of an old shoe. The room was at the level of the next street. I pretended I was in jail and looked out through the bars, watching people's feet as they passed. Shoes with hard soles clicked against the concrete sidewalk. I never could figure out why women wore high heels, especially when I saw them walking at ground level. I imagined the heel slipping through the bottom of a woman's shoe and stabbing her like a spear.

I walked downstairs and spotted a box of books on the floor. There I discovered a high school American history text from the 1950s. I wanted to buy it and asked Aunt Megan, "How much does it cost?"

"Oh, a quarter," she said.

"Granddaddy, can I buy this history book for a quarter?"

"Yeah. Reading's good for you. I never learned. Had to work hard on the farm all the time, help make a

livin' for my family. Wish I'd learned. Know a few words
– *d; o; g;* - *dog*. Not much more than that. Here's your
quarter."

I took the quarter and paid Aunt Megan, then I
took the book. Granny said, "Put that back in the car
before you lose it," and I did. When I returned, Aunt
Megan was saying, "Isn't it wonderful that a boy's
interested in reading like that. Jeffrey could go a long
way."

"Thank you," I said, and I felt proud. I'd read high
school books, even when I didn't understand all the
words. I'd try to put Granddaddy's life into a year in
history. Granddaddy was born in 1901, so I would look
in a history book to see what happened in 1901. I knew
about World Wars I and II and asked Granddaddy
whether he served. "No, was too young in the first one,
too old in the second. Worst war was that Civil War. I
knew some old people who were soldiers in it. Fought
for the South. My great-granddaddy Patrick, though,
fought for the North. His brother Louis was on the other
side. They were in the same battle and Louis got hurt.
They let Patrick come to his brother and take him back
home. Louis lived, but walked with a limp the rest of his
life. He outlived Patrick, though. Died a couple of years
after I was born."

I thought about how long ago the Civil War
ended - over a hundred years ago. I felt a connection to
that time - and to earlier times. Granddaddy knew
people who fought in the Civil War. They may have
known old people who knew others who fought in the
Revolutionary War. Go a few more steps and you'd find
people who knew Christopher Columbus. I once tried
tracing the chain back to the time of Jesus. It didn't take

many links. Why don't others see this? I wondered. Why do people act like no one ever lived long ago?

Granddaddy and I left the store. Granny stayed until we returned. She and Aunt Megan kept talking about relatives who were on the shadowlands of my consciousness. We were going to walk to the square. It wasn't far, just a block. It was a real square of shops, with the antebellum red brick county courthouse in the center, and the great clock on top of the cupola broken, frozen on 10:50. We passed the barber shop, but there was a crowd waiting and Granddaddy decided not to stop. So we stopped by the jewelry shop, run since 1947 by Granddaddy's second cousin Joe Martin. After he and Granddaddy talked, Mr. Martin would show me pocket watches and an old grandfather clock at the back of the shop. It reminded me of Grandfather Clock on Captain Kangaroo.

Then we crossed the street to the courthouse. It was huge, and I stared straight up, trying but failing to find the top of the columns. We walked up concrete steps to the hall inside, lined on both sides by offices. In the center was a candy stand run by Mr. Avery Wallace. He had been running that stand since the 1930s and looked to me like he had been living since the 1830s, with his prune face and bald head. A voice cracked beyond repair asked, "What can I get ya, young man?"

Granddaddy said, "Pick something out and I'll buy you a candy bar. Think I'll get one for myself, too." I picked out a Milky Way and Granddaddy took a Mars bar. He also bought a Coke for us to share.

We walked outside to some benches sitting under ancient oaks. I thought they must be older than the courthouse, the trunks were so thick. On the benches ten old men held cedar sticks, whittling them with knives. Several of them intoned "Hey, Bud," and one old man asked, "That your grandson there?"

"Yeah, that's Jeffrey."

"Glad to meet you Jeffrey," and I shook the hands of all ten men. The aroma of cedar filling the air smelled like wood must smell in a house in heaven. Cedar shavings floated to the ground, hypnotizing me. I was in another world, of people doing something just because they wanted to do it, not because they had to. I wondered if I would live in such a world when I was old.

I remembered that these men were old. Granddaddy told me last year that one was ninety and that most of the others were in their seventies and eighties. Some of them would not live much longer. Two of the men who whittled last year were dead. I overheard one man telling Granddaddy about another death in the past month. "Just dropped dead cutting the grass. Wife found him. So sad. He was about the youngest of us - sixty-seven."

I tried not to think about Granddaddy's being old. I also hoped the men would keep whittling year after year, that others would come and whittle so the benches wouldn't be empty when I grew up. I didn't want part of heaven to pass away. I watched Granddaddy's face, saw the wrinkles grow clearer in the shade trees' shadows. He was negotiating with one of the other men to sell one of his pocket knives, and they agreed for five dollars. Then he told me, "Let's walk about a bit and find some lunch."

We walked the entire square and could not find a place we liked, so we turned back toward Aunt Megan's store. On the same street we found a sandwich and hot dog shop, and there I ordered a hot dog. It was wonderful, the best hot dog I ever had - on white bread, two split dogs, tomato, lettuce, salad dressing, mustard. I felt as warm as the food digesting inside me.

We walked another block, crossed another street, and found an old variety store about to close. Granddaddy discovered some matchbox dogs - plastic dogs in boxes with the name of the breed on the box. They were a dime apiece. Granddaddy picked out a beagle. I took a beagle, too, but I was also surprised to find a white Spitz. I had to buy it. I named it "Fuzzy." The beagle's name I could figure out later.

As we left the store, I took my dogs out of the boxes. They were so shiny the sun's reflection from them blinded me.

We found a grocery store with some cans of soup, spam and Vienna sausages on a table on sale half off. The cans had been dropped, bent, but seemed okay. Granddaddy picked out six cans of Vienna sausages and bought them. I expected he would share some with me soon.

Back at Aunt Megan's store, we said our goodbyes and left for the IGA grocery store on Mason Boulevard. Granddaddy knew the owner and it was a popular spot with older people in Randallsville. Time was moving on toward late afternoon, five p.m., and I knew the day in town would soon come to a close. I examined the fresh fruit and vegetables and checked the items on the shelves in each row. I wanted to savor every moment. The store and everything in it were part of those sacramental moments, those images of something in eternity I couldn't quite grasp. I wanted to hold each moment in my head, keep it as an heirloom, like the book I had bought today that I would set on the table by my bed.

    With groceries bagged and in the truck, we got in. I asked Granny if I could sit in the bed, and she, with some reluctance, agreed. I lay down in the hard metal bed. I did not feel sick. I just wanted to close my eyes.

CHAPTER 9

As I walked through Granddaddy and Granny's field as a middle-aged man, I smiled, with childhood memories of that same summer warming me in spite of the cold. Low on the western horizon a dark line of clouds drifted in. I wanted to reach The Thicket before snow or sleet came - but the memories kept flowing.

I remembered how crops in the garden started to mature, and red and ripening tomatoes began to dot the windowsill over the kitchen sink. The shells of beans and peas filled out, and Granddaddy, Granny and I picked them. Granny and Aunt Jenny would shell them or break green beans with a snap. Corn grew taller than my height, and even Granddaddy would disappear between the rows. Cucumbers helped to fill salad bowls, and ripe cantaloupe was on the table at every breakfast. Watermelons grew at a record pace. Every raindrop and every ray of sun brought life and growth.

I lived in these daily routines, hedges against

change and death. But Death would often sneak into my thoughts like a snake sneaking into a hen house to swallow eggs. Death hid in the safest of rituals, coiled and ready to strike.

When I was a child, the second Tuesday in July offered me a special treat - my grandparent's monthly trek to the big flea market on Maiden Lane in Randallsville. But before they got there, Granddaddy and I needed haircuts. After dropping Granny off at Aunt Megan's store, we drove to the Andrews Barber Shop on the square.

The barber shop was one of my favorite places. I was fascinated by the striped pole outside and wondered what it had to do with cutting hair. I had been going there for three years, and the old Coke machine was in the same corner, the same photos were on the walls, the chairs and tables were in the same places. The calendar changed from year to year, but it was always the same type of calendar - a Rexall Drugs almanac, the same kind that hung above Granddaddy's bed.

Mr. Andrews was in his sixties, with short, black hair that had just begun to gray. He was tall, and towered over both me and Granddaddy. He had opened his barber shop at that same location in 1946, although he had been a barber since he was in his twenties, working at other shops around town. He was a fixture on the public square, as stable as the courthouse cupola.

As Granddaddy and I walked into the shop, Mr. Andrews said, "Well hello there Bud. Hi, young man. I guess it's been a month."

"Hi folks," said Mr. James, the other barber. I never knew their first names.

"Okay, young man," Mr. Andrews said. Come on

up here, and we'll take care of you. You want a flat top again?"

"Yes sir," I said.

Mr. Andrews wrapped a sheet around me to protect my clothes from falling hair. Then he added a collar.

Mr. Andrews noticed my discomfort and asked, "Too tight for you? Here, I'll loosen it a little," and it was better, though still uncomfortable.

The chair, however, was great. If chairs were made in heaven, this would be one of them. I sank down into it. If I didn't have to hold my head up, I would have fallen asleep.

The haircut also felt good, especially in the summer. I figured with a flat top the wind would blow between the hairs, creating tiny wind tunnels that would cool my head.

I heard the whirr of the electric clippers. Mr. Andrews knew how to use them without pulling hair, and I didn't feel any discomfort except around my ears. The space between the top of my ears and head was narrow, and the clipper blades had to fit between them. Mr. Andrews negotiated the narrow passageways with skill, and the small ordeal was soon over.

The rest of the cut went quickly. Mr. Andrews liked to talk as he cut.

"You ready for school to start?"

"No, sir! I wish summer could last forever!"

"I think every boy who comes here says that. But you'll see your friends again in the fall and learn some new things at school. And you get off Saturday and Sunday. Christmas will be here before you know it."

I thought barbers had a different sense of time

than other people. I remembered getting my hair cut in February during a cold spell. It was cloudy, but since it did not snow or ice, I still had to go to school. It was so cold I could not play outside very long.

"How do you like this cold weather, young man?" Mr. Andrews had asked me.

"I hate it. It's dark, it's cloudy, and it won't snow, so I don't get out of going to school. It's just bad."

"Snow's not good. Makes people slip on the highways and have wrecks. Yes, it's dark and cold now, but that just makes you appreciate more the good weather coming in spring. You know, in a little over a month, people will be plowing their gardens again."

He had made it sound as if spring were around the corner. And when March arrived, I heard Granddaddy fussing again that L.T. was drunk and had forgotten to plow his garden, and I finally understood what Mr. Andrews had meant. February had passed like a fast car on Randallsville Highway, and spring already arrived. The weather was getting warmer. Daffodils dotted the front yard and their patch in the field.

What was the barber's secret? Had he seen so many seasons pass that they flashed by like lightning? Perhaps time didn't affect him like other people. That would explain why things remained the same in the barber shop. Did barbers understand eternity?

The memory faded, and I was back in the barber shop in July. Mr. Andrews had just finished cutting my hair. He held a mirror in front of my eyes and asked, "Is this about what you wanted?"

"Looks good," I said.

Then Mr. Andrews picked up a machine that massaged a person's back and neck. I had tight muscles from holding my head in one place too long. The machine loosened my knotted neck and back muscles. Mr. Andrews kept it moving around the neck, shoulders, and back for at least a full minute, but I always wished the massage would last longer.

Mr. Andrews pulled off the sheet, and I got down. Granddaddy would pay for both our haircuts before we left. Mr. Andrews asked me, "Do you want something from the drink machine?"

"Yes, sir. A Coke." Mr. Andrews took the key he had to the machine, unlocked it, pulled out a glass bottle of Coke, and gave it to me. "That's your gift for the day, young man."

"Thanks a lot, Mr. Andrews!"

"You're quite welcome. Bud, it's your turn."

Granddaddy walked up and sat in the chair. "Same as before, Bud?" the barber said.

"Yeah."

"How that's garden of yours doing?"

"It's been too dry. I water it every day, but that ain't good as rain. Stuff's gonna start dyin' if it don't rain soon."

"We'll get some rain, Bud. Big thunderclouds in the sky every day. They just rain somewhere else. One day one of those clouds will be right over your garden."

"I hope so, Mr. Andrews."

Mr. Andrews finished Granddaddy's haircut. "That'll be $3.00 for the two of you." Granddaddy pulled out three one dollar bills and gave them to Mr. Andrews.

"Thanks for coming. See you in a month, Bud. Young man."

We left, picked up Granny, and drove to the Murphy Heights Shopping Center parking lot where the management set up tables for the flea market every Tuesday and Wednesday.

There were six rows of tables that seemed to go on forever. There people would bring stuff to sell. Much of it was junk - worn out tools, faded clothing, empty bottles of perfume and other trashy things. But now and then in the midst of all that junk a person could find treasure. I walked with Granddaddy down each row, looking to my left and right. I surveyed the material on each table, looking for books or other items I liked. At first there were slim pickings despite the overflowing tables.

Granddaddy stopped at Jim Morton's table. Mr. Morton was a thick, heavy man with close-cropped gray hair. From his accent, I figured he was a Yankee. He had been a soldier in World War II and liked to tell stories of fighting with Germans at the Battle of the Bulge. "I'm telling you, that was a mess. Krauts all over the place, coming out of nowhere. We were damn lucky to make it out of there alive. Here, take a look at this German helmet."

Every time I went to the flea market, that helmet was on Mr. Morton's table. He wanted fifty dollars for it - that was a lot of money. Granddaddy would have to sell fifty big watermelons to get that much. In the portion of the helmet that covered the forehead was a bullet hole. "Yep," Mr. Morton said, "found it on a dead Nazi. Took it home as a souvenir. Army didn't like that, but I didn't get caught. Try it on, young man."

I laughed. Mr. Morton had never invited me to try on the helmet before. I took the helmet and put it on, but it was too big for my head and sunk down over my eyes. Then Granddaddy tried it on. It fit.

"How do I look?" Granddaddy asked.

"Scary," I answered. We both laughed. Granddaddy took off the helmet and returned it to the table.

"Take care, Mr. Morton," Granddaddy said.

"You too, Bud. Young man. Anytime you want to come by and look, you're welcome."

As we passed by the other tables, my mood darkened. I couldn't get my mind off the helmet with the bullet hole. I knew Nazis were bad, and that it was probably a good thing an American soldier killed the enemy. I thought about the Nazi soldier, alive and well and healthy one moment, dead the next. I imagined the man's brains splashed on the inside of his helmet, gray mixed with red. I did not see any stains on the helmet when I examined it. Mr. Morton must have washed it. Maybe traces of the soldier were still there. I chilled at the thought of my head touching the remains of a dead man.

I struggled to focus on the items on each table. One table had two rows of paperback books for a dime apiece. Most of them were books with pictures of men holding partially undressed women with large chests. I also found a copy of H.G. Wells' *The War of the Worlds* and an *Encyclopedia Brown* mystery. Granddaddy had given me a dollar to buy whatever I liked today. I paid, took my change, and kept looking around.

Granddaddy had stopped by a table full of knives. He was always searching for new knives and sometimes would bring some of his own to sell or trade. I did not understand the fascination. What could you use pocket knives for other than whittling? I tried to carve soap with a kitchen knife once, because a book said that carving soap was easy to do, but I discovered that it was easier to cut the end of a finger than a bar of soap.

I heard Granddaddy's loud voice: "That durn knife ain't worth twenty dollars."

Then another old man's voice. "It's worth more than that. Try buyin' this new for anything less than fifty. You won't find it any cheaper, Bud. This knife's a bargain."

"I'll give you my knife and ten dollars for it."

"Heck no, your knife ain't worth two dollars, much less ten."

Granddaddy walked away and joined me. He was mad. "Durn crooks, tryin' to rip people off. They ought to go to the penitentiary for that."

Whenever I heard Granddaddy talk about bad people going to the penitentiary, I imagined it as an underground dungeon where people were locked in stone rooms, water condensing and dripping from the walls, rats crawling over a filthy floor. I vowed I would not do anything so bad that it would get me thrown in the penitentiary. It was worse than being in the city jail in Randallsville. I once overheard Aunt Jenny talking about Granddaddy getting drunk when he was young and being taken to jail and how Aunt Liz had gotten him out.

I had heard stories of Aunt Liz's kindness, but she died of cancer before I was born. Granddaddy told me about her funeral in Nashville, how hundreds of people had come to the church and flowers were lined across the front and sides of the funeral parlor. That reminded me that Granddaddy and Granny were older than Aunt Liz had been when she died. A lot older. Again, I tried to think about something other than death, but my thoughts returned to Granddaddy's drinking.

I had never seen Granddaddy drink. I was glad he stopped. The preacher said drinking was a sin that would send a person to hell. Granddaddy's stopping drinking gave the devil one less reason to get Granddaddy.

Granddaddy once had another bad habit - he told me he used to smoke cigarettes when he was young. "Nasty habit. I stopped doin' that long time ago." The preacher never said much about smoking, since half the men in the church would sit smoking on the porch benches after services. I wondered if the preacher would say anything if they were sitting on those same benches drinking whisky.

We reached the middle of the second row. There I found a table full of treasure. Old coins were laid out in glass cases, snug in their white cardboard and plastic folders and laid out by date and coin type. Pennies were on top, then nickels, dimes, quarters, half-dollars and dollars. There were other coins too - ten and twenty dollar gold pieces. They shone yellow in the sun, looking valuable. My mouth fell open when I saw the prices on the packets: $150.00, $200.00. I never even dreamed of having that much money.

I had eighty cents left and was glad that I wouldn't have to pay any tax at the flea market. That made sense to me. I did not understand why someone would charge ten dollars for an item and then add in the tax. Why not list the item's price including the tax? That way it wouldn't seem like you were paying extra.

I found two coins I wanted - wheat pennies. I always collected the wheat pennies I found in my change. Because they had a different design on the back, they seemed older than they actually were. At the table, I found a 1909 for thirty cents and a 1910 for twenty cents. I approached the man at the table and said "I want these two."

"Sure, young man. Fifty cents. Nice to see you've started collecting coins. I've been doin' it forty years; wish I'd started young as you. Hope you enjoy 'em."

"Thanks, sir," and I put the coins in my jeans pocket, trying not to bend the folders as I walked. I caught up with Granddaddy, who had bought a knife at the next table. "Look at this knife, Jeffrey. Looks good, don't it?"

"Yes, sir," and I was impressed. The blades were encased in brown plastic with the color of hardwood. The two blades looked polished and oiled. Granddaddy took a piece of paper and showed me how the blades would cut it clean in two.

"You find anything?"

"These coins," and I took them out of my pocket and showed them to Granddaddy. He looked at the dates. "1909, 1910. I was eight and nine years old then, livin' over on Mr. Crowder's place. I had four sisters, one older, three younger. Tess was the oldest. She was fat. Died five year ago. Had diabetes. Her man, Tennessee Jim Watson, gave her shots every day."

"Every day?" I said. "That would hurt."

Granddaddy frowned for a moment, then said, "She had to have them to live. You're willin' to hurt a lot if you want to live. She was a mean old woman, though. Beat her boys with a radiator belt. They both ran off soon as they were old enough. One lives up in Pennsylvania, the other boy's in California. Both grown and married now. Billy in California's been married five times. Guess his mama ruined him."

"That's a long way away for them to move. Why was she so mean?"

"Don't know. Always was. Daddy tried to beat it out of her, but it just seemed to make her worse. When she was a girl she'd flip her sisters' ears until they turned red. Got a beatin' for it too. Still kept doin' it."

I considered my own temper, hot as the wood stove full of burning coal in winter. I remembered when R.J., a boy who lived a few yards down the Randallsville Highway, came over to play. R.J. told me that my Uncle Lawton looked weird. My face turned bright red. I picked up a stick and began to beat R.J. until Granddaddy pulled me away. R.J.'s mother came over and said, "You keep that crazy boy of yours away from mine or I'll call the sheriff." Granny got mad, said, "I bet your boy put him up to it!" R.J.'s daddy had to pull his mama away, and Granddaddy had to pull Granny away. It was up to Aunt Jenny to take care of my whipping. I had to pick my own switch.

I focused on Granddaddy as he looked over some old tools. I thought of how badly Granddaddy treated Granny. Even though he never hit her and only hit me that time I threw mud balls at him, the evil was still there. Could evil be passed on? I didn't remember my mama, but I supposed Granddaddy's temper had been passed on to her. And Granddaddy's granddaddy and great-granddaddy must have had bad tempers too. How far back did it go? Granny had always said that the Irish were hot-tempered. Were my ancestors hot tempered 2000 years ago? Was I cursed to have a hot temper too?

I was polite around adults, but around other kids, I felt angry and superior. They never talked about history and science. All they cared about was winning ball games at play period. Sometimes I wished I could be away from them to read on my own instead of going to school. It was already July, and I knew that in two weeks the sales for school supplies would start.

I took my mind off the approaching threat of school and followed Granddaddy to the other tables. I spent another quarter on a picture book about the planets and that left me a nickel. I could find some candy to buy later.

After the flea market, we went to the IGA store. I wondered why the more I wanted to freeze time the faster it seemed to pass. I looked up at the clock in the store. It had a large face and big hands. I could see the minute hand move, which surprised me. I knew the hands must move, and I saw the second hand go round its constant circle. But seeing the minute hand move? I wondered if time were speeding up before my eyes.

When we arrived home, I enjoyed a late supper of meatloaf, mashed potatoes and gravy, and black eyed peas. The only dessert was ice milk, which Granddaddy and Granny loved. I tolerated it. It was cold and sweet, but not like ice cream. I crunched ice crystals as I ate, and the taste was like water mixed with milk and a little sugar. "How'd you like the flea market today?" Granny asked me.

"I loved it. I bought two coins and three books."

"You're goin' to read them, ain't you?"

"Oh, yes, ma'am. I love to read."

"Good. You know school starts in about a month."

"Yes ma'am, but I don't want it to start so soon."

"Boys and girls never do. I had to stop goin' to school when I was twelve. My mama died and I had to help Daddy take care of my sisters. Be glad you're goin' to school and keep at it."

"I will."

After supper, I sat outside in a glider with Granddaddy. He turned to me and asked, "How would you like to take a long bike ride tomorrow? R.J.'s mother said she'd let him go. Your granny apologized to her, and she's feelin' more friendly now. Don't go beatin' him with a stick again, Jeffrey."

"No sir. I sure won't."

That night, snug under my sheet, I had a vague sense I was about to dream something unpleasant. I couldn't make the thought more specific so I went to sleep and had a pleasant dream about buying books and old coins.

CHAPTER 10

As I opened my eyes to cold drizzle, the memories of childhood faded for a moment. I walked faster, wondering if my entire life had been a flight from reality. Then I remembered that bike ride I took with Granddaddy. It was a memory I could relish.

The morning after the trip to the flea market, I got up at seven sharp. I picked out a pair of white shorts and a white tee shirt to reflect the sun. After breakfast, I put suntan lotion on my legs, arms, neck and face. Then Granddaddy and I went outside. He did not bring water since he had no place to put it. We would buy drinks when we stopped at the country store, about six miles along.

We walked to the garage and pulled out our bikes. Granddaddy worked on old bikes and fixed them.

His bike had a heavy frame. It was a 1940s model with 26-inch tires. I rode a new bike I received for my birthday. I just graduated from a sixteen-inch to a twenty-inch. I rode it around the yard, rode in circles around an abandoned gas station near the intersection of Bramble Road and the Randallsville Highway, but I wasn't allowed to ride more than a half mile away by myself. Bramble Road was a gravel road, narrow and winding. Cars would fly around curves, often in the middle of the road. Randallsville Highway was too full of traffic for me to safely ride there by myself.

Granddaddy and I sat in the gliders and waited for R.J. to come. Soon he arrived on a beat-up bike with twenty-inch tires. R.J. was poor. He was not trashy, though, and avoided dirty words. He lived down the road with his mama, who was nice most of the time, and his three-hundred-pound daddy, who was mean most of the time. They also owned a mangy bulldog, who was so persistently mean that I didn't often visit them. Their house had a playroom in the attic that was a nice cubby hole where R.J. and I could play with matchbox cars or with a space ship we pretended to launch to a mysterious planet.

Although R.J. rarely came by - once every other month was common - I was glad to see him. Today I walked over to R.J. and said, "I'm sorry for hitting you last time. That wasn't right."

"Well, I said mean things about your uncle, but I didn't mean nothin' by it. I like your kinfolk. Your uncle's kind of neat in his dark sunglasses and bald head. And he's funny, but in a good way."

"You want anything to drink before we go?" Granddaddy asked R.J., and we went inside for a glass of water. When we came back, Granddaddy asked, "Well, are we goin' anywhere or not? Let's go!" and we were off.

The first part of the trip was treacherous, for we had to ride a half-mile down the Randallsville Highway. We rode around the curve on the gravel drive past the sugar maples and stopped at the intersection. Cars and trucks flew by. Granddaddy was in the lead, watching for cars, and in about two minutes he found a clear spot. We turned right on the highway, making it halfway before the first group of cars came.

Granddaddy didn't like to ride when cars were coming. He would listen for them, and when he heard one, he would have us pull over and stop. We waited for the vehicles to pass and start up again. We all waved at the drivers. Most waved back.

We only had to stop three times before we reached Farris Road where there was not as much traffic, and we could enjoy the breeze from riding. The wind rushing by us was so loud that we couldn't talk without shouting, so we only talked during rest stops. When one of us tired, we found a shaded area where trees overhung the road to stop and stand in the grass bordering the ditch.

R.J. and I chatted at the first stop, under some hickory trees, where we picked up hickory nuts and threw them as we talked.

"Who do you figure you'll get as a teacher this year?" R.J. asked. Both R.J. and I were entering fourth grade. This meant moving from the Gilead Primary to Gilead Elementary. The elementary school had been a high school many years before. It was in an old building made of rock.

"Don't know who I'll get," I said. "Don't know but one of the teachers there, and that's a lady who goes to my church, Mrs. Clarkson. I hope I get her. Last year I had Mrs. Pruitt. She was nice."

"You didn't hear 'bout what happened to Mrs. Pruitt?" R.J. asked.

"No, what happened?"

"She was cleanin' out her classroom for the summer, and she done kneeled over, dead. School janitor found her layin' by her desk. Heart attack or somethin'. She weren't even sixty yet."

"That's terrible."

"You weren't gonna get her again anyways. But I'm sorry she's dead too. She sure were a good teacher. Sure hope we git a good 'un next year."

"Looks like Granddaddy's getting on his bike again," I said. "Time to ride."

We took off out of the shade into sunlight. I felt dark inside despite the bright day. Mrs. Pruitt. Dead. How could it be? Heart just gave out on her. And Granddaddy would soon be sixty-seven. On the 23rd. He could die too. Please forget this news, I thought. It's a sunny day. Bicycle riding, Granddaddy and R.J.... I didn't have a chance to complete my thoughts, which seemed to be an omen, for Granddaddy's bike toppled over, and he rolled into tall grass in the ditch. Sick at my stomach, I felt as if I were riding in slow motion as I rode toward the scene.

Granddaddy sat up, and before I had a chance to speak, he said, "Dad gum rock! I hit one, and it threw my bike like a horse."

To my amazement, Granddaddy stood up, brushing himself off. The grass had broken his fall.

"Let's rest a bit," said Granddaddy.

I felt as if someone knocked the wind out of me, and I wondered if Granddaddy had told me the whole truth about the fall. I slowly began to feel better and was fine when we started riding again and Granddaddy went on ahead.

We rode around several curves, hugging the shoulder to avoid any hidden cars, and reached a steep hill. At the bottom, we stopped to rest again. None of our bicycles had gears. I thought gears were for cars. Bikes you just rode. But I had no doubt we would make it up the hill, especially since less than a half-mile past the hill was a country store where we could buy cold Cokes.

It would take fifty yards for us to get up to speed. I pedaled as fast as I could. Then we reached the base of the hill. I was surprised that a bike that was going so fast could slow down nearly to a stop just like that. My muscles ached. Granddaddy was still pedaling hard and was well ahead of us, and I wondered whether his old heart could take it. We made it to the top and stopped to rest and sat down in the ditch, careful to watch for poison oak and for snakes. R.J. told me, "Last Sunday I got saved."

"At church?" I asked.

"From my sins. Jesus saved me."

"But you're too young to be saved. You don't have any sins yet."

"Not what my preacher said. He said we all sin, and it was time to be saved. Said to ask Jesus to forgive us and accept him as our pers'nal savior. And I did. So I'm saved. Then I got baptized."

"You can't be saved before you're baptized," I

said. "You're baptized, then you're saved. But you have to be twelve anyway."

"No, you don't. I'm saved, and I won't never fall neither."

"How do you know? You might kill your teacher one day and go to hell."

"Even if I did I'd repent and still be saved."

"Well, my preacher said the Baptists are wrong on that 'once saved, always saved.' He said they're wrong to say you're saved before you're baptized. He said Baptists weren't worshipping in the true church, and God would send them to hell."

"But my preacher said you Church of Christ folks believed that you can work your way to heaven. He said people who tell themselves that are bound to go to hell."

"Yeah, but how would he know?"

"Your preacher's wrong. He don't believe the Bible."

"Well, your preacher don't ever read the Bible."

"Boys, stop it!" Granddaddy interrupted. "Let's get on our bikes and go to that country store."

We agreed to that and rode to the end of Farris Road, turned right at Sawdust Road, and made it up and down a more gentle hill to where we could see the store sign – "Benny's Country Store." There was a Coca-Cola logo on the window behind the gas pumps. Best of all, there was an "OPEN" sign in the door. We parked our bikes in the gravel lot and stepped inside.

This time I bought an RC Cola. Granddaddy liked Diet Rite. I kept trying to like it because Granddaddy did, but I never could get used to the taste. R.J. bought a Coke. The store owner pulled up some chairs, and we sat down.

"You boys havin' a good bike ride? It's a pretty day for it, that's for sure."

"Yes, sir," we agreed.

"Haven't seen you 'round here," he said to Granddaddy. "My name's Benny Hall. I've been runnin' this store twenty years. Where do you live?"

"Off the Randallsville Highway, other side of Farris Road. Fifteen years now. Farmed cotton there before I retired. I'm Bud Wilson."

"Pleased to make your acquaintance, Bud. You must live in old Billy Boy Benson's house. Real pretty house. You buy it?"

"Nope. Been rentin.'"

"Always wondered who lived there. Billy Boy's mother, Miss Betty, lived there, but she passed."

"Yeah, he built the house for her."

"Terrible way she died in there, though. Had a stroke, crawled out of bed. Pulled herself up long enough to reach the phone. They found her with the receiver in her hand. They had a time pryin' it loose. Tore Billy Boy up so bad, he couldn't bear to live there. Moved to Nashville. You must be a good man. He wouldn't rent to no scoundrel."

I tried to squelch that image of the dead woman grasping a phone, and I wandered around the store. Canned items were lined on wood shelves, clean and painted white. A red refrigerator, looking like a metal trunk, with rounded edges on the top, had a Coca-Cola logo on the front. In a section of the shelves near the front door sat cans of motor oil and brake fluid. I returned to listen to the conversation, and Granddaddy spoke.

"I try to be good as I can. Wife and I have enjoyed

livin' there with my grandson. He lost his folks when he was two-years-old; Jim and Ruth Conley."

"Yeah, I heard about that wreck. Tractor-trailer driver was drunk. Stuck him in the state penitentiary for eight years for that. Weren't half what he deserved. He'd been caught drivin' drunk five times before and had run into a house. They still wouldn't take his license away."

"If they hadn't put him in the penitentiary I would have taken care of it."

"And you'd been right too. Man's gotta protect his family. If the law won't do it, who else will?"

"That's right. Thanks for your hospitality. We'll be on our way."

"Much obliged for you stoppin' by. Next time you're on a bike ride or just happen to be drivin' by in yer car, feel free to stop. You'd sure be welcome."

"Thank you. Good bye."

We left, refreshed by our drinks. We turned onto McCormick Road, a rural road with hardly any traffic, where we passed woods and hay fields. The ditch was overgrown with brambles. The road grew more hilly, and we passed hills with patches of cedar and bare spots dotted with large limestone rocks. The land flattened, and we found a field with a flat outcrop of limestone that stretched for a hundred yards. It was dotted with prickly pear cactus and flowers that I had never seen. I yelled "Let's stop here to rest," and we stopped at a shady spot.

R.J. and I walked to the rock and pretended to be astronauts exploring an alien landscape. R.J. called me over and said, "Hey, look at this fish!" On the surface of the rock was a fossil fish, clearly marked. We wanted to remove it and ran to Granddaddy. "Come over here, see this fish! Can we get it out of the rock?"

"What you boys want? I want to stay in the shade." We pulled him away from the shade and dragged him to the fish. "Fish lived a long time ago, I reckon. Can't get it out. Rock's flat. Even with hammer and chisel it would be too hard. Just look at it a while. You can't take it home, and don't come back and try or you'll have rock fly in your eye and blind you."

We were disappointed but knew that Granddaddy was right. After a few more minutes of exploring, we returned to the shade to cool off. Then we went on our way.

We reached the end of the road and made a right onto Andrews Road. After a large curve a familiar building appeared. "That's my church!" I said. It looked different viewed from the back. There was a propane tank behind the Sunday school rooms. The field where we children played after church seemed smaller. Even the trees looked backwards.

I steered my bike to the left and stopped in the gravel in front of the church until my mind adjusted. Now things were where they were supposed to be. The others followed me, and we rested in the shade of the same tree under which Uncle Lawton and Aunt Jenny liked to park.

"This is nice," R.J. said. "My church has one of them paved lots, and I don't like it. Don't have no yard either to play in. Maybe I'll come by one Sunday night, and we can play outside."

"That would be good," I said, hoping that R.J. would come to see his error before he reached the age of accountability. Otherwise he would stay a Baptist and go to hell. I worried about my other granddaddy, the one I called Grandpa Conley. I didn't see him much, but I cared about him. He was Baptist, too and I knew he would go to hell if he didn't change and become a Christian. There was still time as long as he was alive. He had heart trouble. His wife, my grandma, was healthy as a horse. She was also Baptist. Maybe she would have more time to find the truth.

We found another tiny store up a dead end lane. This time we bought Cokes and packs of crackers for lunch. Granddaddy bought Diet Rite and a can of sardines. R.J. and I didn't understand how he could eat sardines, especially when it was hot. We ate and drank outside, threw our trash in a rusty metal trash can, and left the store. After a couple of miles, Granddaddy stopped in an isolated area. "I'm going to take a leak," he said. "You two'd better do it too before you bust from all this Coke." Granddaddy went off by himself, and R. J. and I found spots where we were sure no one could watch through a crack in the trees.

We returned to our bikes and rode a while on gently rolling hills, making a right on Two Mile Lane where we reached a creaky wood bridge. It was dark, even at two in the afternoon. Some people said the ghost of a woman who jumped into the creek and drowned haunted the bridge. They said she had been jilted by her lover. Here I could believe anything. We decided to walk our bikes across the bridge. The iron girders were rusty and looked like the spires of a haunted Victorian house. The cold from the water below had crept to the bridge, and we felt chilled, even on a day in the high eighties. We sighed together as our fear melted on the road across the bridge. We left the shade, rode into sun, turned left on Hendricks Road, and made the long peddle back to the Randallsville Highway.

It took six more miles. We reached the highway and turned right, watching for cars. There weren't any, so we rode a few hundred yards and turned right at the other end of Bramble Road, our journey almost over. Now we knew we could make it. I was surprised that Granddaddy could ride so far. He had to be strong. Strong enough to live a lot more years, for sure.

We finally reached the other side of the gravel drive at home. We rode past the corn, beans and peas in the garden on our right, straight to the garage, where Granddaddy and I stashed our bikes. R.J.'s mother was already there.

"Hope you had a good time. Time to go home, R.J. You'll need a bath. But you'd better get somethin' to drink first."

While R.J. was inside getting a glass of water, she placed his bike in the back of a rusty Chevy pickup. R.J. returned and got in the truck bed too. They waved goodbye and drove home.

All I wanted now was water. I drank two and a half glasses. It went down like liquid energy, and though my legs still hurt and I was awfully tired, supper tasted better than ever, and I was happy to have cold cantaloupe. There was real ice cream, too, for dessert.

I went to bed early that night, before nine.

CHAPTER 11

In the field, a much older version of me began to get cold. I realized that my memories would soon grow grim and chill me to the bone, so the feeling fit my mood. There were still a few good memories to go, however. I pulled my arms into my coat, walked to a brush pile near a limestone outcropping. I stopped at a spot under some small oaks where the leaves made a bed. I lay down there, covering myself with tall dry hay I found near the rocks. This reminded me of my favorite spot in my grandparents' house when I was a child. The day after the bike ride had been a good day to sit next to Granddaddy's bed, rest and listen to him play.

Granddaddy picked up his guitar, strumming each string to make sure it was in tune. He made some adjustments and began playing chords and picking out songs. He settled on *The Ballad of Floyd Collins*. I heard it many times before, but I wanted to hear it again. It was all about a young man, Floyd Collins, who enjoyed exploring caves in the 1920s. One day he was inside a small cave in Kentucky called Sand Cave, trying to discover a passage to Mammoth Cave. On the way out, a rock fell on his leg. His family found him a day later. People brought him blankets and food while trying to figure out a way to get Collins out. But every time rescuers would try to save him, rocks began to fall in the passageway, and they had to withdraw. Although they dug a cross shaft down to his location, by the time they finally reached him they found he had died of exposure.

It was a sad song, but I loved it. Every time I heard the song, I hoped they would find a way to get Collins out. The ending always stayed the same. I could not understand my fascination with the song. Was it because Granddaddy was singing it? What it because it was another sign of sameness in his world? I just knew I liked to hear it.

Granddaddy began to sing:
Oh come all ye young people and listen while I tell,
The Fate of Floyd Collins, the lad we all knew well,
His face was fair and handsome; his heart was
     true and brave,
His body now lies sleeping in a lonely sandstone
     cave.

I was lost in that Kentucky cave. I felt the excitement of entering the dark passage, shining a light to try to find something no one had seen before. I slipped on the slick sandstone floor but moved deeper into the cave, hearing the drip of water that indicated a new chamber. I found the chamber, but my lantern was getting low. I squeezed my body into a passageway. I dropped my lantern, which went out. Then I heard the sound of rock releasing itself from the ceiling. I tried to turn but it was too late. The cold, wet rock landed on my leg, trapping me in the shaft.

> *Oh, mother don't you worry, dear father don't be sad,*
> *I'll tell you all my troubles in an awful dream I had,*
> *I dreamed I was a prisoner, my life I could not save,*
> *I cried, "Oh must I perish within this silent cave?"*

I imagined Collins feeling a burst of searing pain followed by numbness. He waited, knowing people would miss him. Rescuers came - but how could they lift the large rock off Collins's leg without harming themselves? Collins was cold and damp. Hope began to seep away like the heat from his body.

> *The rescue party labored, they worked both night and day,*
> *To move the mighty barrier that stood within their way,*
> *To rescue Floyd Collins, it was their battle cry,*
> *"We'll never, no we'll never, let Floyd Collins die."*

Fresh blankets that men carried to him were wet within an hour. He sneezed, knew he had a cold. A cough followed, and he shivered with chill after chill rocking his body. Would they ever find a way to release him? He felt himself fading away, fading away....

> *But on that fateful morning, the sun rose in the sky,*
> *The workers still were busy, "we'll save him by and by,"*

> *But oh how sad the ending, his life could not be*
> *saved,*
> *His body was then sleeping in the lonely sandstone*
> *cave.*

The song ended with a warning about the Judgment Day:

> *Young people, all take warning from Floyd Collins'*
> *fate,*
> *And get right with your maker before it is too late.*
> *It may not be a Sand Cave in which we find our*
> *tomb,*
> *But on that day of judgment, we too must meet*
> *our doom.*

I felt more haunted than sad. I wondered why most ballads were dark. Dark, but filled with a longing for things to be different. Even the reference to judgment fit in. Life could end any time, so a person needed to be ready.

I asked Granddaddy to sing another song. Instead, he played *Home, Sweet Home*. I wanted to cry. I did not know all the words, but the title and the music made me sad. I wondered how I could be sad and happy - both at once. I felt as if home could be lost at any time. That everything I had known could pass away without warning. The thought of it broke my heart.

After that song, Granddaddy sang a song that was not so sad. *Gamblin' Man*. I knew Granddaddy didn't gamble, but he liked to sing the song anyway. I imagined the man in the song moving from state to state to find places to play cards or roulette. I had seen some spy movies on TV that showed people gambling. I was not exactly sure how gambling worked but Brother Noland said it was a sin. I liked the song because when I heard it

I felt whisked away by a musical magic carpet to distant lands - *I've gambled down in Mexico, and I've gambled up in Maine.*

Granddaddy stopped playing the guitar and put it back in its case. He wanted to play some records. He had a record player that could play old 78 records as well as slower ones. I was fascinated at how quickly the 78s spun and would sometimes get dizzy watching them. I knew where Granddaddy kept his records: they were in the third drawer from the top, right side, of his dresser. He pulled them all out. Most were old Victrola 78s, with a picture of a dog listening to the old-fashioned horn speaker. Below the picture were the words, "His Master's Voice." Granddaddy also owned a few 45s with their big holes in the middle, and a couple of 33s whose slow spin could put me to sleep when I heard a calm song.

We started with the 78s. There was one Granddaddy loved but I didn't. It was a slow recording by a band of the song, *When You and I Were Young, Maggie.* It was way too sad. The only reason I could bear it was that I knew lighter fare lay ahead. Granddaddy put the record on. I dreaded the beginning. After a short introduction by the band, a lone violin intoned the melody, which sounded to me like mourning itself. I thought about the title and heard time and youth slip away into the decay of old age and death. I recalled every loss I suffered. My brother's and parents' deaths seemed sadder now, and I wished I could remember them. My dead great uncles and aunts, great-grandparents and Fuzzy. All came back in a blur of loss. Fortunately it was over just before I needed to run out of the room, bawling.

Thankfully, Granddaddy decided to switch to some 45s. I heard a recording of *Babes in Toyland*, which raised my mood, and I began to forget about the previous moment. Then Granddaddy played a couple of Jimmie Rogers records, and finally a 33 album, *Sing Along with the Honky Tonks*. They were singing songs from the 1890s. To me, the old songs sounded cheerful. By the time I heard, *Hail! Hail! The Gang's All Here!* the memory of my sad mood was erased.

I got up and returned the records to their correct drawer. There I found a coin magazine, *Coin-age*, I had not noticed before. I asked Granddaddy if he could take a look at it. He did, and gave it back to me. When I opened it, I found that it had prices for American coins from all periods of the country's history. I looked up prices for the coins I bought and discovered I had been charged a fair price. I was amazed that prices for some newer coins were much higher than prices of older coins. In 1943, people used steel pennies. They were cheap, too. I resolved the next time I visited the flea market I would look for a steel penny. A 1943 copper penny, though, was worth thousands of dollars. I suddenly wanted to check Granddaddy's change for a 1943 copper penny, although I probably wouldn't find one.

I decided to go outside before supper. Over the years, uncut bushes had grown around trees, and where the branches were high enough, there were paths. I explored every path I could find, examining the plants, looking over the ground. I learned many years ago not to examine poison ivy. That was the worst itch in the world, and soaking in a solution of Blue Stone did not help that much. Those leaves, and poison oak leaves, I would avoid. Although I was afraid of snakes, they usually stayed in the garden or in the back yard around rocks. I never found one in the bushes.

At the junction of bushes and trees, there was usually a small clearing. Overhanging branches of small trees would form a roof of sorts that could keep me dry in case of light rain. If the rain were heavy, it would drip through the branches, and I would have to run inside.

Today I found an old steel can with the label rusted off. Most likely a soup can. I tried to squeeze it, but the metal did not move. I decided to drop it and leave it. I would find that can the next time I came here. I liked to find things in the same places. That helped keep my world straight and orderly.

Granny's voice called out "Jeffrey! Supper's ready!" I ran to the house and almost slid into the table. Supper was leftovers from dinner, but that was all right. There was still salad and French dressing left.

We watched the news at six. I liked to watch the world news. Granddaddy and Granny did not object but were not as interested. Each night the news had a chart on the screen with a body count from Vietnam. I figured that if the Americans were killing that many enemy soldiers they would win the war fast. I watched the news about antiwar protesters, but did not think much about them. Granddaddy's only comments concerned the length of their hair.

"Looks ugly. Long hair's supposed to be on a woman. Can't even walk on the street in town and tell from the back whether you're lookin' at a man or a woman. Durn hippies. What in the world's gotten into young people these days?"

Granddaddy said that every time he saw hippies

on TV. I preferred to focus on news stories about space flights and astronauts. I hoped I could go to the moon one day.

After the world news, the three of us sat outside on the stone steps. The mosquitoes were biting, and I kept smacking various parts of my body on which they landed. Once I wondered if old people like my grandparents had tough skin that could block mosquito bites, but when I saw Granddaddy and Granny slapping mosquitoes I knew the bugs could bite through their old skin too. Were there no advantages to getting old?

Lightning bugs began to fly. I had often gone out with a salad dressing jar, poked air holes in the top, and caught as many lightning bugs as I could find to make a lamp. I took it inside into my dark bedroom and watched the yellow flashes. When they began to fade, I opened the lid, stepped outside, and let the bugs out. I wished there were fewer mosquitoes and more lightning bugs.

"We'd better get inside before we get ate up," said Granny. We went in. Granddaddy turned on his radio, and I walked in the bedroom to listen. The phone rang, and Granny answered it. "Hello, Lou," she said. That was her distant cousin, Lou, who lived down Farris Road. She called every day, sometimes twice. More lady talk.

Granddaddy had two radios. One had transistors, and he and Granny used to listen to the news and Shop and Swap in the mornings. The other was a black tube radio. Granddaddy would listen to it with the lights out. The dial glowed yellow and the tubes inside glowed orange. They made me feel warm.

Granddaddy turned the station knob until he

found a preacher to whom he liked to listen: Herbert W. Armstrong of the Worldwide Church of God. I liked the brass music at the opening and close of the show, which to me sounded grand and inspiring. Armstrong's arguments were beyond me, but I enjoyed listening to the deep, sonorous voice of the old preacher.

After that show ended, Granddaddy listened to WSM for a few minutes. He liked the older country songs. He also enjoyed hearing Flatt and Scruggs, Grandpa Jones and Stringbean. He did not care for newer country singers. Granddaddy had once met Uncle Dave Macon, an early Grand Ole Opry star, when he was young, and he was among the people surrounding Uncle Dave when he visited Randallsville and played impromptu on the square.

Hovering by the radio, Granddaddy twisted the dial slowly, searching for stations. I liked to do this too, to see how far a station's signal would go. We found WWL in New Orleans, WGN in Chicago, WCBS in New York. So many miles away, I thought, and we are hearing them now, in this room in our house in Tennessee.

The soft glow lulled me toward sleep, and I made my way to bed. I had a familiar dream about exploring a cave and finding a new passage filled with stalactites and stalagmites. In this dream, I always got out safely.

CHAPTER 12

As the mature me stopped to catch my breath in the field, old memories kept coming like frames from a movie. I was pulled back to a day when Granddaddy and I played a game. That day, I was swinging on the tree swing when Granddaddy called my name. My feet dug into dust as I stopped the swing. "I brought some chairs out to the pine tree," Granddaddy said. "It's goin' to be hot one today. Let's sit in that little spot under the pine and watch the Highway."

We had done this before, but I never tired of watching different cars and trucks go by. Today, Granddaddy had something else in mind.

The pine tree was surrounded by smaller hardwoods that created a ceiling of leaves. The floor was made of soft pine needles. It was a cool place to sit in the hottest days of the summer.

Granddaddy said, "Let's play a game. We'll both guess the color of the next car that passes by. Whoever guesses right the most wins."

I said, "I guess the first car will be red."

"I pick blue" said Granddaddy. We both laughed when the car was a green Oldsmobile. We guessed again.

"White," I said.

"Green," said Granddaddy, and a white Plymouth passed by. "You win this time, but I bet I'll win next time."

We continued to guess and were soon tied at five-five. We decided to break the tie once and for all. I guessed "blue" and Granddaddy guessed "red." A blue Ford truck flew by that looked a lot like Granddaddy's truck. "I win," I said.

"Yep, you sure did. Let's keep looking at cars."

A Cadillac passed. "Rich men drive that," said Granddaddy. "Like my sister Allie and her husband Len. They buy a new Cadillac every two years. Trade the old one in. Len makes plenty of money. He's an interior decorator. They have a house down in Florida where they spend the winter."

I only saw Len and Allie at Christmas, but I liked it when they visited. I imagined visiting Florida with them, riding in their Cadillac. When they arrived, I would see the ocean and the waves. I thought of Florida as a faraway and exotic place and Len and Allie as rich lords living on a manor. Len wore a suit over a turtleneck shirt and Allie wore expensive dresses. I knew it was the kind of life I never had. But I did not covet their lives. I was happy where I was. Visiting Florida would be nice. Not living there, not even for the winter. This was home.

Under the pine tree, Granddaddy and I continued

to watch cars. A large trailer truck passed by loaded with cars on three different layers. "How can they stay up there?" I asked.

"I suppose they have 'em chained down so they don't move," Granddaddy answered. There were red cars, blue cars, white cars, all shinier than any cars I had seen.

A concrete truck passed, its cylindrical chamber churning the mix. Pickup trucks passed that looked the same whether they were Chevys or Fords. Motorcycles buzzed by with their loud motors and helmeted drivers.

"Those things are dangerous," Granddaddy said. "Lots of people get thrown from motorcycles. Thrown like a horse. That helmet won't help them - they fall, break their necks. Don't ever get one of those things. It will kill you for sure."

"No, sir," I said, though I thought it would be exciting to ride one fast, to feel the wind blowing hard against my face. Then I imagined riding down the gravel of Bramble Road, the tire striking a rock the wrong way. I had done that riding my bike. I was thrown from the bike. Lucky for me I only bruised my leg. If a motorcycle hit, going so fast - there is no telling how much damage that would do.

Mr. Denny passed by in his tractor. Granddaddy and I both waved. He waved back but was on his way to cut hay and couldn't stop. A few boys on bikes rode by, but they were not friendly and didn't wave back. Later, we saw a group of men in leather jackets riding on motorcycles. Some of them waved. I knew that a motorcycle gang had passed. It must have been a nice motorcycle gang.

Granddaddy stared off into space, as if he were

lost in his memories. "My first car was a Model T Ford. Bought it for $200. Most cars today cost more than $2000. Things sure are high. But that was a good car. They made 'em better in those days. Best car I had was an old Ford Packard. Had that eight years. The truck I have now's pretty good. Ford. Good for ridin,' good as a farm truck. Used it out in the field before I retired. I remember the days when most folks had to ride in horse and buggy. Only rich folks had cars. Farmers couldn't afford tractors. Mules would pull plows. Stubborn animals. I remember an old mule that refused to pull a plow. Daddy tried every which way to get that durn thing to move. Old black man from down the road came by. Said, 'I can get that mule to move. Get me a two-by-four.' And he took that two-by-four, broke it over that mule's head. Mule started movin' then."

I tried to imagine a world different from anything I knew. I had seen horses and mules, but Granddaddy had given up farming years before, and I barely remembered back to when he still grew cotton. Somebody else rented the field from Mr. Benson and owned the cows. Only the garden remained to link me to the old ways when people grew their food instead of going to the grocery store. I pictured Granddaddy as some kind of pioneer or settler. Sometimes I thought those times were better.

Granddaddy continued, "Things are easier now than they were then. Lots of people grew cotton in those days. They picked it day after day when it was ready, bale it up, take the bales to the square on wagons, and sell it. My daddy and I did that for years. Pickin' cotton was hard work. Cut your hand to pick it. Had to wear gloves in the hot sun, and your hand would still get cut.

You had to wear overalls in the heat. You think it's hot now - imagine all those clothes on you, you're hot and sticky, and you had to keep goin.' Only way you could make any money. I was lucky. The last three years before I retired I'd rent a machine to harvest cotton. That's the only way I got out of that work, boy.

"Back then, garden and canning didn't take care of everything. You still had to buy salt, things for the house. If we had a bad year in the garden we had to buy food."

"How did you get meat?" I asked, watching a truck filled with cows go by.

"We had lots of pork meat. Hogs. When it got cold, it was hog killin' time. Bunch of folks would come over to help. We'd help them when they killed their own hogs. Big job. We'd shoot the hogs with a rifle. They'd kick after they were dead."

"How can they kick when they're dead?"

"Reflex I guess. They'd do it, though. We'd hang them up, get the hair and skin off, gut them. Some folks would take the organs and use them. People were poor. They had to use everything. We'd get some country ham, cure it in a smokehouse. We'd make bacon, sausage, souse meat - you name it, we made it. There's nothing like hot country ham on a cold winter day. Like I said, hard work, but worth it."

Granddaddy paused as a tractor passed by. It was L.T., the old man who loved alcohol too much and who plowed and disked Granddaddy's garden every year. "Hey, L.T.," he shouted.

"Hey, Bud. On my way to the store. See you later!"

I figured that L.T. was on his way to the liquor

store to buy whisky. Granddaddy turned to me and said, "Don't ever drink that alcohol. You'll end up a drunk like L.T.

"Let's see, where was I? Meat - well, we had chickens too. Lots of them. Gathered eggs every morning, Would get pecked sometimes doin' it. Fresh country eggs are good for breakfast."

I was not convinced. I hated eggs. I hated their taste. I hated their scent. I hated how they looked. I thought they looked like something that came out of a sick animal's mouth. Granddaddy and Granny would eat eggs for breakfast most mornings, along with bacon or sausage.

Granddaddy continued. "We'd wring the chickens' necks. Twist 'em right off. Boy, would they flap their wings. Would run around if you didn't get hold of 'em."

"Chickens ran after they were dead? With no heads?!"

"Oh yeah. Would run plumb cross the road if you let them."

"So that's why the chicken crossed the road. Because he lost his head!" I laughed.

Granddaddy did not get it; he simply went on. "We'd pluck them and clean them, then we'd fry them. Fried chicken's good."

"Now beef, we'd bring the beef cows to a slaughter house and have them take care of the meat.

"Milk we got from cows - that milk we buy in the grocery store wasn't made in no factory. Comes from cows too. Then we'd have to get up at five every morning to milk. All the children. We grab each tit and squeeze the milk into a bucket. It was rich, buttery, not like milk today. We could make buttermilk out of it, then use that to make buttermilk cornbread or biscuits. We churned butter. That butter was better than anything store-bought today."

I sat quiet for a few moments. A convoy of ten cars passed by. Above, a jet plane flew high in the sky, leaving a white plume of cloud behind. Telephone poles and electric lines stood along both sides of the highway. They looked like alien ships from a hostile planet. I closed my eyes, smelled the scent of fresh pine needles. I pretended I had gone back in time, before airplanes, before cars had replaced horses, before tractors replaced mules. I imagined fresh air and wide fields, woods still unspoiled by the cans I constantly found by the road. I heard the sounds of wagon wheels creaking as families rode toward the square in Randallsville.

The sound of a tractor-trailer truck passing by interrupted my thoughts. I had a fleeting image of it smashing into a car, but I managed to return to my previous train of thought.

I figured I had it easy compared to folks in the past. Garden work wasn't that hard. In the old days I would be picking cotton and there would be no time left to play. There would be no way I could explore the world of my home like I could now. It was nice to ride in the back seat of a car to the square or to places with Aunt Jenny and Uncle Lawton. Lights that someone could just switch on at night were good, too. There would also be no "guess the car color" with Granddaddy. I assumed all wagons were painted black. No guessing there. Granddaddy said all Model Ts used to be black. I was glad cars were painted in different colors today.

"I reckon it's about time to go inside for dinner,"

Granddaddy said. He took both chairs and carried them to the garage. I followed him there and inside the house. Granny said to Granddaddy, "Mr. Conley just called. Said he was going to Wilsonville today to that hardware store that had the pipes for the stove."

"Why you get to talkin' to him about that. It's July. We won't be usin' that stove until October, at least."

"He knows the way up there, and he's wantin' to go this afternoon. Jeffrey needs to see his other grandpa too. Hardly sees him at all anymore. He'll be by at two to pick both of you up."

"All right. Guess it won't hurt to take a long ride in the country."

The pipes that connected the stove to the chimney had been worn over the years by smoke and age. Granddaddy was afraid that smoke would get in the house rather than going up the chimney. The pipes had to be replaced. Few places sold stove pipes any more, but Grandpa Conley knew of a shop in Wilsonville, a small town about fifty miles away. It was in hill country, and some people considered the people in Wilsonville to be white trash. Granddaddy figured they were just poor people who were a little poorer than other poor people. He never had a problem with that.

At 2:00 sharp, Grandpa Conley arrived as scheduled. He was driving a '57 Chevy. The car seemed small, especially in the back seat, but I fit. Grandpa Conley was ready to go, so he and Granddaddy got straight in the car. "Hello Bud. Good to see ya again. Hey, boy. Haven't seen you in don't know how long! You're going to be in which grade this fall?"

"Fourth," I said.

"Good Lord! Fourth grade!   I swear you're

growin' up too fast. Gettin' tall, too. All that food they're feedin' you must be makin' its mark."

"Guess so, Grandpa." I called my father's father "Grandpa" or "Grandpa Conley" to distinguish him from Granddaddy. "Granny" was married to Granddaddy." "Granny Marie" was married to Grandpa Conley. I thought it was funny that Grandpa Conley's first name was Elvis. I doubted Grandpa could swing his hips like Elvis Presley.

CHAPTER 13

Looking back on that drive with Granddaddy and Grandpa Conley so many years ago, I sat down again in the hay and started to cry. I knew that memories of death would haunt me soon, but the memories kept flowing like tears.

I remembered Grandpa Conley, who had died suddenly of a heart attack when I was fifteen. I was never as close to Grandpa Conley as I had been to Granddaddy Wilson, but the loss still hurt. I recalled the last time Granddaddy and Grandpa Conley spent some time together.

Granddaddy and Grandpa Conley got along well, but they did not visit each other often. Perhaps their visits reminded them of their dead children, my mama and daddy. When Grandpa Conley came by, it was usually because Granddaddy needed a carpenter or painter. Grandpa Conley did both kinds of work and usually took less than average wages for his labor. He was six years younger than Granddaddy and had, like Granddaddy, enjoyed the bottle a bit too much when he was young. He had stopped drinking five years before, and my memories of him were all from his later days.

The day came when Grandpa Conley and Granddaddy searched for chimney pipes to connect the wood stove to the chimney. Once we were on our way, Grandpa Conley started talking to me. "You know, before he met your mama, your daddy took a spell of wantin' to join the Navy. He read up on ships and submarines. Thought he would like to be on a submarine. Well, we let him join, and they put him on a ship rather than a submarine. Probably a good thing, too. He was so seasick he couldn't get out of bed. Most sailors get over it. Your daddy never did. They kept him on the ship, though. He enjoyed stoppin' at ports and meeting the girls. Almost married a girl in England. Don't know what ever happened to her. Your daddy was a good boy. So you'd better be a good boy too."

"He's all right," Granddaddy said. "Hardly ever gets in trouble at school, at least to hear him tell it. He makes good marks too."

"Good for you, Jeffrey. Keep it up. Hey, Bud, which part of the highway did you work for the WPA?"

"The underpass toward Randallsville, and then we paved about five miles north from there."

"I was fifteen miles away, toward Oakmont. On the part they paved over later. The old Randallsville Highway."

"Sad to see it go four-lane. I'm told it was an old

wagon road before the Civil War.

"They have to change everything, make everything *new*." Grandpa Conley frowned. "But I s'pose they needed those four lanes. It was gettin' to the point it took a half-hour to go the last five miles into Randallsville. Tryin' to stop progress is like stoppin' a runaway freight train. You step in front, and you'll be run right over. Life's that way. Old folks have to die and get out of the way so the young folks can take our place. It's one big cycle. That's why it's such a shame when young folks die, like Jim and Ruth. God durn drunk driver! I was gonna take my .22 and blow his head off, but Marie stopped me. Told me it wouldn't do nobody any good for me to go to jail or be put in t'electric chair. Made sense, so I put the gun away."

"You two won't die," I said.

Granddaddy and Grandpa Conley were silent for a few seconds. Finally, Grandpa Conley said, "I hope it's a long way off. But Old Man Death's gonna get us. Going to ride up in his black wagon, and we'll shake his bony hand. We all die, Jeffrey. Fact of life. I ain't in no hurry to die. Nobody is. I know your folks weren't. But we never know when it'll happen. You have to be ready, though, when it comes, because God's gonna raise us up. That's the good news. The bad news is if we don't do right and believe in Jesus we'll go to the bad place."

"That's right," Granddaddy said. "When you're old enough, Jeffrey, get baptized, and keep livin' a good life like your mama and daddy. Live yourself a good life, and you'll see 'em again in heaven."

"I'll sure try."

"Good. That's good," both my granddaddies said, speaking in unison. Then Granddaddy turned to

Grandpa Conley and said, "You go to the Baptist Church, don't you?"

"Yes sir. First Baptist Church of Lawrence. Go every Sunday."

"That's good. I go on Sunday morning, and when I can make it, Sunday nights and Wednesday nights."

"Doctor doesn't want me driving at night, so I just go on Sunday morning. Don't the Church of Christ think I'm going to hell for bein' Baptist?"

"Preacher will say things like that, but I don't know. I watch Billy Graham on TV whenever he comes on. He's a Baptist, but there ain't no way he'll be going to hell. So I don't think you're going either."

"Wish your preacher said as much."

"I believe most of what the preacher says if he can find it in the Bible," Granddaddy replied. "I worry enough about goin' to hell myself."

"Goodness gracious, Bud. You know you're goin' to heaven. What you done so bad that it'll send you to hell?"

"I drank a lot when I was young."

"I drank a lot when I was young and old. When I was middle-aged, too. Then I stopped, just like you did. Good Lord's already forgiven us for that. You need to believe in forgiveness. God's not some policeman waitin' to give you a ticket."

I interrupted. "My ears hurt."

"Pop your ears," Grandpa Conley said. "Do like you're yawnin.' We're going up and down big hills. Changes the pressure on your eardrum."

I tried to yawn, and I heard my ears pop. For a while it would be okay. Then they started hurting again, and I had to keep popping them.

I looked out the car window. We were riding through wooded hills. In the valleys were small houses with peeling paint. Some seemed to lack any paint at all. To me, they looked like shacks, and I could hardly believe people lived in them, though some stared out from doorways or windows as we passed. Were these the poor white trash that people had told me about? Granny didn't like me to use those words. She said when she was young some people had called her poor white trash, and she never used those words for anyone else.

I saw some black families in houses that looked as bad or worse. Granddaddy never let me use any bad words about black people, although I had heard them a lot in school. Granddaddy once told me, "They're folks just like us. Good Lord made us both from Adam and Eve. I don't ever want you sayin' anything bad 'bout somebody because of the color of their skin. A lot of black farmers helped us when we were barely gettin' by." I tried to follow his advice.

"Well, Bud, we're 'bout into Wilsonville. Such as it is," Grandpa Conley said.

The town stretched only three blocks before houses faded into fields of hay. A few shops dotted the side of the highway. Behind them were houses that looked better than those along the way. They were small, white, wood-frame homes, but their paint was not peeling.

We pulled into a dirt lot by Frank's Hardware and Fireplace Supplies. It was a large building for such a small town, rectangular, wood, much longer than it was wide. Several ceiling fans inside kept the air flowing. I thought the whirring sound would put me to sleep. An urge to explore kept me awake. The three of us reached a wall lined with fireplace fixtures and stovepipes of various sizes. Grandpa Conley had already measured the length and diameter of the pipes needed. Four pieces: One to go straight into the stove, another to go straight into the side wall to connect to the chimney, and a curved piece to connect the two. A round piece of metal with wavy edges would fit around the pipe in the wall to prevent smoke from leaking. I carried that piece to the counter. Granddaddy paid for them at the front of the store. "Any place to eat around here?" Grandpa Conley asked the clerk.

"Yes sir. A couple of places on the other side of the highway. A hamburger place and a place with good country food. Just keep your car parked here and walk. Not much traffic in this town. You won't have any trouble crossin.'"

"Much obliged."

The man was right. There was no traffic to speak of, and we crossed the empty highway. I wanted a hamburger. Granddaddy had no problem with that. "We get some country cookin' at home. Your granny ain't no good at makin' hamburgers. Your mama and daddy sure made good ones."

We entered a tiny restaurant with three tables. Only one of them was taken. The hamburgers were good. I had a big one with a thick slice of tomato, lettuce, and pickles, as well as mustard and mayonnaise. The only problem was flies that the owner kept trying to shoo away with a swatter. "Dad gum things come every day. Try to keep them out. Bet I killed fifty of 'em after closin' time yesterday. More of them every day. It's like a cycle. You cain't stop it."

"It's alright," Grandpa Conley said. "Your

hamburgers are sure good."

I stared at the ceiling fan. Flies come, flies go, I thought. People come, people go. An endless cycle. And we die like flies. Were my parents' flies in God's eyes? What about Granddaddy? Granny? Grandpa Conley? Uncle Lawton, Aunt Jenny? The great uncles and aunts? Me? I want things to stay the same. I want everyone to live forever. I don't want to die like my parents. We have to be better than flies, squished and replaced by other flies. The world just ain't right otherwise.

We finished our food and returned to the car. To me, the road seemed longer going back, and the curves seemed to go around on themselves. Were we really going anywhere? I knew we had to be. The scenery changed, the hills flattened, the houses had more paint.

"Hey, Jeffrey," Grandpa Conley said. "What'ya say you and Bud and Anna come over to our place. We'll let the women gossip in the living room, while the three of us go fishin.' How's that sound?"

"That sounds great!" I said. I fished with Granddaddy on Raymond's Creek and caught a few tiny perch I threw back and one catfish big enough to keep. Grandpa Conley had a boat, and he was planning to take it to the lake. He had life jackets, too, so I knew I could go.

"Well, I'll have to figure. Maybe one Saturday in the fall when it's not so hot. Alright with you, Bud?"

"Yeah, sounds good to me. We'll catch us some big bass."

I wanted to go out on the lake right away, but Granddaddy said it was too hot. Otherwise, the sun would cook me into a pot roast.

The rest of the trip home proved uneventful.

When we pulled up the drive, Granddaddy asked, "Would you like to stay for supper or have a drink of tea?"

"Nah, Bud, don't think so. Marie will give me hell if I get back late. Good to see ya 'gain, Bud. Jeffrey, you be good, boy. You're gonna do just fine. Bye."

"Bye, Grandpa Conley" I said, and I waved as he pulled off.

Hell and death. I thought about bugs flying in a circle around the outside light. Some got too close and fried themselves. I felt part of that circle, as if it were turning for me or for those I loved. I couldn't forget the images of hell that the preacher's sermon had conjured up, couldn't forget the fact that my parents were dead, couldn't forget that my grandparents were old.

When I got to bed at ten, I had trouble getting to sleep. The room spun around. This was not unusual since I had been in a car that sped up hills and around curves. But the spinning reminded me of circles and circles reminded me of what the man in the restaurant had said.

CHAPTER 14

As the memories of that long ago drive faded, my head spun as if reliving the effects. I opened my eyes, and my dizziness slowly disappeared. The wind kicked up again, and I tightened the hood on my coat. The earth seemed empty despite the passing of traffic on the Randallsville Highway and the rush of starlings as they left their perch on electrical lines crisscrossing the field. Sometimes I wondered what life would have been like if my twin brother had lived, if my parents had not been killed. I returned to that ninth summer of my life to the day Granddaddy, Granny and I visited the places where my brother and parents rested.

Early one Saturday morning I heard Granny call, "Get dressed and come to breakfast! We're going to visit the cemetery!"

My body jerked with a lurch of excitement. I remembered visiting my parents' graves, but if I had ever visited my twin Michael's grave, I had forgotten it. I found my jeans from the day before and a clean shirt, and quickly put them on. Breakfast went fast and by eight I was sitting between my grandparents in the cab of their truck.

We were visiting Michael's grave first, and rode over rolling hills for what seemed like forever. The longest trips I remembered were to Sears in downtown Nashville, thirty miles away. This journey was far longer, and I felt lost in unfamiliar territory with its strange roads and shifting scenery. We moved from farmers' fields full of wheat to wooded areas that shaded the truck. We crossed the bridge over Long Point Lake, and I could see fishermen's boats below. Some of them were moving fast, skidding across the water, leaving behind foamy white streaks.

Then, as my stomach started to turn sour, we made a left onto a dirt drive by a wood sign that said, "Crews Cemetery." Granddaddy said, "We're here!"

We left the truck and walked on grass filled with the morning's leftover dew. The graveyard seemed ancient, some standing stones so old that they were caked with green moss. Weathering had reduced others to scattered shards. On a few, the letters had worn off, and I was sad that perhaps no one knew who was buried there.

I followed my grandparents to a group of graves with the last name "CONLEY" inscribed in each stone. "This is where your daddy's folks are buried," Granddaddy said. "Look at those for a while, and we'll clean up 'round Michael's grave."

I was tempted to go to Michael's grave right away, but I saw Granddaddy and Granny brushing it off and decided not to bother them. I scanned the other Conley graves. One caught my eye.

ALVIN CONLEY
June 7, 1930-July 9, 1939

That boy was my age when he died, I thought.

Meanwhile Granddaddy had finished cleaning Michael's grave and had walked over to me. I asked, "Why did Alvin Conley die so young?"

"He was playin' 'round a mule-drawn wood cart loaded with logs. His mama warned him to stay off, but when she wasn't lookin' he sneaked right back out and onto the cart. One of the two mules pulling it twitched and the logs fell right on poor Alvin. They took him to the hospital in Nashville, but his head was all busted up, and he died that same night."

"That's awful."

"Yep. Sure was. You need to be careful and do what grownups say."

"Yes, sir, I will."

I recalled a time when I was five and went outside to play. Granddaddy had recently hauled out an old refrigerator and set it by the pear tree in the front yard. I was fascinated with opening the door and staying inside an enclosed space. One day I walked toward the refrigerator, located the handle, opened the door, and stepped inside. The hollow felt close and comfortable, so I closed the door, hearing it slam. I thought for sure I was safe, hidden from the world.

Almost immediately, the door opened, and

Granddaddy pulled me out. He yelled at me, "Don't you ever get into that 'frigerator again. Hear? You'll run out of air and die!"

Granddaddy's harsh voice frightened me and I started to cry. Then Granddaddy picked me up and said, "I just don't want you to get hurt. Me and your granny love you." I wrapped my arms around Granddaddy's neck as we went inside. Later, Granddaddy removed the refrigerator latch and filled the inside compartment with tools, leaving no room for a curious little boy.

I might have died then, I thought, and I trembled from a chill even though the air was still and hot. Then a strange question came to my mind: If that door had shut, and I ran out of air, how long would it have taken my heart to stop? I held my breath and timed it with my Timex. Thirty seconds. So it would have taken longer than thirty seconds. I was still calculating when Granddaddy interrupted me.

"We're at your brother's grave." Granddaddy took off his hat, and he and Granny both bowed their heads. I bowed as well, looking at the letters on the stone:

MICHAEL CONLEY
May 20, 1959-May 20, 1959
Our Baby

The sight of my own birthday next to Michael's name made me feel strange. Seeing the death date transported my mind to a place I was afraid to go. My thoughts raced ahead, out of my control. I imagined myself in a coffin, nothing left but a pile of bones and pieces of cartilage, my flesh rotted away years before.

Why did God let me live and not him? Why couldn't we have both lived? What would it have been like to live with a twin?

I dropped to my knees and looked at the ground behind the stone, a low patch of indented earth the only sign of a casket underneath. I lay down there, my head resting against the cold granite.

"What are you doin', Jeffrey?" Granny said.

"I'm trying to be with my brother."

"Get on up, Jeffrey."

"I just want to be with him a while."

Granddaddy walked over to my side, leaned down, and said, "Stay there, but just a few minutes - we have to go soon to see your parents' graves."

I didn't know whether Granny would agree, but she didn't say anything. I lay with my eyes closed, imagining shrinking, lying beside Michael's bones on the casket's ice-cold floor. I tried to talk with him, told him "I love you, brother, and hope you're happy in heaven. One day I'll meet you and we'll play together."

I heard a child's voice, maybe a boy about my age. I opened my eyes, but only the blue summer sky appeared. When I stood up, my grandparents were walking toward the truck, and I caught up with them.

"Are you all right, Jeffrey?" Granddaddy asked.

"Yes, sir," I said. I climbed in the cab, focusing on the window at the road. I willed myself not to look back when my grandparents got in and they drove away.

After traveling for about an hour, we stopped at a tiny, unpainted wood building with a hand-painted sign labeled "AUNT SUE'S COUNTRY KITCHEN." Inside were a few worn wood tables and chairs, and an old lady in a blue polka-dotted dress and her white hair in a bun seated us. "I'm Sue - menu for today's on the blackboard."

We looked up by the counter and saw a blackboard with a few items scrawled on it. There wasn't much choice other than meatloaf, mashed potatoes, butterbeans and cornbread. I didn't mind. I liked those things and preferred eating food I was used to. I had always been afraid of trying something new.

It must have taken a half hour or more for our meals to arrive, along with milk. When I tasted the food, I figured it had been worth the wait. Almost as good as Granny's cooking - but not quite.

When we finished, Granddaddy paid Sue, who rang up the bill at a dusty black cash register on the counter. On the wall there was a sign that said "Grade C." I didn't know what it meant, but the food was better than "C" - I'd have given it an "A."

We drove back toward Randallsville, cut over before we reached the town to the Randallsville Highway. There we drove another five miles until we reached Greenlawn Memorial Gardens. Granddaddy said, "I can remember when all this was farmland. I guess it was about nineteen and fifty-four when they broke ground for the first graves."

To me, any time before I was born was long ago. Since that cemetery was laid out five years before I was born, it seemed old. Granddaddy continued, "When your mama and daddy died, this was new and close to your Grandpa and Grandma Conley, so they decided your folks would be buried out here. They have these newfangled flat markers. I don't like 'em much, but they'll do, I guess."

We got out of the truck. Randallsville and Gilead

were both growing towns, and the cemetery had spread out over the years as more and more people were buried. Flowers were sticking out of pots and the rows of graves seemed never to stop. I knew I wouldn't remember where my parents' graves were located in the confusion of almost identical markers, so I waited for my grandparents to find their own way. They seemed to be arguing over the location of the grave.

"I think it's over there, by that oak tree," Granddaddy said, his hat hiding what I knew was a red face.

"No, it's not - it's by that tulip tree 'bout fifty yards to the left."

"Don't you tell me I'm wrong, woman. Jeffrey, come with me."

I thought Granny would tell me not to go, but instead she said, "Oh, go on, Jeffrey - you'll find out I'm right. Nothing like an old fool."

"Don't call me a fool, Woman. You know what Jesus said about folks calling people fools. They burn in a devil's hell!"

Granny grew silent, and I followed Granddaddy to the spot he suggested. We found graves of Millers, Joneses, Plummets, Randalls, but no Conleys. I walked toward the left, trying to find the place Granny had noted. Instead, about half-way between the two locations about which Granddaddy and Granny had argued, I found my parents' graves.

They had a single marker, with a carved scroll between their names. The inscription on the scroll read, "Together Forever." The names seemed like names of strangers to me.

James E. Conley
April 5, 1939-January 14, 1962
Ruth Ann Conley
March 15, 1941-January 14, 1962

Granddaddy and Granny arrived. They replaced some faded artificial flowers with a new set. We stood in silence. I wished I had known my parents, but I had no memory of them and couldn't really miss them. Maybe it was a good thing, I thought. If I had remembered them, it would have been too hard. An image formed in my mind: the photo on top of the piano at home of my daddy holding me as a baby. Mama was standing beside Daddy and me, and Mama and Daddy were both beaming. Then I pictured the accident, my parents' torn bodies, and wondered how they must look now, decayed in the grave. My stomach turned, and I stared at the silent sky, hoping to find some sign that there was more to a person than a skeleton in a casket.

CHAPTER 15

One of the scariest memories of my childhood began to haunt. In my whole life I had not known a night like that one. Like every other boy, I suppose, I occasionally had nightmares about falling or about monsters chasing me, ready to snatch me just as I woke up. But that night - a warm night in late July in the summer of my ninth year - was the sum of all horrors I had ever experienced. Every dream I remembered, and every dream was a nightmare. I was afraid to go to sleep, but my body forced me to fall asleep, only to fall into another set of terrors.

In the first nightmare, an old man with long white hair and a beard sat on a throne. In his right hand was a string attached to the earth, which he was spinning in a circle. He slung people off the globe, and they flew screaming into empty space. Their dead bodies littered space, and babies fell from the sky. The old man never grew tired of spinning the world. He enjoyed it. On his face was a malevolent smile. The face drew closer to me until I heard a deep, evil voice: "I'll sling you off one day, boy. Just like your daddy and mama. Don't think your granddaddy's safe either. I'm taking him next month." The smiling, leering lips were about to touch me when I woke up, too frightened to scream. I couldn't forget the dream and sat up for a long time before my tired body forced me back under the covers.

I dreamed again. I was walking outside on a dreary, cold winter day. The pear tree was bare. I walked past it to the side of the garage, looking for something - I had no idea what. A vague threat, as if something were about to pop out of thin air to attack me, chilled me until I shook. I closed my eyes, but the threat grew. I walked behind the garage next to the fence, which was covered with leafless vines. Even the evergreen plants were bare. Every step was like walking through thick mud. I didn't want to move, but was drawn forward. Something was waiting around the corner, something that I did not want to see. I imagined every demon and monster I had seen on TV. I turned the corner, my eyes unable to blink.

Something was hanging by the coal pile. A small tree stood there I had not seen before. A rope held the object up. I saw the side of what looked like a person's shirt. When I drew nearer, I found it was Granddaddy's shirt, the one he wore in the winter, blue, checkered with red. I could see the outline of Granddaddy's black Fedora hat that he wore in cool weather. Some force kept me moving, moving to the front of the man with Granddaddy's hat and shirt. I stopped, held in suspense, unable to move. The man hung with a hook through his hat. Then the head raised itself up and a grinning skull spoke with Granddaddy's voice, "Goodbye, Jeffrey. God's going to take me to hell."

I woke up whimpering. My heart was pounding so hard I wondered if a nine-year old boy could die of a heart attack. I started to cry. "I don't want him to die, God, please let him live. I can't lose him. I love him, God, please don't take him away. Don't send him to hell." Thus I cried and prayed myself to sleep.

The nightmares kept coming. There would be no mercy. I found myself walking in the field on a summer day. It was sunny and pleasant, and I felt nothing could go wrong. In the distance a man lay on the ground. It was Granddaddy. I ran to help. I looked down as his eyes rolled to the top of the head, unseeing. Granddaddy was dead. His shirt unbuttoned on its own. His nipples were almost as pale of the rest of his body. Skin, flesh and bone ripped apart in the center of the chest exposing a silent heart. I felt pulled to the heart. I put my hands around it. It was cold, as if it had been refrigerated. I tried to squeeze it, hoping it would beat again. It was rock hard, unmovable even when I squeezed as tightly as I could. The ground opened up and swallowed Granddaddy's body. A mound formed over it. I stood on the mound as a gravestone grew out of the earth. The inscription read:

David "Bud" Wilson
July 23, 1901-August 25, 1968

This time I screamed as I awoke. No one heard me. The bathroom doors were closed on both sides, and the walls were thick between my bedroom and my grandparents' room. "It's just a dream," I kept saying to myself. I had bad dreams before that didn't come true, dreams about Uncle Lawton dying in a plane crash, about Aunt Jenny being thrown from a horse - but Uncle Lawton never flew in airplanes and Aunt Jenny wouldn't be caught dead riding a horse. Dreams. That was all. Just dreams.

I got out of bed, went to the bathroom. Every step felt pregnant with threat. I crept back to the table by my bed, picked up my watch, and held it to the night light. It was 12:30 A.M. Good. After midnight, I thought. I decided that meant it was safe, and I would be able to sleep without nightmares until the sun rose. I was wrong.

I opened my eyes and found myself standing on a ledge. In the distance I saw the old, bearded man again, holding a book in his hand. A line of people were waiting to see the old man. It was Granddaddy's turn. A voice of thunder rang from the bearded man's red lips.

"You were mean to your wife. You yelled at her, cursed her. Made her cry. That was evil. You are evil. All the good you did doesn't make up for it. I won't forgive you. Depart from me, ye cursed, into everlasting fire, prepared for the devil and his angels. Go to where the worm dieth not, and the fire is never quenched. Go to where there is weeping and gnashing of teeth."

Then the old man's finger pointed at Granddaddy, who turned away and fell down, down, into an abyss. I found myself on another ledge full of molten lava. For some reason, my feet didn't burn. Below the ledge was lava, bursts of flame, the odor of sulfur. People were naked and stuck up to their necks in the massive burning lake. The screams of the damned were so loud I had to cover my ears. Then I saw Granddaddy.

His face looked the same as it had when he was alive. He was wearing his horn-rimmed glasses. I uncovered my ears and found I could only hear Granddaddy's voice. He was moaning and crying, talking to himself. "I didn't treat her bad, God. You're wrong. I tried to treat her right. You know that, Lord. I thought I might go to hell, but for something I did wrong. For the drinkin,' for slappin' my daddy, for being rebellious when I was a boy. Now I'm lost forever, in this hot, dark place. Not a drop of water to cool my burnin' tongue."

I tried to get off the ledge to comfort Granddaddy. There was no way down, so I shouted. No sound came from my mouth. I screamed a silent scream, and no one heard. Finally, I jumped. I fell, fell, fell, but not into hell.

My eyes opened and I found myself in bed, wide awake. I checked my watch again. 2:30 A.M. I prayed that the sun would come up before I had another dream. It didn't.

In the last dream I floated in darkness, talking with Granddaddy. Without warning Granddaddy's face began to shimmer and fade. His voice died in the darkness like an echo. Then the rest of his body shimmered. I tried to grasp it but my arms flew past each other in the air. A puff of wind hit my face, then faded away in the distance. Granddaddy was no more. Not in heaven, not in hell. On earth, his body was just a shell. But the Granddaddy I loved was gone for good.

I woke up and cried until one side of my pillow was soaked with tears. I turned the pillow to the other side and continued to weep. I got up and sat on the floor by the night light. It was unseasonably cool, but the light, with its faint yellow glow, brought me some comfort. I remembered the night before Easter Sunday, a night I had managed to forget. I had been watching Davy and Goliath, a Claymation show sponsored by the Lutheran Church. I loved the opening theme played by trumpets, the hymn, *A Mighty Fortress is our God*. We didn't sing that song often in the Church of Christ, but when I heard it, I always made the connection - the Davy and Goliath song.

Davy was a young boy and Goliath was his pet dog. They lived happily with his parents and sister. In the episode I had seen, Davy was playing with his grandmother in the attic, looking for interesting items. Later they played catch outside. It looked like fun. Grandmother looked healthy. She and Davy would have many more chances to play again in the future.

The next day, Davy was playing baseball with his pals. When he arrived home, his parents and sister looked sad. Davy asked, "What's wrong?" His father answered, "Grandmother died this morning."

The shock made my stomach feel like a rock. How could this woman die? She looked fine the day before. She wasn't hit by a car. Can a healthy looking person's heart stop that fast? Could my own heart stop that fast? I kept watching the show, hoping that there was some mistake.

There wasn't. Grandmother was really, truly, sincerely dead. Davy's dad talked to Davy about Easter and the resurrection, but that was no comfort to me. All I could see was death. To me, death was nothingness. You never saw the person again. That was because the person was gone. Dead like Rover, dead all over. When would I die?

I ran into the kitchen. Granddaddy and Granny followed. "What's gotten into that boy?" Granddaddy asked. I kept asking, "When will I die?"

CHAPTER 16

The images in my mind faded and the cold reality of my grown-up present intruded. I stopped at the edge of The Thicket and sat on a rock. I shivered in the cold drizzle, but bad memories flooded my mind so quickly I had to stop and rest. I covered my ears with my hands and shut my eyes, but the sounds and sights of the end of summer of my ninth year kept running through my mind - the summer Death seared my heart like a hot iron on raw flesh. Now the scars threatened to rip apart and tear me once again.

One day in mid-July, for a reason unknown to me, Granddaddy was riding his bicycle around the house on the grass. I saw him reach the side of the house by the basement door. His legs seemed to labor, then they stopped, and he fell down. I rushed to help him, but he got up. "Dad gum bicycle. Fallin' down like that. What in the world did it do that for?"

I took that question as a signal that I better keep clear and not mention the fall to Granny - nor to anyone else. At first I wasn't too worried. I had fallen off my own bike enough myself. Then at dinner something worse happened.

Granddaddy was eating a can of sardines in mustard. I had grown to like the taste, although I hated to bite into scales and bones. Granny and I were eating bowls of vegetable soup. Granddaddy said, "My arms are numb."

"Numb?" I asked.

"Yeah, it's like the feelin' went out of them, specially my left arm."

Granny walked over to him and said, "It's cool in here and you haven't been outside in an hour. You're sweatin' too much. You need to lay down on that bed in there."

"Don't want to lay down, woman. Ain't that bad."

Then he said something that tightened my throat. "Chest feels funny. Something sittin' on it. Maybe I ate somethin' sour."

"Maybe you oughta go to the doctor," Granny said. "Remember Mr. Hubert Jones from church. Last summer he said his chest felt funny, and he was havin' a heart attack."

"Told you, I ain't going to no doctor."

"Yes, you are. I'm callin' Aunt Jenny to pick you up."

Aunt Jenny worked for an accounting firm in Randallsville, but she lived near work and liked to eat lunch at home to save money. She was home when

Granny called and arrived in less than fifteen minutes. During that time, Granddaddy had gotten worse. Sweat dripped from his forehead, and he sat down on the floor. When he tried to lie down, he struggled to catch his breath. I was scared he would die before he got to the hospital. I sat on the floor by Granddaddy, my eyes wet. "Don't worry Jeffrey," he said between gasps of air, "this is just a spell of sickness. I'll be over it just like that. We'll be riding bicycles again before the summer's over."

Aunt Jenny came inside and when she saw Granddaddy's condition, she and Granny carried him to the car to take him to the hospital. Ambulances were slow and the nearest one was too far away. I had to come along since Granny was going too, so I sat in the back seat, listening to Granddaddy's labored breathing. We made it to Randallsville, to Senter County Hospital, and drove up to the emergency entrance. A doctor stuck his head into the waiting area, took one look at Granddaddy, and immediately ordered the attendants to put him on a stretcher and wheel him back. Granny, Aunt Jenny, and I had to stay in the waiting room.

I was afraid that the doctor would come out any minute to tell us that Granddaddy had died. A woman came out to get information about Granddaddy. I tried to focus on the book of Bible stories on the table next to me. I had seen a book like that one before when I went to the clinic to see the doctor. I looked through the pictures and read a few of the stories. I started near the beginning, at the story of Adam and Eve.

I continued to wonder how one sin would cause God to bring death on everyone. Now that Granddaddy was affected, it was personal. *God, you're bad*, I thought.

You kill people. All the time, in the Bible, you kill them. Just because of one little thing Adam and Eve did. Now you're trying to kill my granddaddy. But I love him, you see. That should matter to you. But you're a bad God and don't care. You just want people to be perfect. You scare them. You scare me most of the time. But I'm not scared now. If you kill Granddaddy, I'll hate you forever. If you send him to hell, I'll hate you more. I wish I could beat you up with a stick like I did R.J. that time. You're nothing but a big bully. You're bigger than everyone else, and you like to hurt them and kill them.

These thoughts seemed right to me, and they felt good. God had taken my parents, my brother, my dog, and now the bad God was going to steal Granddaddy. I took the book of Bible stories and stashed it under the table where no other child would find it. Then I shut my eyes and tried to remember the last few days with Granddaddy. I was recalling the car game when the doctor walked in. Granny and Aunt Jenny did not let me listen to the conversation. When they returned, I looked up at them.

"He had a bad heart attack," Granny said. "They don't know whether he'll make it."

Aunt Jenny went to the telephone and started calling relatives and friends. Uncle Lawton got off work and arrived within a half hour. The great uncles and aunts were on their way.

"Doctor said we could see him, but just for a minute. He went out and hasn't woke up. Heart ain't strong enough to keep his brain goin.' They got him upstairs now, up on the fifth floor."

Granddaddy had been moved to the Coronary Care Unit. Granny, Aunt Jenny, Uncle Lawton and I took the elevator up there. Granddaddy was in a room by himself. The nurses only allowed two people at a time to see him. Uncle Lawton said, "Anna, you and Jenny go in. Jeffrey, you stay with me. You don't need to see him in this shape."

"But I want to. I might not see him again."

A nurse overheard the conversation and said, "It's okay. I don't think it would hurt. It might even be good for him to see his grandfather."

Uncle Lawton replied, "I'm not sure 'bout that." He thought for a moment, then said, "Okay, Jeffrey, you can go in with them. But he won't look like himself. I hate for you to see him this way, but you saw him at the house anyway, so I don't reckon it would be any worse seein' him now. You talk to him, let him know you're there."

Granny, Aunt Jenny and I entered the room. I thought it looked like a mad scientist's laboratory. A tube with a needle was in Granddaddy's left arm, connected to a bottle of fluid. Wires were on his chest, and a machine was beeping out the beats of his heart. Every few seconds a beep seemed out of place, and I was afraid Granddaddy would die while I was right there in the room.

Granny went to him, sat down in a green chair by his bed. She didn't say anything, but just looked at him. I didn't understand why she didn't say anything.

Aunt Jenny walked to Granddaddy's side and said, "Hi Daddy. It's Jenny, I'm here. You get some rest. You get better soon so you can go home. Okay, Jeffrey, come over."

I walked over, kissed Granddaddy on his cold cheek. He was pale, more pale than he had been in the house when he first had the heart attack. I gulped to swallow the lump in my throat, then spoke.

"Hi Granddaddy. I love you. Get well. I want you home."

I walked toward Granny and Aunt Jenny. I glanced at the monitor and saw the peaks of each heartbeat. Suddenly the peaks turned to squiggly lines and an alarm went off. A group of doctors and nurses ran into the room with a big cart and a nurse said, "You all have to leave. Now!" The nurse led us from the room and back toward the waiting room. I looked back at the cracked door and saw what I thought was someone pounding Granddaddy's chest. I wanted to run back, tell them, "Don't hurt my granddaddy!" Maybe this place is a mad scientist's lab, I thought. Maybe they're doing some weird experiment on him. But I don't know why they'd hit him. Why did his heartbeat turn into squiggly lines. What did that mean? Was Granddaddy dying? Maybe he was already dead.

We sat down in the waiting room, next to Uncle Lawton. Aunt Jenny was crying. "What happened?" I asked. She just patted his shoulder and didn't answer. I knew then that the next time the doctor came into the room it would be bad news. Maybe the worst.

Twenty minutes passed. The same doctor came in who had spoken to Granny and to Aunt Jenny before. He was a young man, in his thirties. I noticed that he was sweating, as if he had been working outside.

He looked at Granny and said, "Your husband's still alive, but barely. His heart went into a rhythm that would kill him if we didn't do something immediately. Basically, his heart stopped beating. We were able to shock his heart into a better rhythm with an electric

charge. But it doesn't look good. Not good at all. I'm
sorry. We'll keep doing our best to help him."

"Thank you, Doctor," Granny said. I thought she
bowed her head, just for a few seconds. She looked at
me and said, "I hope he lives, Jeffrey. I know you love
him so much. I don't know I'm s'posed to feel other than
that - I know you need him to live."

I looked at her funny. I didn't understand
everything she'd said. I knew Granddaddy had been
mean to her, and I didn't know if she still loved her
husband. But Granny would not want me to be hurt.

It was getting towards evening, and after Granny,
Aunt Jenny and Uncle Lawton had talked to the doctor,
Aunt Jenny said, "We have to go home. We can't do any
good here."

I tried to protest, but Uncle Lawton stopped me.
"The doctor told us the truth - if we stay here it ain't
going to make a bucket of warm spit's difference
whether he lives or dies. They won't let us see him again
tonight. We might as well sleep the best we can in beds."

I wanted to stay there with Granddaddy. I
whimpered all the way home, trying not to be heard.
Aunt Jenny and Uncle Lawton were staying overnight at
the house. Uncle Rick and Aunt Susie and Uncle Bob and
Aunt Debbie would stay at a nearby motel.

By the time the group of four arrived, the great
aunts and uncles were there, waiting for Granny to
unlock the house. They had brought food of all types,
knowing that Granny wouldn't be up to cooking. It was
late but I wasn't hungry. Granny made me eat some
cheese crackers. I kept those down, although I still felt
sick. I asked if I could go to bed. Aunt Jenny said, "Yes,
get some sleep. We'll all go back to the hospital

tomorrow."

I put on my pajamas and climbed into bed. Light streamed through the bottom of the door, and I heard the murmur of sad talk in the living room. I did not say my prayers, though I felt guilty and wondered if God would punish Granddaddy if He didn't get prayed to. I didn't think that would be fair, but God did not play fair. I was too angry to think and too tired to cry, so I went to sleep at nine and didn't wake up until eight the next morning.

When I awakened, the sun was shining, and I heard the same mockingbird that sang every day all summer. I did not remember any dreams, which I took to be a good sign. I was thinking about helping Granddaddy in the garden after breakfast when I remembered yesterday. I had to get up and dressed fast, for all the family members were planning to make it to the hospital as soon as they could. There had been no phone calls last night, which meant that Granddaddy was still alive. I sighed. Maybe he would get better.

I ate some bacon and tomato biscuits. I wanted to be strong when I saw Granddaddy. I didn't feel as sick as I did the night before. The previous day, I had lost hope. My dreams had seemed like a prophecy. Today the timing of the dreams seemed like a coincidence. It just happened that way for no reason, I thought. Granddaddy might recover despite the dreams.

No one talked much on the way to the hospital. When we reached the fifth floor waiting room, the great aunts and uncles had already arrived. This time the doctor spoke to everyone, including me. "He's a lot better today. But as you know, he had a bad attack. We gave him a test called an electrocardiograph. It records the electricity his heart puts out. It showed that about a fourth of the bottom left of his heart was killed by the heart attack. This is the part of the heart that pumps most of the blood around the body. If he lives through the first week, he'll probably survive. But he'll be weak because his heart won't be able to pump as much blood. He won't be able to get around like he used to."

"He won't be able to go on bike rides?" I asked before Granny had a chance to hush me.

"No more bike rides! Nothing that can put a strain on his heart."

"What about that garden of his?" Granny asked. "He has a big garden."

"If he has a garden at all, it will have to be small. I wouldn't recommend him doing any hoeing, especially in hot weather. You can see him now, two at a time during visiting hours, but the boy can come in with two adults if you'd like. Mr. Wilson's awake and alert now. Earlier this morning, he was asking for his mother. But now he seems to know where he is and what's happening around him."

Granny, Aunt Jenny and I entered the room. Granddaddy's bed was up at an angle to help him breathe. The monitor still beeped out his heartbeat but it seemed more regular than before.

Granddaddy's voice was so weak I had to strain to hear it. "Hello. Glad you came. Heart almost gave out on me. Doctor says I gotta slow down. I don't want to, but I'm an old man. Old and sick. Can't sleep good here, either."

Granny talked with Granddaddy for a few minutes, followed by Aunt Jenny. "Okay, Jeffrey, it's your turn," Aunt Jenny said. "Go and talk to Granddaddy." I could not understand why people talked funny when folks were sick. When Aunt Jenny talked like that, I thought she sounded like my school teacher.

I approached Granddaddy but remained standing rather than sitting in the chair by the bed. Bars were raised to keep him from falling off. He was still pale, but not sweating. He was breathing easier too. "Hello Jeffrey. Didn't think I'd be stuck in the hospital. You be good to your granny. I ain't no 'count for nothin' now. Can't ride a bike any more, can't work in the garden like I used to. Don't want to be stuck in bed. All this mess happenin' on my birthday too. You know I'm 67 today!"

In the midst of the chaos, no one had remembered Granddaddy's birthday. He never celebrated it anyway, and he did not care for others to celebrate it, either. "Just another year older," he'd say. "It don't mean a durn thing other than that."

"I know you'll have more birthdays," I said. "You won't be stuck in bed forever. You'll get better and we'll go fishing. We'll get Grandpa Conley over, and we'll go to the lake on his boat, and we'll have fun."

"Yeah, we can do that."

Aunt Jenny said, "Jeffrey, we have to go and let other people see him. We'll get to see him this afternoon. Tell your granddaddy goodbye."

"Bye Granddaddy. See you later."

"Bye, Jeffrey."

We left the room. Everything was white in a hospital. The walls, the rooms. The doctors wore white coats. Nurses wore white uniforms and hats. Granddaddy wore a white gown. It was too white, too clean. There were no other colors. No green of grass and trees, no red of clay dirt. A world without colors was a world gone wrong. But a world with sickness and death was wrong, too. Change and decay were all around me, and there was no way to hide from it, no way to forget.

Uncle Rick walked over and said, "We're going to make our way home, and so are Bob and Debbie. Call if anything changes. We'll be in on Sunday as usual. Are Bud's sisters and their husbands coming?"

"Yes," Aunt Jenny said. "Frank and Lucy are trying to get somebody to watch those dogs of theirs. You know how they are about them. But they should be here to see Bud tonight. Len and Allie are driving in from Nashville. It's hard for him to get away from that interior design business."

I was glad that everybody was coming. I liked to ride in Uncle Len and Aunt Allie's Cadillac. It rode so smooth. Uncle Frank and Aunt Lucy lived down Bramble Lane, but they visited only once a week at most. Granddaddy had never been that close to any of his sisters, other than Aunt Liz, the one who had died of cancer. Plus, Uncle Frank used lots of bad words, which offended Granny and Aunt Jenny. When Uncle Frank came by, he drove a huge red Ford truck, and he'd bring the beagles he used for rabbit hunting. Uncle Frank was originally from Canada, and he and Lucy used to live in Detroit. I liked to talk to him.

At the hospital, it was getting toward noon, time for lunch. Uncle Lawton decided to try the hospital cafeteria, since it would be quick and convenient. We made our way down to the second floor, found the cafeteria. It looked old. Very old. I wondered when the walls had last been painted. I ordered a hamburger and french fries. They were always good.

At least they had always been good until now. I bit into my hamburger and almost spit it out. It was the worst hamburger I had ever tasted. It tasted better than brussels sprouts, but anything tasted better than brussels sprouts. I told Uncle Lawton, "This hamburger tastes terrible."

"My hot dog isn't much better. Probably should have gone out to the Big Boy to eat - I have to be back to work this afternoon to get some business done." Then a wicked smile crossed Uncle Lawton's face. "Hey, Jeffrey, do you know why your hamburger tastes so bad? Because it's made of horse meat!"

I had heard rumors from my classmates at school that all cafeteria hamburgers were made of horse meat. That would certainly explain why cafeteria hamburgers tasted so bad. Horses tasted terrible. They were for riding, not for eating.

Granny snickered. Aunt Jenny glared at Uncle Lawton and said, "Don't you tell that boy lies like that! You know those hamburgers are made of beef!"

"Sure they are," Uncle Lawton replied. When I tried to take another bite, Uncle Lawton neighed, sounding exactly like a horse. I tried but failed to keep from laughing, and I spit out my horseburger in the process. Laughing opened me up, released some of my grief, like steam from a pressure cooker.

I finally got that horseburger down. I hoped the fries would taste better. They did, although they were greasy and needed salt. Uncle Lawton tried to convince me that the grease was made from possum fat. Granny snickered again and said, "You know what you're full of, Lawton."

Lunch was over. I wondered why the meal was

called *lunch* at school and *dinner* at home. On Sunday, it didn't matter - people always called it *dinner*. I never understood why people called the same thing by different words all the time. Life would be simpler if people used one word for one kind of thing.

Uncle Lawton left for work, and Granny, Aunt Jenny and I returned to the waiting room. The next visiting hour was at two. I found a Field & Stream magazine and started thumbing through it. I liked the photos of nature, though I wasn't in the mood to see dead animals. 2:00 came quickly, and the three of us went into Granddaddy's room. He still looked very pale, but he was asleep. We stood over him a moment in silence, then went home. There was another visiting hour at seven, and we would return then.

Aunt Jenny had to go back to work. Granny and I didn't have a ride until Uncle Lawton came to pick us up in the evening for the 7:00 visiting hour. It soon became a mini-routine, and after a few days, I knew the world had changed for good. For the next eight days we came every evening. On Saturday, we could visit Granddaddy once every visiting hour. His sisters finally stopped by with their husbands, but they didn't stay long, and I only had time to say "Hello" to them.

Sunday dinner was depressing without Granddaddy, though the food was still good: meat loaf and the usual assortment of vegetables. The salad was still there, with French dressing, and the chess pie was delicious. More relatives came than usual, with all the great aunts and great uncles from Granddaddy's side of the family present. Uncle Frank brought a couple of the beagles he used as rabbit dogs into the house and fed them table scraps. He came over to me and said, "If your granny lets you, why don't you ride your bike down the road to my place. I have a basketball goal set up in my front yard. Buddy Conway, the kid next door, is about your age. He's a good kid. You people have lived so close to us, and we haven't really gotten to know you like we should."

"I'll ask Granny about the bike ride," I said. I knew it would be good to get away from this place of sickness for a while. And I liked to play basketball, although I wasn't very good at it.

After dinner, I sat with the men outside. Later, when they went inside, I sat on a glider by myself. That's when I started to cry. I brushed a wasp away and ran to the field, ran to The Thicket without stopping. I wanted to have that same feeling I had when I walked with Granddaddy to The Thicket in June. I lay down in the same spot. I swung on the vine. I stared at the farmer's field across the fence. It wasn't the same without Granddaddy. I lay on my stomach, head resting on my arm, sobbing. I hoped Granddaddy would be able to walk to The Thicket after he came home.

The next day the doctor finally said, "I think Mr. Wilson can be discharged tomorrow. Make sure he gets plenty of rest. And don't let him eat all that bacon! Too much fat in his diet is not good for him. Buy skim milk. He shouldn't eat too much red meat. And no more eggs."

I was thrilled that Granddaddy was coming home, although I hoped that I would still have whole milk to drink. I hated skim milk. It tasted like water. But I would drink skim milk the rest of my life if I had Granddaddy back. Tomorrow things would almost be back the way they were. The world would be right again.

CHAPTER 17

Homecoming day for Granddaddy was on the Tuesday of the last week in July. I woke up at 6:30 that morning and stayed awake. Outside it was cloudy, and darkness in the distant west threatened rain. There wasn't going to be a celebration. Granny wanted things to be as quiet as possible. "No need to disturb a man with a weak heart," she said. Uncle Rick, Uncle Lawton and Aunt Jenny were going together to the hospital to pick him up. Uncle Frank was coming in his truck just in case they needed any more help moving Granddaddy. I was to stay home with Granny. At least two men were needed to move Granddaddy since he couldn't get around too well.

I fidgeted. I wanted to go but knew it was best that I didn't. I hoped that Granddaddy would be able to walk or sit when he got home. I hoped he would be able to talk. At breakfast, I sat in the kitchen and talked with Granny.

"I hope Granddaddy gets better. I was scared when he was in the hospital."

"He's too mean to die," Granny said. "They talk about people bein' stubborn as a mule. Your granddaddy's more stubborn than that. Old coot."

"You don't like Granddaddy," I said.

"He's mean to me. I don't like him, but I care about him enough to have stayed with him, didn't I? Both his sisters been divorced once. Allie was divorced twice before she met Len. Guess she found somebody rich 'nough for her. They all got their daddy's temper. Your granddaddy never hit me. I'll give him credit for that. But he's yelled at me and cussed at me in the thirty-one years we've been married. Don't know if he'd be happy if he weren't fussin' 'bout something.' Used to get drunk when he worked at Schmidt's. They let their workers drink what they made. Reckon it was so they could get away with payin' 'em less. I don't know how many Saturdays he was in jail and his poor sister Liz havin' to come down and pay to get him out. Stoppin' drinkin' was good for him, but it didn't get rid of his temper.

"But he really loves you, Jeffrey. He's half a child himself. I'm glad you got to play with him and help him in the garden. I love you, too, Jeffrey. Just hard to show. I don't like to talk much. Found that talkin' too much got me yelled at. So I stopped. Aunt Jenny's been good to you too, whippin' you when you needed it. I'll clean this up. You can go outside and wait for your granddaddy to come if you want to."

I sat out in the glider. I was surprised that Granny could talk so much. I knew she had suffered due to Granddaddy's torments. She was being nice. She did not want me to say anything bad about Granddaddy. I knew she was telling the truth when she said she loved him.

I looked forward to the time when Granddaddy would sit by me and talk with me. I looked up at the pear tree. In two weeks, the pears would be ripe enough for me to eat. I could get more pears at Uncle Lawton's store, too. Soon it would be time to go to town to buy shoes and school supplies. Registration would take place in a month. I wanted to delay school. I hated the idea of staying in school all day while Granddaddy was lying sick at home.

Almost an hour had passed before Uncle Lawton's car pulled up. Granddaddy was in the back seat. I ran to the car as Uncle Lawton and Uncle Rick helped him to his feet. They hadn't needed Uncle Frank's help at the hospital, and he went home, saying he and Lucy would stop by later. Uncle Lawton and Uncle Rick lifted him up the concrete steps, walked him to his room, and lowered him into his bed. It was warm, so Aunt Jenny pulled all the covers away but a sheet. He was dressed in loose fitting pajamas to keep him cool. Aunt Jenny propped two pillows under him so he could sit up. He was awake but groggy.

His speech was slurred as he spoke. "Glad I'm out of that durn hospital and back in my own bed. I'm goin' to sleep a little before supper."

We left the room and Uncle Lawton pushed the door to. I wanted to go outside, but rain had begun to fall. Thunder in the distance grew louder - the storm was getting closer. It was not safe to go out.

I decided to go upstairs, where my parents and I had stayed in my first year of life. I climbed stairs that creaked with every step. On the way up to the left was a door opening to a crawl space I had hoped to explore one day. But Granddaddy told me to stay out, said some of Mr. Benson's stuff was stored there. "Don't ever mess with somebody else's property."

I reached the top of the stairs. Boxes of all sizes and shapes littered the floor. In one corner was my old wood high chair, the figure of a bear painted behind the seat. I turned to the left, walked to the side of the house facing Bramble Road. The panorama of crops in the garden was blurred by heavy rain. Corn stalks stuffed with ears ready to harvest bent in the thunderstorm's wind. A streak of lightning flashed over Bramble Road. A crack of thunder followed a second later. I shivered with fear, but this was a good place to hide. It would not be long before Granny and Aunt Jenny would miss me, and I would have to come down.

Below the window was a trunk. I used to imagine that it contained a skeleton. When I gathered the courage to open it, I found only my baby clothes. I climbed on the trunk and lay down, facing the window. The rain began to abate, then it stopped. Stray rays of sun burned their way through the clouds, illuminating the rows of potatoes. I remembered helping Granddaddy clear them of potato bugs. I resolved to do that myself from now on. I would do my best to make sure Granddaddy's garden was a success. I didn't think I could hoe too good, but I could pick cucumbers, tomatoes, peas, beans, corn, cantaloupe. I could do anything to harvest but dig potatoes. In two weeks, I would help pick watermelons. They were huge this year, and I expected them to taste extra sweet. I didn't think Granddaddy would be up to taking them to the square to sell. I hoped to eat enough to make up for it. I recalled last August, Granddaddy picking the black diamond watermelons, hosing them off, polishing them with a cloth, before loading them in the bed of his truck to carry to the square. I liked to rub their smooth surfaces with my hands. Granddaddy would sell all of them to the group of old whittlers. I wondered if Granddaddy would be able to go to the square. Maybe if Aunt Jenny or Uncle Lawton took him he would.

"Jeff-REY!" Granny called. I ran downstairs and found Granny looking out the door.

"There you are! What in the world were y'doin' in that hot upstairs? Your granddaddy's at the table! He's goin' to eat dinner with us. Come and sit by your granddaddy."

I was overjoyed. I ran into the kitchen and came close to slipping on the slick floor. Granddaddy was on the end of the table nearest the door. I kissed him and sat at my usual spot between the wall and the table.

Other than being hunched over a little, Granddaddy looked pretty good. Some pink was returning to his face. He was moving around some, too, his fingers fiddling with the silverware. There were signs that all was not back to normal. His head and shoulders hunched over and his forearms rested on the table. The doctor said he could still eat sardines, and he gulped them down. I was afraid he would choke and was grateful when he finished his meal.

"How are you feelin' today, Bud?" Uncle Lawton asked.

"Oh, a little better I reckon," Granddaddy replied, his voice stronger than before. "Still weak. Can't walk too good. Doctor said it's hardening of the arteries. I'm gonna get around though. I can't stand just lyin' around."

"Don't you go too fast and wear yourself out. You know you got that weak heart now."

"If I just lie around, I'm gonna die for sure. If I die, I'd rather die walkin' than lyin' in bed."

Aunt Jennie and Uncle Lawton left the next morning. After breakfast I went to my grandparents' bedroom but found the bed empty. I searched in the bathroom, afraid Granddaddy had fallen out. Just as I was about to call Granny, I looked out the window and noticed a familiar form in the glider. I decided I wouldn't let the screen door slam when I walked outside - there was no need for Granny to worry.

"I told people I wasn't gonna lay down all the time," Granddaddy said. I was glad because Granddaddy was going to fight his sickness.

"Tried to walk to the garden, but felt weak. I'll get there though. I just have to get stronger."

"The doctor said you have to slow down."

"Yeah, and I've slowed down. But I don't have to slow down to a stop, do I? I want to go to church this Sunday. I'll complain until Jenny lets me. I'm her daddy. She'll do what I say."

I knew Granddaddy would go to church Sunday. Aunt Jenny knew he would drive her crazy if she refused to take him, and drive Granny crazy too.

"I'll miss the bicycle rides," I said.

Granddaddy's eyes watered a little. Then he recovered and said, "I will too. Some things an old man can't do any more. It's just part of life. Like drivin' a car. Doctor won't let me drive no more. Can't even drive to Mr. Parker's little store up Farris Road. Lawton or Jenny will have to take us, and I don't know how they can do it since they both work. I'm sorry. I'm an old, sick man, but I'm gonna do what I can. Right now I'm gonna go inside and get some rest. See if you can help me up."

I stood up. Granddaddy put one hand on my shoulder, supporting the other on one side of the glider. He stumbled, and I feared he would fall, but he was able to stand. He walked in slow motion to the back door. I stayed by his side. I opened the screen door as Granddaddy plodded his way up the concrete steps and back to bed. He was sweating and panting when he got inside. He crept toward the bed and sat down hard. I placed a pillow under him for support.

"Don't tell your granny 'bout this. It's a good thing she's a little deaf," Granddaddy said. He closed his eyes to go to sleep. I looked at him to make sure he kept breathing, then cracked the door as I left the room.

I hoped that Granny had not looked out the window and seen us. I felt a lump of pride start in my throat and expand into my chest. It felt like a heat that would flow into Granddaddy's room and keep him warm and alive. I was proud that Granddaddy tried to keep doing things, even if the doctor said it was dangerous.

I walked outside to the sugar maples and sat on the wood swing. The leaves were green for the most part, but had lost their dark color. The edges of some had begun to fade to a sickly yellow. The wind picked up, and one leaf began to fall. I got up and chased it, blowing on it. It kept falling, and I tried to catch it. A gust lifted it away from my reach, and it landed six feet away. I lay on my stomach, resting my head on my folded arms. I cried a long, long time.

CHAPTER 18

As I knew he would, Granddaddy kept his promise and badgered Aunt Jenny until she agreed to let him go to church. He was still stooped over at breakfast but looked better afterward. After breakfast, Granddaddy didn't emerge from the bedroom for a long time, and I was worried, but eventually he walked out the door. He was dressed in a dark suit and a gray tie.

"You're gonna burn up in that. First Sunday in August, goin' to be ninety degrees outside."

"I'll wear what I want to, woman. I want to look nice today."

"You know you're goin' too fast. Goin' kill yourself."

"Ah ain't gonna kill m'self. Let me be."

Uncle Lawton helped Granddaddy down the steps and into the back seat. He leaned Granddaddy's head back. When we were on the road, I could not hear above the car noise. I wanted to make sure Granddaddy was still breathing, but I couldn't check to see if his chest was moving because of the car motion. For the first time in a long time, I said a prayer. "God, please let Granddaddy stay alive. Please. In Jesus' name. A-men."

I took Granddaddy's hand. It was cool. I wondered if I should say anything. The car windows were rolled halfway down. It was already hot outside. Maybe it was just the breeze that cooled his hands. I checked my own hands and found them cool. I looked at every stretch of the road, hoping we were close to church. I was relieved when we passed the log cabin and pulled into the gravel lot, parking under the shade of the oak in our usual spot.

As soon as we stopped, Granddaddy's head bent forward. He'd dozed off. He raised his head and said, "Guess we're at church now." I laughed from relief as Uncle Lawton helped him out of the car. We reached the porch where some old men were sitting in their usual spots.

"Hello, Brother Bud! Didn't 'spect you back so soon! Heard you were pretty bad off, but glad to see you're better."

"I must be too mean for the Good Lord to take me. Good to be back."

"We're pretty mean ourselves and Old Asa here, he's ninety, so he must be meaner than you. You take it easy."

"See you after church."

Granddaddy slept through the sermon, or anyway kept his eyes closed. The sermon was all about the prodigal son. I had heard that story before in various versions, and I was more interested in watching Granddaddy. The preacher didn't pound the pulpit as he usually did when he saw someone asleep in church. I guessed the preacher thought God would forgive Granddaddy because he had been sick.

The invitation song began. To my surprise, Granddaddy pulled himself up to stand as the congregation sang, *All things are ready, come to the feast!* It was a stirring melody and I felt like marching. We sat down to sing the song before the Lord's Supper, one verse of *Break Thou the Bread of Life.* I liked the song, but it made me hungry. I wished I could eat one of the crackers or drink a cup of grape juice. I felt good when Granddaddy took both.

The closing prayer ended. Lots of folks came by to shake hands with Granddaddy. With Uncle Lawton's help, he made it back to the car. Uncle Lawton said, "I think we need to get you a cane to help you walk on your own."

"Ain't gonna use no dad gum cane," Granddaddy said. His face was red, and I was glad of that - better than being pale.

"What's the difference between your walkin' with a cane and me helping you to the car?" Uncle Lawton asked.

"I told you, I ain't gonna walk on no cane!"

"Alright, but if you fall down and bust yer head, don't blame me!"

Uncle Lawton tried to light a cigar, but Aunt Jenny stopped him. "That cigar smoke will kill my daddy. Wait until you get outside."

"I guess you're right."

We made it back home in one piece for Sunday dinner. On the table was a feast: roast beef, meatloaf, black eyed and Crowder peas, lima beans, corn on the cob, mashed potatoes. There were cucumbers in salted vinegar, salad and a jar of my favorite French dressing. Desserts included Coca-Cola cake, pecan pie and coconut cake. All of my great aunts and uncles were there. Uncle Rick, Aunt Susie, Uncle Bob, Aunt Debbie, and on Granddaddy's side, Uncle Len and Aunt Allie. The sound of whimpering beagles outside alerted me to the presence of Uncle Frank and Aunt Lucy.

There were too many people to seat all at once, so folks had to take turns eating. A few of the men took their plates outside, but I ate in my usual cubbyhole. Granddaddy sat at the head of the table. His head was drooping again, but he seemed to like the food.

"Bud, you sure look a lot better since I saw you in that hospital bed," Aunt Susie said.

"I'm feeling better too. In a week or two I might be back in the garden."

"You always did love that garden," said Aunt Debbie. "You grow good stuff, too. Bob and I are going to pick and shell some lima beans today."

"You're welcome to them," said Granddaddy. "We can't eat but so many, and Anna can't can like she used to. Too much trouble. Easier to buy food for winter at the grocery store these days."

I felt like things were getting back to normal. I told God thanks for keeping Granddaddy alive today.

"'Bout time for you to be startin' school?" Aunt Lucy, who had just come into the kitchen, asked.

"Yes ma'am," I said. I was tired of relatives reminding me of the inevitable.

Aunt Jenny said, "Jeffrey, tomorrow after I get off work I'll stop by and take you to the shoe store on the square. It's that time of year again."

"Yes, ma'am."

I knew that buying new shoes was a sure sign of school starting. But I also loved going to town. It was another chance to see the square, the courthouse, those familiar places that helped make up my world.

I joined the men outside after dinner. Granddaddy was sitting in a small glider, head bowed. Uncle Frank came by.

"I talked to your Granny, and she said you could ride your bike to my place this Wednesday. Lucy and your grandmother have been talking to each other more since Bud's been sick. Come by about nine, before it's too hot. I'll ask Buddy Conway, the boy from next door, to come over and we can shoot some baskets. Then I want to talk to you. Tell you how the world works. Your granddaddy getting sick made me think of this. You know he's not in the best of shape, even though he's better now. I know you want him to live forever, but none of us will. Come by Wednesday. We'll serve you lunch too."

"Thanks Uncle Frank."

I was excited about riding my bike so far. I knew this week was going to be much better than the last two.

"Good. Oh, and your granddaddy asked me to take the both of you for a haircut on Tuesday. He said it's a week early but he wanted to get it over. He said your hair grows faster than Johnson grass. You'll fit in my truck, but you'll have to sit in the middle, just like you do in your granddaddy's truck. Me, I don't have enough hair on top to cut, but I guess the barber can trim a little off the back."

"I'm glad you can take us."

"I retired early from working at an auto plant in

Detroit. Got tired of living up there. Wanted to go down here, where I could afford to live in the country and hunt rabbits. Your aunt wanted to be closer to her people, too. That's a mixed blessing. But I do love living here."

He walked over to the pear tree where he had tied his two beagles. They yelped and ran to him, licking his face. Then they ran to me, attacking my face, too, with their fast flicking tongues. I laughed more than I had laughed since I'd played with Fuzzy. The dogs went to Granddaddy, but he wasn't as pleased to see them. "Git off me, you crazy dogs. Gonna lick me clean to death!"

"Get off him, Patches, Tiny," Uncle Frank said. The dogs obeyed, and afterwards he took them and tied them up again.

I did not remember much about the rest of the day except that things felt right. Everything was moving back into its proper place. I attended evening services at church with Uncle Lawton and Aunt Jenny. Granddaddy and Granny stayed at home. After the services, I played with Johnny McRae. The Conwell boys tried to pick on us, but I didn't care. This was a good day, and they were not going to mess it up. Then I stood in the gravel lot looking out toward the west, the reds and oranges of heat lightning illuminating the distant sky. Lightning bugs flashed in a staccato rhythm. In the growing night, triangle tops of cedars were black on the western hills. Aunt Jenny called for me to come to the car.

After we arrived home and Aunt Jenny and Uncle Lawton had left, I sat in the kitchen. Granny asked if I wanted a snack. Granddaddy had gone to bed. I wanted cheese crackers, and Granny pulled the Velveeta from the refrigerator. I found crackers in a round container marked "FLOUR" in a cabinet. Granny cut some pieces of cheese and poured milk. I thought the light in the kitchen was bright enough to keep the night out. I enjoyed the snack, kissed Granny good night, said a prayer for her and for Granddaddy, and fell asleep.

I woke up Monday morning refreshed. I was ready to help with the garden. Granddaddy was up for breakfast too, and his head didn't droop, although his arms still moved slowly as he ate. He did not have eggs, but he did have sausage biscuits with tomato slices.

I told him, "I'm going to get the potato bugs off today."

"Good. I'm proud of you. Don't let yourself get too hot out there. Come in for water when you need it."

I rushed to the potato patch, pulled each bug off and stomped on it. I was proud to be able to help Granddaddy. I finished all three rows in less than an hour, then found a bucket in the garage. I harvested cucumbers and tomatoes, brought them into the house, and washed them in the sink.

"You got a lot done today!" Granny said. "I'll can some of these tomatoes. The cucumbers will be good on salads, and I'll put some in salt and vinegar too."

I felt prouder than ever as I drank two glasses of water from the faucet. I was doing my part for Granddaddy. I looked for other ways to help, but couldn't think of any, so I ran outdoors again to explore. I saw something shiny sticking through the ground near the pear tree. I took a trowel from the garage and started digging. Before long a 1955 quarter lay before me. Granddaddy had told me that they were made of silver before 1965. I decided not to spend it, but to add it to my coin collection. I thought the quarter was a sign that my luck was changing for the better. Granddaddy would get stronger, and maybe he would live until I was twenty-one after all. Maybe God was not so bad after all.

I played alone outside. Granddaddy rested but was awake enough to talk with me in the glider in the afternoon. He told the same stories I had heard before, but that was fine. I was happy to hear Granddaddy's voice and didn't care if I heard the same stories a hundred times or more.

Aunt Jenny got off work at 4:30 and arrived to pick me up just before five. The shoe store was only open until seven. "Get in the car, Jeffrey. We want to have plenty of time to pick out a pair of shoes."

I got in the car. I had big, wide feet. Every time I went to the shoe store, I had to try on at least three pairs of shoes before I found a pair that would not rub my feet. The problem got worse every year.

When we arrived in Randallsville, Aunt Jenny drove around until she found a parking space a block away from a store that sold Buster Brown shoes. I liked the picture of the dog on the sign. Buying shoes before school had become a yearly ritual, although this was only the ritual's fourth year. It rarely took long for me to get used to things.

Aunt Jenny and I entered the store. I relished the scent of new leather shoes. I wanted the same kind of brown Buster Brown shoes with laces I had worn the previous years. The store clerk asked me to remove my right shoe. He placed my foot in the metal sizer to determine my shoe size. I liked the snug feel of the bars as the clerk moved them against my sock feet. "You have big feet, young man," the clerk said. "Wide, too."

I was certain the first pair wouldn't fit, and I was right. The shoe was too tight on my right foot. There was no need to walk around the store to know it.

"I'll find the next size up," said the clerk.

The next pair was too long. Aunt Jenny felt my big toe, and it ended more than an inch below the tip of the shoe. "I'll see if I can find a half size in wide. Hard to find, but I'll try." About three minutes later he came out with a shoe that I guessed would be just right. It was. It didn't rub against the sides of my feet, and it was not too long. I was glad to have a good pair of shoes. They smelled good and fit so well I thought I could skip around the square. But I was also sad. Time flew by like the motorcycles Granddaddy and I saw on the highway.

"We need to go to Fred's to find some school supplies," Aunt Jenny said. This was another ritual. Although it reminded me of school, I knew it was something repeated year after year, just like church every week, just like the Lord's Supper at church. We went inside. I got some large pencils, a writing pad, an eraser, a bottle of Elmer's Glue-All and a lunch box with a picture of the Beverly Hillbillies on the front.

We left to go to Penny's off the square, where Aunt Jenny found me some new shirts and jeans. I hated to try clothes on in the dressing room. But it did no good to protest. Aunt Jenny would say, "I don't want to buy clothes and have to drive here and take them back because they don't fit." Soon enough, thank goodness, that part was over.

Aunt Jenny decided not to drive forty miles to Nashville to the Sears to buy me dress shoes. She told me, "I'm going to buy your dress shoes here, if we can find a pair that fits."

"No!" I said. "I want to go to Sears to get them like we've done before!"

"I don't have time to go there with your granddaddy sick! Remember he's my daddy. We'll go to Sears when he gets better. We're going to look for dress shoes here."

I felt guilty about being selfish, and I followed Aunt Jenny to the shoe section. She found some black dress shoes in the same style I liked, without laces, and the clerk located a pair that fit me.

With the shoes, supplies and clothes I needed for another school year, it was time to go home. I knew there would be one more trip to the square this week, tomorrow, with Uncle Frank and Granddaddy to get a haircut.

On the way back, Aunt Jenny stopped at an Esso station to buy gas, the price marked 24.9 cents per gallon on the price signs above. It was too much out of the way for her to stop by the station Uncle Lawton ran. The attendant pumped the gas, checked the oil, and washed the windshield. I looked around at the city lights. They were colorful, pretty, but different than country lights. I liked the glow of fireflies' flashes, the flares of heat lightning, the outside lights of farm houses I saw out the car window at night. I also liked the flashiness of neon signs and the way the city lit the landscape with an array of colors. Either form of light, city or country, was good, part of the proper order of things.

I lay down in the car. Aunt Jenny took the Ridgeway Highway most of the way back. As we moved away from town, street lights seemed to flash like strobes as we passed them. When there were no more street lights, I observed the passing power lines, and I focused on the corner of the window. I also saw the moon and stars. I pretended the car was a spaceship taking me to another solar system, to a mysterious planet, hot and full of craters and cracked rocks like Mercury. I would leave the ship in my refrigerated spacesuit, cleave samples from standing stones, and watch the sun's corona through my black visor. With that thought, I passed into sleep. Aunt Jenny woke me up when we got home.

Uncle Frank arrived in his truck at ten the next morning. Granddaddy was able to walk on his own to the truck, letting me get in first. I would sit in the middle between them, and it was going to be a tight fit. Uncle Frank was drinking a beer. I worried that he would get drunk and have a wreck, like the drivers I saw on the TV news. But Uncle Lawton had told me that Uncle Frank was one of those people who could drink a lot without getting drunk. I looked at him. He did not seem drunk, so I figured we'd make it to the barber shop alive.

When we entered the shop, Mr. Andrews opened his eyes wide. "Bud! You don't look as good as when I saw you last. Lost a lot of weight. How's things been for you?"

"Had a dad gum heart attack. Was in the hospital eight days. They didn't think I'd live."

"Well, I'm sure glad you did. Good Lord was with you, I guess. You want to get your hair cut first?"

"No, let Jeffrey go. This is my sister's husband Frank Clark. He doesn't mind which barber he sees."

"Please to meet you, Mr. Clark. Mr. Baker over in the other chair will be finished in about two minutes. He'll take care of ya then."

"No problem. Pleased to meet you."

I looked down at Granddaddy from the barber chair as Mr. Andrews cut my hair. Everything was the same. Granddaddy was getting his hair cut as usual. His hair was growing. He was alive. He'd stay alive. First church and now the haircut. These were signs from God. Summer's end would be good.

CHAPTER 19

Uncle Frank drove Granddaddy and me home after our haircuts. "Remember, Jeffrey, be at my place at ten tomorrow."

"Yes, sir."

"Wish I could ride a bike up there myself," Granddaddy said. "When I had the chance I didn't do it, and now I can't."

"Don't worry, Bud. We'll be by to visit."

We were home by dinnertime. The days were becoming more routine. I knew I would keep working in the garden, and I would need to cut the grass when it got long. But Granddaddy was getting stronger. I sat on Granddaddy's bed as he played the guitar in the afternoon, although he wasn't up to singing. Then we played some records, the same ones we had always played.

Wednesday morning was the day of the bicycle ride to Uncle Frank's. It felt like an adventure, since I'd never ridden my bicycle so far by myself before. It would be a mile and half each way. After Granddaddy and Granny each told me again to be careful, I rode down the driveway to Bramble Road where I looked both ways and took a left onto gravel. Holes and rough spots from rain dotted the entire route. The road had two sharp curves, and I stopped at each one, walking my bicycle to the other side. It was a good thing too, for a car whooshed around on the wrong side of the road, and I had to jump into the ditch with my bike. The driver shouted, "Watch out, kid!" and went on.

Granddaddy would call that guy a smart-aleck, I thought. I forgot my flush of anger when I found the spot where Granddaddy said a church had blown down in a tornado twenty years before. I stopped there and searched for the remains, but I couldn't find any. I rode on past fields filled with cows, a few ponds and some stray farm houses. I found Uncle Frank's house from the name on his mailbox. Uncle Frank was outside in the shade with three of his dogs, waiting. A boy about my age was standing beside him.

"Hello, Jeffrey! Meet Buddy. Buddy, meet Jeffrey."

Buddy and I exchanged greetings, and Buddy said, "Come on, let's shoot some baskets."

The three of us shot baskets for a while, then played a game of HORSE. Uncle Frank beat us both, making shots from twenty feet away.

"Hey, you're too good for us," I said.

"That's so you two don't get jealous of each other," Uncle Frank said. "Come in and drink some pop."

"Pop?" asked Buddy.

"Cokes," I explained. "My great uncle's from the north. He lived in Detroit. They call Cokes 'pop' up there."

"People from the north talk funny."

"They sure do."

We were out of Uncle Frank's earshot. We walked toward the back door of the house, finding our way through a pack of beagles eager to lick us and say hello. Aunt Lucy was in the kitchen with open bottles of RC Cola. "Hi Jeffrey. Hi Buddy. Have some pop."

The cold drinks went down good. It was another hot day, and we'd sweated a lot outside. Uncle Frank said, "Why don't you two sit out on the porch and talk for a while. We'll call you back inside when it's time for lunch."

We sat on a swing hanging from a small covered porch. The porch was painted light blue. Buddy said, "Your uncle sure is good at basketball, ain't he?"

"Yeah, he is. I never played him before. Had no idea he could shoot."

"We gotta go back to school soon."

"Yeah. I hope we get good teachers. I'm supposed to get my neighbor, Mrs. Clarkson, as a teacher. Don't know for sure, though."

"I may get Miss Ragan. She paddles kids all the time - for nothing.'"

"I sure hope I don't get her," I said, turning to notice some magazines on a rack beside us. I pulled some out.

"Hey, look at this. Naked women!"

"Oh my Gawwwwd! Look at how long her titties are!"

We both laughed and couldn't stop laughing.

"You know," said Buddy, "some grown women sure look funny. How do their titties get that big?"

"I don't know," I said. "Seems like they start out human like us. Then they mutate to something else."

"Mutate? What's that mean?"

"Change."

"Like a caterpillar changing to a butterfly?"

"No. When a girl mutates, it's more like a butterfly changing to a caterpillar."

We laughed again, and I replaced the magazine where I had found it. I knew that we weren't supposed to look at such pictures.

Aunt Lucy called us from the kitchen. "Boys, time for lunch!" We ate a lunch of ham sandwiches with more pop to wash them down. After lunch, Buddy had to go home. "Mama's expecting me back. She says we have to go to the store to buy shoes and stuff for school."

"Oh, I did that yesterday."

"I hate doing it. I hate school."

"I don't hate school after I've been going a while, but I hate it when it first starts."

"Well, we'll play some basketball again sometimes. I play with R.J. on the Old Highway."

"I know him. Maybe we can all play together one day."

"Sounds good. See you."

After Buddy left, Aunt Lucy cleaned up in the kitchen. Uncle Frank took me outside and sat beside me in the porch swing.

"Jeffrey, I want to talk to you about your granddaddy and about the way life really is. You're going to be a man sooner than you think. A lot of grown people are still kids. They don't face the ways of the world." He paused. "I don't know if you'll understand everything I say. Just listen up. Ask me questions if you don't understand."

"Yes, sir.

Uncle Frank's eyes were gazing off to one side, as if looking into some other realm. "Jeffrey, your granddaddy's in worse shape than he lets on. He's better than he was, but he's still very sick. I know it's hard for you to hear this, but he may not live much longer. I thought you needed to know."

"Yes, sir," I said. I wanted to stop my ears, to stop listening to what Uncle Frank was saying. This week had been fun until now.

"You're going to have to make it on your own, the best you can," Uncle Frank said, as if he were presenting a rehearsed speech. "Here's the truth of things. Everything you see around you has been here in one form or another nearly forever. Nobody made it. It's just there. Over the years, some of this stuff came together to make life. Things you can only see through a microscope first, then plants, then animals. Tiny changes over time. Finally, something that looked like an ape lived a long time ago. From that ape came gorillas, chimpanzees and us."

I protested. "Uncle Lawton says we didn't come from the apes. He says God created Adam and Eve."

"Let me tell you about God," Uncle Frank said. "People who run countries need to control things. It's bad for them and for everybody else when people run around killing each other and stealing. The rulers figured out that if people believed in God, it would scare them into behaving themselves.

"There is no God, Jeffrey. Your preacher and your family mean well. They tell you there's a God, and they really do believe in Him. But this universe is all there is.

We all have to be strong to survive. You'll have to be strong when your granddaddy passes away. You have to learn to depend on yourself."

"I don't understand," I whimpered.

"I'm not trying to be mean to you. I'm trying to do you a favor. Do you think I haven't heard Bud talk about going to hell, how he's afraid of hell, fire seven times hotter than any fire on earth? Your preacher has the poor man scared to death. I'm sure you're scared, too. You're afraid your granddaddy will go to hell. But he isn't going to hell. None of us are. But we're not going to heaven either."

"Then where will we go?" I asked.

"Have you ever seen what happens when L.T. plows your granddaddy's garden? All the dead plants, dead worms, dead mice get plowed under. They help feed next year's crops. When we die, we return to the earth, become part of that cycle. But we don't live on. That's a child's belief, and you're going to have to become a man faster than most boys. You're already lost your parents. Your granddaddy's sick. You've faced a lot in nine years. So you need to know the truth."

"But how does this help me?" I asked? My eyes were wet.

"It helps you to stop worrying about hell. To stop worrying about some God watching everything you do. And it helps you appreciate every moment you have, and the people you love, because you know they won't be here very long, and when they're gone, they're gone for good."

"Yes, sir."

"Think about it Jeffrey. If there is a God, would he have let your parents die? Would he make your granddaddy sick to the point of death, when he knows how much he means to you?"

"Maybe God is bad instead of good."

Uncle Frank smiled. "Do you really want to believe in a god who makes people sick and kills millions every year? You need to face reality. People just came to be. It's the way nature operates. You just make it the best way you can, loving who you can. You love your granddaddy. That's good. That's important. Keep loving him. And when he's gone, keep loving your granny, your relatives, your friends. Those are the ones who'll help pull you through pain, not some God who isn't there to care."

"But I want Him to be there. Sometimes I hate Him. But I prayed for him to help Granddaddy live, and Granddaddy's alive. When he got sick and almost died, I hated God and thought He was bad."

"Yep, you go back and forth. The universe isn't good, isn't bad. We call things good and bad, but these things, like getting sick and dying, are just the ways of nature. It's like gambling. When you gamble, you're either lucky or you're not. We all draw a bad hand in the end. Listen, I went to church when I was a boy, but I stopped believing in God when I was ten. Then, when I was a teenager, I started going to church again. Not because I went back to believing in God, but because I thought I could find some innocent girls that way. Boy, did I, but I won't go into that. I decided it would impress the girls if I were baptized. It was a church that dunked people under water. I didn't know the preacher would dunk me three times: 'in the name of the Father' - dunk! - 'and of the Son' - dunk! - 'and of the Holy Ghost' - dunk! I thought the preacher was trying to drown me, so I bit him. And that was the end of that."

I laughed for the first time in the conversation. But the thought of no God brought with it fear of death being nothingness, of Granddaddy becoming nothing when he died. I would also be nothing when I died. I did not understand how Uncle Frank could find this comforting. At least if God were evil, he might raise people from the dead to torture them. But if God tortured people, they would be conscious. And being conscious was better than being nothing.

"Do you understand what I'm saying, Jeffrey. Please think about it."

"I will, Uncle Frank. Thanks for the lunch and for playing basketball. You're real good at it."

"You'll probably beat me next time. Come back soon, since you're allowed to ride that bicycle on your own."

"I will." I shouted through the door, "Bye Aunt Lucy. Thanks for fixing lunch!"

"You're welcome," I heard. "Visit again soon. You're always welcome."

I jumped on my bicycle and rode home. The world seemed flat and barren. I tried to pray but I couldn't. What if Uncle Frank were right, if there were no God? If only Granddaddy would keep getting better, it might be all right for a while, even if God didn't exist.

That's not what happened. Granddaddy got worse.

CHAPTER 20

I rode home fast, wanting to talk with Granddaddy. But when I came inside the house, Granny told me he was asleep. "He went to bed after breakfast and hasn't stirred since. I think he's okay, but he's been pushin' himself too hard. Goin' to church and goin' to get a haircut. But I s'pose we should be thankful for his stubbornness. Makes him want to go on no matter how sick."

I went outside to the swing. I swung higher and faster than I had ever swung before. The tree trunk seemed to blur into two and my feet touched the maple's bottom leaves. I felt the rush of air with each upward swing and stared at the blue sky that popped up over the bushes when I was up high. The rhythm was comforting. I lost all track of time. I never wanted to stop. I didn't think about anything then. I just saw and felt and heard the wind whish past my ears. But I could not keep going. My legs got tired of pushing me up. I stopped and stared at some dead leaves lying under one of the trees. I picked one up, brown and full of holes. I looked in the dirt below, found fragments of old leaves. I ran to the front yard, to the pear tree and picked a pear that looked ripe enough to eat. It had the proper tangy taste, and I ate it too quickly, tossing the core into the bushes behind the gliders. My belly hurt.

I walked to the bushes by the gravel drive and entered the opening to find my special place. It looked the same as the day I mourned Fuzzy. I lay down, shut my eyes. I thought, Granny was right. Granddaddy was just tired. He tried to push himself too hard. Once he gets some rest he'll be okay. We'll just have to make sure he doesn't work too hard again. He doesn't have to go to church every Sunday. He's not dying. He's not strong like he used to be, but he's not dying.

I walked back to the house, looked at my watch. It was nearly 4:00. I had been outside three hours. I sauntered toward the back door, saw Granddaddy resting in a glider, and sat beside him.

"Ain't feelin' no 'count today, Jeffrey. Almost fell walkin' out here. Put on my old overalls for support. They're hot, but they help me stand up straight.

"I'm worried. Good Lord might take me any time now. And when I was takin' my nap this afternoon, I dreamed of bein' in hell. I had boils all over my body from the heat, and they'd heal. Then they'd burn again. Never felt pain like that before. God was tellin' me that I'm goin' there after I die."

"No, Granddaddy. It was just a dream. Dreams aren't real."

"No, Jeffrey. This dream was real. I'm goin' to die soon, and I'm goin' to hell. Lived too mean of a life."

"But the preacher says ask God for forgiveness and you can be saved," I protested.

"Too late for me. I drank too much, done wrong to too many people. I reckon I've probably been terrible mean to your granny sometimes. I've asked God to forgive me, but He won't. It's too late."

"It's not too late!"

"Yes, it is. I wouldn't had that dream if it weren't too late."

I started to cry. Granddaddy put his hand on my shoulder.

"You just try to live a good life and do good works. That way you won't end up where I'm goin.'"

"But I want to go where you're going. I don't care if it's hell."

"No! You don't ever want to go there! It's a bad place."

"Maybe there's no God and you won't go to hell."

"No God! What's wrong with you, boy? I bet you been talkin' to my sister's husband. Listen to me, Jeffrey. That man ain't got no sense. You know he was from Canada before he moved to Detroit. Got some strange ideas up there. Only a fool doesn't believe in God. Don't you forget that. There's a God. You do what God says, so you don't end up like me."

I was quiet, wiping tears away with my arm. Granddaddy said, "I'm gettin' tired again. Gonna lay down for a while." He tried to get up but couldn't. I tried to help him, pulling and pulling on his arms. Granddaddy was suspended between sitting and rising. I was afraid he would fall. "Pull harder, Jeffrey. I'm about played out!" With one last pull, I got Granddaddy into a standing position. Granddaddy crept back to the steps and made it inside, but slipped and came close to falling before he got into bed. I helped make him comfortable, then ran to my room, locked the doors, and wet both sides of my pillow.

The rest of the week Granddaddy continued to slow down. He slept more every day. One evening, Uncle Lawton and Aunt Jenny came by with a walker. I was heartbroken when Granddaddy didn't protest. He was able to get up again and could move around the house, but he could not make it outside without help.

Later that week, I was talking with Granddaddy when he was propped up in bed. Granddaddy told me, "I think people are like watches. You still have your watch?"

"Yes, sir. Right here." I took it off and showed it to Granddaddy. He gave it back to me and said, "What happens to the watch if you forget to wind it?"

"It stops running."

"That's right. Well, I feel like I'm winding down. Any day now I'm gonna stop runnin.' And nobody's gonna be able to wind me up again. Seems to me that's how the Good Lord planned things. He wound us up when we were born. We kick around, run fast at first, then we slow down a little every day. Spring gets weak, like it does in a watch. And God finally decides we're too worn out to wind us up again."

"You're not in that bad shape, Granddaddy."

"Wish that were true, Jeffrey. Some folks wear out faster than others. My daddy made it 'till he was 78. My Mama was 72. But my great-granddaddy was in his fifties, and my granddaddy was 64. I just turned 67 and it looks like that's all for me. I'm a windin' down, windin' down." With those words Granddaddy fell asleep. It was the last lucid conversation I would have with him.

On Sunday, Granddaddy fell twice. He fell out of a chair in the living room. Neither Granny nor I could get him up. Lucky for us, five minutes later, Uncle Lawton and Aunt Jenny came by to take me to church. Uncle Lawton helped put Granddaddy back to bed. He didn't seem hurt, just weak. "You stay in bed, Bud," Uncle Lawton said. "You're not well enough to stand. We'll prop you up and bring you dinner after church."

Granny told us that she would keep an eye on him while we were in church. Uncle Rick and Aunt Susie were coming for Sunday dinner. None of the other great-aunts or uncles were coming that day. Rick and Susie arrived early, and as I later discovered, it had been a good thing. As soon as they'd walked in the door they'd heard a loud thump from Granddaddy and Granny's bedroom. Granddaddy had tried to get out of his bed while Granny was away. The three of them rushed in, and Granddaddy was sprawled on the floor, holding his hip. They helped him into the car and took him to the hospital in Randallsville. They left a note on the door explaining what happened.

When Uncle Lawton, Aunt Jenny and I got back home from church, we knew something was wrong. Uncle Rick's car was gone and the door to the house was closed and locked. Aunt Jenny read the note. "We have to go to the hospital. Bud may have broke his hip." She heard the phone ringing inside. She unlocked the door and ran to answer it. She made it to the phone in four rings. It was Aunt Susie. They were about to take Granddaddy back home. His hip was not broken. His weakness was due to hardening of the arteries. Too little blood was getting to his leg muscles. The doctors didn't think he would be able to walk - not even with a walker. They suggested that he use a wheelchair to get around.

Aunt Jenny was relieved that Granddaddy didn't have a broken hip, but she cried because she knew that he was an independent man. He liked to do things for himself. The only job he had ever enjoyed was farming since there was no supervisor watching over him. And now he was going to be confined to a wheelchair - or worse, to his bed.

Uncle Rick and Aunt Susie arrived twenty minutes later. They pulled a wheelchair from the trunk of the car and unfolded it. They set Granddaddy in the chair. Uncle Rick and Uncle Lawton had to carry the chair up the steps. I thought Granddaddy looked terrible. He was paler than he had been since he had the heart attack. His eyes were open, but he did not appear alert. He wasn't wearing his glasses, and the bones of his face protruded like a bare skull. He was wasting away. I remembered then what he said about winding down.

I walked over to him and said "Hi Granddaddy."

"Hello, boy. Who are you?"

I wiped my eyes and said, "I'm Jeffrey, your grandson."

"Grandson? Ain't got no grandson. Have two daughters, Jenny and Ruth. They're still in school. Too young to have children."

I ran to the bathroom and threw up, then lay on the cool floor and cried until my head hurt. I could not eat Sunday dinner.

"Jeffrey, are you okay?" The voice was Aunt Jenny's.

"Granddaddy doesn't know who I am."

"Unlock the door, Jeffrey."

I unlocked the door, and she led me to Granny's bed, where we sat down. She said, "You know, sometimes when people get old, their minds don't work right. He's my daddy, and he didn't even know me. He thinks I'm still a little girl and that your mama is alive. To him, I'm just a strange woman.

"What you need to do is hard. Pretend he's right. Pretend you're a little boy visiting his daughters. Say whatever makes sense to him. It will be easier that way. It's hardest on Granny. He thinks she's his grandma." Her eyes began to water, and I began to cry. She pulled me against her heart.

"I wish none of this were happening!" she said. "To see my daddy this way, to see you without a daddy a second time. That's what he was to you. And a good daddy he was."

She held me tight. I heard her heart beating and at first the sound calmed me. But then I thought, it sounds so strong now but one day it will be weak like Granddaddy's, and she will die too and so will I. I shook her body with my sobs. Finally the tension in my body eased.

"You need to eat something," she said, and I agreed. I was unable to cry any more, and I was hungry again. I wondered why my body's calls for food continued even when someone I loved was dying.

I ate two baked pork chops and a small salad, and had chocolate cake for dessert. Granddaddy was having trouble swallowing his food. He was choking with every bite. "He just started that," Uncle Lawton said. "Think we need to take him to the hospital again?"

"No," Aunt Jenny said. "I'll make a regular doctor's appointment. Once he gets the food down he can keep it down."

"Sounds like a hernia to me," Uncle Rick said. "I had one of those. Couldn't get anything down. They did surgery, and I could eat fine after that."

"Doubt they'd do surgery on him, shape he's in," Aunt Jenny said.

Granny went to the phone to call other relatives with an update. A few minutes later, Uncle Frank and Aunt Lucy arrived. He had two dogs in the back of his truck, one of them a puppy. I ran outside to greet him.

"Heard your granddaddy is having a rough time today," Uncle Frank said. But I have something to give you. I think you'll like it."

He picked up a beagle puppy and gave it to me. It was whimpering, but as soon as I held it in my arms the puppy licked me until my face was wet.

"It's your puppy," said Uncle Frank. "You'll have to take care of him. You'll have to feed him, keep him tied up. I bought along a chain. You don't want him chasing cars like Fuzzy."

I played with the puppy, then hooked him up to the chain to see how well he would run. When I was satisfied that the dog was tolerating the chain, I asked Uncle Frank, "What's his name?"

"I call him Cricket, but you can call him anything you want."

"Cricket is a good name," I said.

The puppy was a comfort to me, but he could not erase the pain of what was happening to Granddaddy, who grew weaker and weaker over the next few days, until one morning Granny couldn't wake him up. It was a Saturday, one week before school was supposed to start. Granny phoned Aunt Jenny, who called an ambulance. I was still asleep when the sound of an approaching siren woke me up. I was so upset I wet the bed. Ashamed, I pulled off the sheet, changed my drawers, got into some shorts and a clean shirt, and walked into the living room in time to see a stretcher wheeled into Granddaddy's room. Both attendants appeared to be drunk, and I wanted to hit them. I ran to my grandparents' room and peeked in. One attendant had Granddaddy by his arms, the other by his legs, and they slung him on the stretcher. "We'll get him to the hospital," one of the attendants said with slurred speech. I wanted to yell at the men for treating Granddaddy like meat. Granny called Uncle Lawton since his car would hold everyone.

He and Aunt Jenny arrived twenty minutes later. I lay in the back seat, my new school shoes on the floorboards but my head resting on Granny's lap.

CHAPTER 21

Uncle Lawton drove too fast to the hospital, and I felt car sick. Since Granddaddy had taken a turn for the worse, I was in no mood to pray. Maybe Uncle Frank was wrong about there being no God. Even if there was a God, he was cruel. He had enjoyed torturing Granddaddy, and he would enjoy swooping in on him for the final kill.

The hospital, a tall, red brick building, looked haunted. Before, it had seemed a place of healing, however unpleasant a problem might be. Now it was a place of doom. Every step I took toward the door seemed a step closer to death.

We went to the emergency room. The only news concerning Granddaddy was "They're still working on him." I wondered what "working on him" meant, considering that the last time I saw doctors "working" they were pounding on his chest.

In the waiting room, everyone was silent. I

picked up a fishing magazine and thumbed through it, looking at the photos of big bass but not reading. I shut my eyes and found I could no longer cry. I lay my head back until weariness caught up with me, and I leaned against Aunt Jenny's shoulder.

It was over an hour later that I awoke. A different doctor than the one with whom we had talked last time asked to see the "Wilson family." Uncle Lawton and Aunt Jenny walked out the door with the doctor, a tall, old, skinny man with graying hair. His head was bowed, and I knew the news had to be bad. After five minutes, Aunt Jenny and Uncle Lawton returned.

She looked at me, tears in her eyes. "Your granddaddy is alive, but barely hanging on. The doctor said he'd had another heart attack. His heart stopped, and it took them ten minutes to get it started again. They're not sure if he'll even wake up. He's in bad shape. They're not even sure if he'll get strong enough for them to take him upstairs, so they won't let us see him yet."

She stopped, sat down, and sobbed. I continued to sob, too. This was going to be it - I would lose Granddaddy today. Every time I started to think things would get back to normal, God made Granddaddy sicker. God hated Granddaddy, and I figured that God hated me too. I wanted to kill God. But God was bigger than me. Stronger. So I could not kill him - but I could let him know how I felt.

Angry thoughts filled my head. *God, you're not good. You're mean. You give people hope and take it away. You pretend to make Granddaddy better, but you were really making him worse. You gave him bad dreams about going to hell. I guess you'll send him there. Send me there too. I want to be with Granddaddy. But I bet you won't. I bet you'll send me to heaven and make me forget him. But I don't want to forget him. It's mean to make people forget folks they love. You hate everybody. And I hate you.*

There was a short pause. Then I finished. *In Jesus' name. A-men.*

Uncle Lawton walked to the phone to call family members. "Rick and Susie and Bob and Debbie are coming. So are Bud's sisters and their husbands."

Uncle Frank and Aunt Lucy were the first to arrive. "Damn," he said. "I knew Bud was getting worse, but I didn't expect him to go downhill so fast." Aunt Lucy said, "Why won't they let anybody see him? I want to see my brother before he passes."

"They wanted room to work on him," Aunt Jenny said. "I hate that they won't let us say goodbye." She couldn't say any more.

Uncle Bob and Aunt Debbie arrived a half hour later. I noticed that Uncle Bob was serious. I stood up, and he shook my hand. "How are you doing, Jeffrey?"

"Fine," I answered automatically. "How are you?"

"Fine."

I still failed to understand why people lied when they greeted one another. Neither one of us was fine, but maybe it was a way people kept themselves from going crazy when things went bad. It was like playing pretend. If adults pretended they were fine long enough, maybe they would, if enough time passed, feel fine.

If I got in trouble with Granny or Aunt Jenny, I would walk in the garden to the rusted out wood stoves and pretend that the stoves were robots attacking me on a hostile planet. That made me feel better, even though it never turned me into an astronaut.

What if I pretended that Granddaddy was okay? Would that make it so? Maybe if I pretended hard enough Granddaddy would recover. I imagined Granddaddy getting better. The doctors would be amazed at his recovery. "It's like a miracle," they would say. "He got out of bed the day after his heart attack and walked out of the hospital on his own." He would be able to work in the garden and ride his bicycle again.

We stayed in the waiting room another two hours before the doctor returned. By then, Uncle Len and Aunt Allie had arrived. She was crying and demanding that she be allowed to see Granddaddy, but she sat down when the clerk said that she would have to call security to have her removed from the waiting room.

The doctor spoke to the entire group. "Mr. Wilson is better, but he's not out of the woods yet. We're moving him up to the coronary care unit. He's awake, but he's suffering from dementia. He keeps saying he saw his mother and asks staff members to call her. I imagine she's dead?"

"Oh yes," Aunt Jenny said. "Fourteen years now."

"Just be warned when you go see him that he's not himself."

"He hasn't been himself for a week now."

"So sad to see. Limited blood flow to his brain. Well, we'll have him up there in CCU and hooked up in a half hour."

"Thank you, Doctor," Aunt Jenny said.

Granny and Aunt Jenny made their way to the receptionist. When they returned, I joined them to go to the coronary care unit. I walked behind the group. I noticed that they were whispering. Sometimes Aunt

Jenny or Granny would turn their heads and glance at me. I thought they might be arguing about me. I wondered if they would let me see Granddaddy.

When we reached the waiting room and sat down, Aunt Jenny put both her hands on my shoulders.

"We're going to see your granddaddy when the doctor lets us in. Granny and I want to spend some time with him alone. Not long, just a few minutes. We'll be back soon. Don't worry. It will be okay."

"When will I get to see Granddaddy and talk to him?" I asked.

"Maybe later," Aunt Jenny said.

"Tell him I love him," I said.

"I will," Granny said.

It was past dinner time and before official visiting hours when a nurse walked in and asked for the David Wilson family. The other relatives had arrived. They gathered and formed a group in one corner of the waiting room. The nurse said, "Mr. Wilson's a lot better. The doctor is amazed that a man who was at the point of death this morning is sitting up in bed talking. But you know that he's still not coherent when he talks. He wants to call his mother. Pick out two to visit. The boy, is that his grandson? Good. He can join the group. We'll still consider that two people. I think I can talk the doctor into letting three others see him when official visiting hours begin in an hour."

"Thank you so much," Aunt Jenny said. "You're very kind."

"I just hate to see a family kept out of the room when a relative is so close to death."

We paced down the long hall. I smelled alcohol again. The nurse said, "Here's his room. Remember, fifteen minutes max."

"Go on in, Jeffrey," Granny said. I stepped inside. A skeletal figure lay on the bed. His shirt was off, and white patches were on his pale chest. Wires and tubes were everywhere. The heart monitor beeped an irregular rhythm. I looked at Granddaddy's ribs, skin sunk between them. The bump of Granddaddy's beating heart rose and fell near his left nipple. Sometimes it would pause, as if about to stop, then resume beating again. I remembered the dream of the man hanging by a rope by the garage. The rope was now wires and tubes, the skeleton Granddaddy's emaciated body.

Granddaddy was conscious and propped up in bed.

"Hi, boy. What you doin' here?"

"I've stopped by to visit you today," I said. I'd decided to play along with whatever world in which Granddaddy was lost.

"I've been trying to call my mama. Could you get that phone and dial her number. It's 555-9946."

That was my grandparents' number. I had no idea what to do. I picked up the phone and pretended to dial a number. Then I gave the phone to Granddaddy.

"Hello, Mama. Yeah, it was good to see you again too. You want me to come? Sure, I'd like to. Gonna be a few days before you've got the house cleaned up? That's okay, I'll wait until then. Yeah, I still got the Model T. I'll be seein' ya soon, I reckon. Good talkin' to you, too. Bye."

I hung up the phone. I tried not to cry and swallowed the lump in my throat. I kissed Granddaddy on the cheek and said "Good bye."

"Well, that was sweet of you, boy. I'm going to

see my mama in a few days. Don't know if I'll see you again, but it was sure nice meetin' you. Thank you for helpin' me with the phone. You know, I think if I had a boy, I would want one just like you. Bye."

I turned around and walked out, bumping into Granny because my eyes were misty. "You said what you needed to say?" Granny asked.

"Yes, ma'am," I answered.

"Well, then, you know the way back to the waitin' room?"

"Yes, ma'am."

"Okay, we won't be long. Go to the waitin' room and sit there with the crowd."

"Yes, ma'am."

I returned to the waiting room and sat by Uncle Frank. I didn't know how to feel. It seemed that my nightmare about Granddaddy was coming true before my eyes, yet Granddaddy looked happier than he had been since his first heart attack. Granddaddy was lost in his own world. Was it better to be lost in one's own world? I had been hiding in a world in which Fuzzy was still alive. Granddaddy was lost in a world in which his mama was still alive. Uncle Frank had talked about facing the real world, becoming a man. Granddaddy had never become a man in that way. Granny had always said he had a child's mind. I knew that was true. Perhaps it was better to stay a child.

Aunt Jenny and Granny returned. Aunt Jenny was holding a piece of tissue paper to her eyes. "How's he doin'?" Aunt Lucy asked.

"He's still here," Granny said, "his body is. His mind ain't no good. He thinks he's a young man and he's going to take the Model T to visit his mama."

"Oh, Lord, I hate to see that."

"He's a fighter," Aunt Susie said. "Always has been. I think he'll die when he's durn good and ready. About as stubborn as you are, Sis."

"That's right," said Aunt Debbie. "Inherited it from his daddy."

Just then Grandpa Conley and Granny Marie walked in. "Goodness, what a crowd," Grandpa Conley said. "I heard Bud was about dead this morning, but he's better now. Good to hear."

Granny Marie said, "Hi, Jeffrey. How's my grandson? I know you're sad, but that old man just keeps on goin.' He may make it yet. Come here, give your Granny Marie a hug."

I hugged them both and sat down, listening to the murmur of talk punctuated by laughter. I didn't understand why anyone would laugh at a time like this. It seemed obscene, out of place, like my dream in which I walked naked into my classroom. I felt like I was the only person in the room in my right mind.

I was unable to see Granddaddy again that day. We finally made it home after the evening visiting hour was over. The next two days Granddaddy improved enough to be put in a regular hospital room. When I visited him, he didn't remember seeing me earlier. We repeated the same conversation I had with him before. I picked up the phone, pretended to dial. Granddaddy told his "mama" the same things as before, and said the same kind words to me as before. It had become a ritual.

One morning, before Uncle Frank came to take Granny and me by the hospital, Granny asked me to sit down. "I need to talk to you about something.

"Your granddaddy's not coming home. I can't

take care of him. Jenny and Lawton both work. His sisters can't help him either. He has to have a nurse all the time. We can't afford that at home. The hospital says they can't do anything more. We're going to have to put him in a nursing home. It's a place where people stay when they can't care for themselves any more. You'll be able to visit him. I'm sure Frank and Lucy will see him through the week and Jenny and Lawton will visit on the weekends and some evenin's. I know you wish he could come back here, but it just won't be. I'm sorry 'bout that, but it's the way it is."

I ran outside, sat on a glider, and sulked. I knew Granny was right, but I was mad that Granddaddy wasn't coming home, not even for Sunday dinners. I considered going into my grandparents' bedroom to look at Granddaddy's old things, but that would be too sad - like he was already dead.

CHAPTER 22

Granddaddy was moved to the Cedar Corners Nursing Home on the Friday of the week before I was to register for fourth grade. An ambulance transported him. Aunt Jenny helped Granny pack his clothes. They needed room in the car, so they dropped me off at Uncle Frank's and Aunt Lucy's. Buddy left word that he was visiting relatives in Nashville, but Uncle Frank shot some baskets with me, giving me tips on how to improve. "You're trying to pitch the basketball into the hoop. It's not the best way to make a shot. Put your arms over your head. There.... like that."

I began to make more shots than I missed. Uncle Frank said, "Keep on practicing. Come in and get some pop when you're finished."

I kept shooting the ball, running after it, and shooting again. I felt my pent up energy and pain melt into play. Maybe Granddaddy would find a place where someone would take better care of him. He wouldn't be home, and maybe his mind wouldn't be right again, but he was alive. I would be able to visit, and he wouldn't even mind if we had the same conversation every time. Granddaddy seemed happy, and that's what mattered.

I got tired and went inside for some RC Cola. "How's Cricket doing?" Uncle Frank asked.

"He's doing great. I remember to feed him and give him water every day, even on days we went to the hospital. Granny and Aunt Jenny are proud of me."

"As well they should be! He's a good dog, from good stock. In a way I hate to see him become a pet rather than a hunting dog, but you need him more than I do. You have to grab for what you can in life. A good dog can be a comfort.

"Your granddaddy's doing well enough to go to a nursing home, I hear. That's good. Maybe he'll even make it to Christmas. Lucy wants him to last. He's her only brother, and it'll be hard on her when he passes. He lived a good life, Jeffrey. Worked hard for a living, even when he worked at Schmidt's. He and your granny took you in without hesitation when your folks died. You're lucky to have grandparents like that."

"Yes, sir," I said.

Uncle Frank continued. "You remember what I said last time? It's true. Sure, you'll need to make your own way. You've made a start on that, being so responsible in taking care of Cricket. As far as I'm concerned, you're well on your way."

"Thank you, Uncle Frank," I said, feeling proud.

Aunt Lucy sat down and joined us at the kitchen table. "Ain't that a shame what's happened to Bud. Him going to the nursing home, when he's been so independent all his life. No dignity in such a place."

Uncle Frank, looking miffed, replied, "Jenny and Lawton were thinking of what was best for Bud! They can't afford a private nurse. Even if we all helped, we couldn't afford one. We don't have an extra room so Bud could live with us, and even then we'd need a nurse to keep an eye on him. From what I've heard, he's not all there. He doesn't know where he is."

"It's still such a shame.... such a shame...." Her voice trailed off into a whisper.

Uncle Frank spoke again. "It's not as if any of us had any real choice in the matter. The man's heart's giving out. Hardening of the arteries. We can hope that when we reach his age, we're in as good shape as he was. You know he and Jeffrey and that kid at the end of the road took a twenty mile bike ride one day. That was just a few weeks ago. If I'm fine up to near the end of my life, I'd consider myself lucky. Better than a lot of people."

He turned to me. "Are Lawton and Jenny taking you to see your Granddaddy today?"

"No, sir. They said he'll be pooped from putting his clothes on. They're going to take me tomorrow."

"That's good. We'll probably go by tomorrow morning to see him. It's our grocery shopping day and the nursing home is on the way."

Uncle Frank opened the pen and six dogs ran out, looking like popcorn as they jumped over each other. He said, "Jeffrey, why don't we take a walk with the dogs?"

The dogs were eager to run when Uncle Frank opened the gate to the field. It was rough country, with outcroppings of limestone, bushes loaded with long, sharp thorns, and thistles blooming purple. Hills were strewn with rocks, and we had to be careful not to trip.

Even the dogs ran slow. To me, this was another world, a field different than the one at my grandparents. I was an explorer again.

Uncle Frank began to talk. "Look at all this. It took millions of years to make each piece of limestone and to carve out these hills. None of this was made for us, but here we are."

I had a vision of the world changing over time, rocks cracking, mountains molded by forces I could not understand. I imagined great beasts, dinosaurs standing in the same spot in which I was standing, a bloody Tyrannosaurus battling with a Triceratops. Finally, one day, the Indians came, and then later ships brought people from over the sea. My grandparents arrived in a land of horses and buggies, my own parents were born, then I came to be. Where did I fit into such a vast universe? What could it matter that Granddaddy was lying sick in a nursing home and that he might soon die? Uncle Frank said that Granddaddy would return to the earth, be part of the cycle, but the cycle would go on. If Granddaddy had never been born, it would not have mattered - someone else would die and fertilize the earth.

Mulling over that thought was agonizing, because that meant my parents didn't matter, and neither did I or Cricket. Uncle Frank and his dogs would all be food for the worms, and Fuzzy was already lost in the cycle. I thought about Brother Noland's story of the eagle and eternity. At least the preacher believed that the world mattered.

We walked across one field, then crossed a rusty, barbed-wire fence to a wooded area. It was tough going, but I pretended that I was exploring planets, each one more exotic than the last. But then I thought that none of them mattered, and I felt smaller than one of the specks of dust that floated in sunbeams every morning.

I was getting tired, so we made our way back to the house. Although the dogs loved to run, they were hot and wanted water, so they returned to their pen without complaining. Uncle Lawton's car had already pulled up.

Granny said, "We got him settled in his room."

At home, I ate some cheese crackers and a bowl of vegetable soup. I had the whole afternoon to myself. I pondered playing some records, but I did not have the strength to see my grandparents' bedroom. I decided to check out the watermelons in the garden. I loved watermelon, especially when it had time to chill in the refrigerator, and it was the time of month in which Granddaddy would pick the ripe ones. He liked carrying them to the hose to be washed. Granddaddy'd thump a melon with his forefinger. If it sounded hollow, it was ripe. If there was a dull sound, the melon was green. Some melons he sat aside to sell, but the others were for eating at home. When the melon had cooled off, Granny would cut it after supper. I liked the sound of the ripe melon splitting when Granny stuck the knife inside. She would cut half of it, put one half in the refrigerator, leaving the other half to eat. Then she'd divide that half into three pieces—I received a third. It was more than enough for me, and I loved the cool, sweet taste of the watermelon, seasoned with salt.

The only drawback was the seeds. Watermelons were full of them. The top two inches were almost seed-free. After that, I'd pick as many seeds as I could out of the melon with a knife before cutting off the next piece.

But I was unable to find all the seeds. I'd bite a piece of melon and have to spit out five seeds in my mouth. It was worth it, though.

In the watermelon patch, I knew to look for the melons on which the stem had turned brown. I found three. When I thumped each one, I discovered that two of them were ripe. They were huge and heavy black diamonds, dark green with darker, difficult to see stripes across them. I plucked the stem off the first melon, and tried to pick it up. I raised it a foot off the ground, then had to put it down. I decided to roll it and the other melon to the hose where I would wash them off.

Once I got the melon started, I rolled it over the barrier between garden and grass and stopped beside the hose. Then I did the same with the other melon. I turned on the water, which was hot because the hose had been in the sun. The water cooled after a minute or two, and I sprayed each watermelon, turning them around until they were clean. I knew they would get some dirt on them when I rolled them to the house, but I would take care of that with a paper towel.

I rolled each melon to the edge of the concrete steps at the back of the house. I cradled the first in my arms and set it on one step at a time. Then I cracked the screen door and rolled the melon on the mat where people wiped their shoes. I did the same with the other melon. By then, my back was sore. I took two paper towels and wiped the melons again. When I was finished, they looked as shiny as the ones Granddaddy polished.

Then I rolled the melons into the kitchen. Granny was inside cutting some carrots. "What in the world did you bring in Jeffrey? How'd you lift those things? You did good. I'm proud of you. We'll start eatin' one of these after supper." She was stronger than I thought, and lifted one melon and put it in a dishpan where she'd cut it later. The other she took and parked on the floor between the refrigerator and storage cabinets. I looked forward to supper.

We had pork chops and green beans, but since I was waiting for the watermelon, I did not overeat. As soon as Granny pushed the knife into the melon, it split open, revealing the rich red fruit. I knew it would be sweet, and I was right. It was the best watermelon I had ever tasted. And Granddaddy had grown it. I wished he had been there to share it, to taste the results. I decided to enjoy it enough for both of us.

The next day I was fidgety. I wanted Uncle Lawton and Aunt Jenny to hurry up and arrive so I could ride with them to visit Granddaddy. He might not understand what I said, but I wanted to tell him that he grew good watermelons. They finally arrived at four, and we drove to the nursing home.

It was a low brick building next to the post office. Old people were sitting in rocking chairs under an overhang. They all said "Hello" as we walked inside.

I gagged as soon we entered the lobby. The smell of alcohol was mixed with the stench of urine - and worse. An old, bent over man in a wheelchair looked like he was chewing all the time. A lady next to him was babbling in an unknown language. The nurses were not as friendly as those at the hospital. I didn't know if they were real nurses. Some of them looked mean.

We walked around a corridor into the hall where we found Granddaddy in his room. On the way we passed by a room where a woman was hollering. I had no idea why. I looked at her and she was lying in her bed. There was no one else around. No one seemed to care.

I was thinking that Granddaddy was locked up in a dungeon filled with crazy people and mean nurses, but when we reached his room, he lay quietly in his bed. It was raised so he could sit up. He wore pajamas, and I noticed that his clothes were piled neat in a plastic set of drawers. Granny said, "Hello. How are you feeling today," and Aunt Jenny said, "Hi Daddy." For a few seconds, he looked as if he were focusing his eyes on the people in the room. Then I heard a weak voice say, "I can't get food down."

Uncle Lawton had told me on the way that Uncle Rick had been right about Granddaddy having a hernia. It made it hard for him to swallow. The doctors didn't want to do surgery because he was too sick. I thought Granddaddy had been left alone here to die. I was mad, not only at Granny and Aunt Jenny, but also at the doctors. They were afraid to help somebody who was dying. They had given up and wouldn't have anything to do with him anymore. They were not real doctors. Real doctors would take care of someone even if he was going to die.

"Hello," I said.

"Hello, boy."

"Do the nurses treat you good here?"

"Yeah," Granddaddy said. For some reason, he seemed content with his care. It was as if he had ceased to fight. He was no longer stubborn.

He wouldn't say much more. We sat on each side of his bed and stayed for a few minutes. They allowed me to remain a minute longer. I could not think of anything else to say. Finally I remembered. "You know your watermelons this year are the best we ever had. You grew good ones."

"Good," Granddaddy said, but I didn't know whether he had understood.

"I hope you feel better," I said. "I'll see you later."

"Good." That was the last word I heard from Granddaddy. I looked back as Granddaddy closed his eyes. I would never see him alive again.

CHAPTER 23

The day was overcast and threatening rain, but I looked forward to church. The Sunday school lesson was about the destruction of Jerusalem by the Babylonians. The Children of Israel had been worshipping idols, but I was sad to read about the temple's destruction. I was disappointed that there would no longer be any kings of Judah. I imagined the widows whose husbands were killed in battle. I thought of the people being sent away from their homes into exile.

At church we sang *Sweet Bye and Bye* and *What a Friend We Have in Jesus*. I would have to tell Granddaddy. I felt that since everything was in place in Granddaddy's room at the nursing home, things would be all right. Maybe he would get stronger. Maybe he would be strong enough so the doctors could fix the hernia and he could eat. Maybe his mind would come back, and he would recognize me again.

Uncle Lawton smoked his cigar on the way back. I hated it, but at least it smelled familiar. When we arrived at the house, Uncle Rick was on the phone, dialing a number. His face was red with frustration.

"Who you trying to call?" asked Aunt Jenny.

"I've been trying for the last thirty minutes to find the phone number for your church. I'm sorry. Bud died this morning."

"No!" I cried, and I wanted to run away. "I'm sorry, Jeffrey," Uncle Rick said. "The nurse told me he was able to keep a little breakfast down about eight. At ten, he was asleep in his room. An hour later they checked on him, and he was gone."

I ran into my grandparents' bedroom and lay on Granddaddy's bed, pulling out a pillow and hugging it. My body shook with hard sobs that I could not control. I was still sniffling when I raised my head. Everything in the room was a reminder. The almanac calendar on the wall, the record player on the table by the bed. The odor of Old Spice and talcum powder that still filled the air. Granddaddy's things, small tools, odds and ends, were on the dresser next to a closet. Some of his larger tools - hammers, screwdrivers - were still sitting on a tall trunk by the window. I could almost hear Granddaddy's guitar playing *Home, Sweet Home*. This thought started me crying again, and I tried not to shake too much.

Finally, I stood up and saw Granddaddy's hats lined against the wall. On the left was his straw hat, the rim eaten away by heat and sweat. Granddaddy wore that hat when he worked in the garden. The hat in the middle was one he'd wear to the square. It was a lightweight, gray Fedora that was cool in the summer. Then there was the black Fedora he wore to church and to town on cold days.

Then I realized that those hats would be empty. I put my hands to my head, making a sound that was a mix of crying and screaming. The world wasn't right. It would never be right again.

I ran outside just as Uncle Frank and Aunt Lucy pulled up in their truck. It had started to rain, and wet drops fell on me that were not my tears. I began to walk around in circles.

The truck pulled next to me and Uncle Frank said, "Jeffrey, what you doing out here in the rain?"

I took a moment to get the words out and said, "He just died!"

Aunt Lucy said, "Oh no. We've got to go and call Len and Allie. We'll be back here later."

It rained harder, and I walked into the garage. I stumbled over Granddaddy's bicycle that was lying on the dirt floor. I walked over to the truck and lay in the bed, which smelled of old hay and cow manure. I remembered the times we had gone to the square, chatting with old men on the courthouse lawn, buying a candy bar, visiting Aunt Megan's store. I sat up, looked inside at the driver's seat, imagined Granddaddy's wrinkled hands holding the steering wheel.

This could not be real. The phone call must have been a mistake. Why would Granddaddy's stuff be in such good order if he were dead? He had not died. It must have been someone else. I was excited. Yes, Granddaddy was alive, not in heaven or hell, but on earth. I ran into the bushes, found his place and sat, feeling happy, having happy thoughts. I know he's still at the nursing home and will get better, and he'll come home. We'll work in the garden together, ride bikes again, go the flea market to look for coins.

I ran to the swing that Granddaddy had put up three years before. How could he be dead, I thought, if I can feel him on the swing, see him in his hats, smell the Old Spice in his room? I rushed inside again to Granddaddy's room. Everything was in order as before.

I went to his spot at the table for Sunday dinner. The talk was hushed, and the air felt heavy. I overheard pieces of conversation.

"When are you setting up visitation and the funeral?"

"Tomorrow, I guess. It's Monday. Everything will be open."

"Where's he at?"

"Took him to Crandall's. That's where he wanted the funeral. Crandall's a good man. He won't cheat you."

"We'll pick out a casket tomorrow."

"He'll be buried in Greenlawn."

"You'll get a notice in the paper?"

"As soon as we make the arrangements."

"Everybody been called?"

"I think so, and some of them said they'd call others."

"You know, he's better off now. He didn't suffer long. He would have never been happy bedridden."

"No, he wouldn't."

I finished my dinner as quickly as I could because I wanted to get out of there. They could not see what I saw. I knew that they were mourning for nothing. Granddaddy was still living, just like Fuzzy!

But denial didn't help, and reality reeled me in. I ran to my bedroom, locked myself in, collapsed on my bed, and cried until I had to throw up.

After I had finished in the bathroom, I went outside. Uncle Frank was in the garage, sitting on the hood of Granddaddy's truck. I joined him.

"Damn, I thought your granddaddy would make it longer. I'm sorry this happened so soon."

"Thanks."

Uncle Rick walked over and stood next to them.

"Well, Bud's dead," Uncle Frank said.

"Yep," said Uncle Rick.

"Hell, just a month ago he was working in his garden. I thought he'd last another twenty years."

"Well, you never know. My uncle worked as a longshoreman. He went to the doctor for a company physical. The doctor said his heart would last forever. A week later he dropped deader than a doornail. Forty-six years old."

"That's young."

"Sure is."

We sat in silence, listening to the sound of the rain on the garage's tin roof.

No one at the house attended church that night. I did not fall asleep for hours. I wondered if I would get dehydrated from the tears that kept falling. If I lost too much water, I would die and be with Granddaddy. Then I thought, *What if Uncle Frank is right and Granddaddy's just gone? Or what if he's in hell? I may have hated God, but I believed the preachers who said that children of my age would go to heaven if they died.* Then I thought, *Maybe they're wrong. If God is bad, he might enjoy sending children to hell. Even babies. But if God were bad, wouldn't he want good people in hell and bad people in heaven? Where did that leave Granddaddy? He was a good man, but he was mean to Granny.* I wasn't sure what to think about God or heaven or hell or Granddaddy's fate. I remembered the car game by the side of the road and cried myself to sleep.

Aunt Jenny took her remaining vacation days from work to arrange Granddaddy's funeral. She picked up Granny and me and drove to the funeral home. Mr. Crandall, the owner, was dressed in a black suit. His black tie was long and thin. He was middle-aged, balding, slender and pale. I thought he looked like one of the vampires I had seen in the horror movies I would watch sometimes on Channel 5. His voice sounded fake.

"Ladies, I'll show you into the casket room. This model is...." He went on, describing metal caskets, pine caskets, walnut caskets, all of them expensive. I thought they looked comfortable inside, but could not understand why a dead man would need to be comfortable. Granny and Aunt Jenny agreed on one of the cheaper metal caskets that cost $750.00. I wondered why it cost so much to bury someone. Plus, Uncle Frank had said when a person died, he'd fertilize the earth. But somebody sealed up in a casket wouldn't fertilize anything. I knew no one would dig up the caskets years later to look at the bodies inside. I loved Granddaddy, but I didn't want to see him rotting. That thought made me sick, and I asked Mr. Crandall where the bathroom was. I found it and retched again. In my mind, I kept hearing, "Granddaddy will be rotting like a dead dog. He will be a skeleton, just like Fuzzy. A skeleton with clothes."

When I got back, Granny and Aunt Jenny were discussing funeral arrangements. The visitation was tomorrow from six to nine and the funeral would be Wednesday at 2:30. That would give me time to get registered for classes at the elementary school before I attended the funeral.

I imagined the body lying in the casket. I dreaded seeing it tomorrow evening at visitation. *It.* That word scared me. Why didn't I think of the word *him* rather than *it*?

I walked outside in the twilight, watching the lightning bugs. It was cooler than normal, reminding me that fall was on the way. I had no idea how I would be able to survive school this year. There would be no more summers, none like this, none so real.

CHAPTER 24

The morning of the visitation, I went outside to feed Cricket and fill his water dish. I unhooked his collar and played ball with him in the back yard. Afterwards, Cricket nuzzled his head on my chest, and I put his arm around him.

"I wish you got to know Granddaddy," I said. "He was a good man. He even played with puppies like you. I wish you had known Fuzzy too. But he might have taught you to chase cars, and that would not be good. I guess you and I will have to get by the best we can."

Cricket began to lick my face, and I petted the puppy for a long, long time before I hooked him to his chain. Then I went inside the house and took a bath. It was a warm day, but I preferred the water hot. I liked to soak and think. The water was comforting, but I felt as if part of my spirit had been stripped away. My foundation. Granddaddy was the rock I thought would never break. A preacher might say that I was sad because I had built my life on someone other than God.

But what was so bad about that? I could not see God. I could not smell or hear Him. I could see Granddaddy, smell him, hear his voice. God never spoke to me. Even when I read the Bible, which was supposed to be God's word, I sensed that it was written to other people, not to me.

I wondered whether Uncle Frank was right. But I could not bear the thought of Granddaddy being gone forever. Uncle Frank did not want to believe in God. I did. It did not matter to me whether God was good, evil, or somewhere in-between. I needed to believe in God. If I stopped believing in God, everything would fall apart. Even an evil God would hold things together, if only for his own evil purposes.

I put on a pair of shorts and a pullover shirt. Aunt Jenny told me not to wear my suit and tie until I had eaten. There was plenty of food that relatives and church members had brought. I felt guilty that the food tasted so good.

The rest of the afternoon I walked in circles. I walked in circles in my bedroom. I walked in circles around the backyard outside. I took my bike and rode it back and forth to each end of the driveway. I often behaved this way whenever my feelings were too strong. It calmed me.

After supper, I washed up in the bathroom and put on my good suit and tie. I stepped into the new dress shoes Aunt Jenny had bought at Penny's. When Granny and I were in the car with Uncle Lawton and Aunt Jenny, I felt a lump in my throat. That lump grew larger and larger the closer we got to the funeral home.

When we arrived it had moved down to my gut, having passed through my pounding heart. I didn't know what I would find behind the door that led to Granddaddy's casket. How would he look? Would he look like himself?

We entered the visitation area. I signed my name on the guest register. I never could write well in cursive, so I printed my name neatly. Flower arrangements were all around. I read the cards on some of them: "Love, Lawton and Jennie," "Bob and Debbie," "In sympathy, Harrell's Corners Church of Christ." Boxes of tissue were on every table in the room. Granny walked up to the casket with Aunt Jenny. They stood over the body for a few minutes, then sat down on the front row.

Uncle Lawton turned to me and asked, "You want to see your granddaddy now? Come on up with me."

I looked over the body and knew it was Granddaddy's. He was dressed in a suit and tie as if for church and he wore his horn-rimmed glasses. He looked peaceful and relaxed. He looked better dead than he had looked the last few weeks of his life alive. His nose was hooked and he looked like some the photos of Irish people I had seen in my social studies book. It was as if death brought out features I never noticed before. I looked at his chest and thought I saw it rise. My head was swimming and I went to the front row and sat down by Granny. Aunt Jenny moved to sit on the other side.

People began to wander in. I recognized some church members. As they walked by the casket, they spoke their condolences to Granny and Aunt Jenny. Sometimes they would come up to me and say, "Sorry about your granddaddy." Then Uncle Rick and Aunt Susie arrived, as did Uncle Bob and Aunt Debbie. On

Granddaddy's side of the family came Uncle Frank and Aunt Lucy, and Uncle Len and Aunt Allie.

The uncles and aunts greeted me formally, as if I were a grown-up. I saw other relatives I had never seen before and probably wouldn't see again unless somebody else died. I was happy to sit down with the relatives I knew. The sound of conversation grew louder, reached a peak about eight, then quieted down. Brother Noland came and told me how sorry he was. I thanked him.

Finally, people began to leave for home until only Granny, Aunt Jenny, Uncle Lawton and I remained.

"I don't guess anyone else is coming," Aunt Jenny said. "And it's getting late. We have a busy day tomorrow, with school registration and the funeral."

Registration for school! I had forgotten all about it. Usually I would have been anxious. I would ordinarily use the last weeks of summer to prepare my mind for the great change. Why did I have to register on the same day as Granddaddy's funeral?

The next morning, Aunt Jenny drove me to school. The parking lot, designed for teachers and staff, was full when we arrived, so she parked on the street. Aunt Jenny and I took a walkway up a steep hill to the front door. Parents were lined up and it took time to get inside. Aunt Jenny kept glancing at her watch. We reached the registration tables, and Aunt Jenny had my immunization records and the paperwork was done. My teacher, as I had expected, would be Mrs. Clarkson from church. I saw some of my friends from the previous years - Scott Grundy, Paul Davis, who would sometimes tell dirty jokes, and David Akers. I waved at them as they left the line. We would all be in the same class.

Aunt Jenny and I made it home past school traffic and stopped school buses in plenty of time for us to get ready for the funeral, but I realized I had forgotten to feed Cricket. I rushed outside with some table scraps and filled his water dish. Then it was time for another bath, dinner and a trip to the funeral home. I had made it through visitation with only a few tears. I knew I would cry later when I heard Granddaddy's favorite songs at the funeral.

Once we reached the funeral home and walked inside, I stopped by the casket again and looked at the body. I noticed Uncle Len and Aunt Allie setting up a camera stand, with an old-fashioned flash. I stood aside as they photographed the body. Aunt Jenny said, "They always do that. Every funeral."

I spoke with my relatives. I had never seen Uncle Rick or Uncle Bob in a suit and tie. I was even more surprised to see Uncle Frank in a suit and tie. Uncle Frank walked up to me and said, "We have a half hour before the funeral. There's food and drinks in the lounge."

We went inside a small lounge. I saw a dignified looking old man in a black suit and tie. I did not recognize him, but Uncle Frank did. "L.T.!" he said, "how have you been doing?"

"I've been doin' just fine," L.T. said, sounding sober. "Sorry to hear 'bout ole' Bud."

"Yeah, we knew he was in bad shape. We didn't expect him to go so fast, though."

"I'll miss plowing and disking his garden."

"Yeah, Jeffrey here can help with a garden, but he's a little young for one that big. Maybe he can hoe up a little patch and grow tomatoes next year."

"I'd like to do that," I said.

"Okay, I'll come over and help you set some tomato plants. But you have to take care of them. Don't let Cricket dig them up."

"I won't," I said. The conversation cheered me, but the funeral was only ten minutes away.

"We'd better get out there. They're going to seat the family soon, and I'm a pallbearer. See you later, L.T."

"Yeah, I'll see you 'round, Frank."

We walked back to the visitation area. Mr. Crandall was about to instruct the pallbearers, and another staff member was preparing the family to walk into the funeral parlor. I lined up after Aunt Jenny, who would sit next to Granny. Granddaddy's sisters and their husbands were also in the line. Other people were finding their way to the pews. After instructions were given, the family was seated. Mr. Crandall and the other man closed the casket, moved it to the parlor, and opened it again. They invited family members to come up and have a last look at the body. The sisters came up first with their husbands. Then Aunt Jenny, Granny and I looked. I was about to cry but tried to keep my eyes clear so I would remember seeing Granddaddy one last time.

When we sat down, the men pulled the lid of the casket shut. I heard sniffles in the audience when the lid went down. I did not want to be heard, but I couldn't help it. It only got worse when the music started up - a tape, a choir singing *What a Friend we Have in Jesus*. My eyes watered when I shut them. My nose was running, and Aunt Jenny gave me a tissue that was soaked in seconds. Then the song ended, and Brother Noland came forward to present the eulogy.

"We are gathered here today to remember the life of David 'Bud' Wilson, born July 23, 1901, died August 25, 1968. We do not know how God will judge any man, but we know that we have a responsibility to do His will. From what I know about Brother Wilson, he made preparations to meet his God, and that should be of some comfort to us.

"The writer of Hebrews says in 9:27, 'It is appointed unto men once to die, and after this the judgment.'"

Brother Noland continued but I was angry. How could he preach Granddaddy's funeral without talking more about Granddaddy? Why did he talk about judgment so much? Why not words of comfort, words about heaven? The God of Brother Noland was a mean God, always looking to find some reason to send a soul to hell. This was the God I hated. I did not want to hear any more. I shut my eyes, wiping away tears.

Mercifully, Brother Noland's talk was short. The tape started again and a choir sang *Sweet Bye and Bye*. I remembered being at church, hoping the song leader would choose Hymn 154 so Granddaddy would be happy. The audience stood, and I wiped my eyes to avoid stumbling into Granny. The pallbearers carried the casket to the hearse. Then Aunt Jenny and Granny got in their car, which the staff had pulled behind the cars of the pallbearers, and we all began the eight mile drive to the cemetery.

The cars had their headlights on, and drivers on both sides of the road pulled their cars over. A police officer stood at an intersection and saluted. We turned into the cemetery lot, less than a mile from home. From the road I could see Mr. Parker's store. We curved around to the left to the place where Granddaddy's body would lie. The pallbearers moved the casket over the grave, and slowly the staff lowered it into the ground with straps. I felt an icy chill when I thought about Granddaddy lying in the cold earth.

The family sat in chairs provided under a canopy. Most people had to stand. Brother Noland read Psalm 23, "The Lord is my shepherd..." and said a closing prayer. Family and friends then said their goodbyes. Billy Jackson, one of Granddaddy's cousins who visited once or twice a year, asked me, "I figure your granddaddy went to heaven, don't you?" And I said, "Yes, I'm sure," not knowing what I really believed.

CHAPTER 25

The workers began to cover the casket with dirt. Grandpa Conley and Granny Marie stayed to watch. They invited Granny and me to visit them one day.

"If I can get somebody to take us, we will. You're welcome at our place, too," Granny said.

It was time to go. I looked across the highway, my thoughts already stretching toward home. I gathered the strength to turn away from the grave and walk to Uncle Lawton's car. At the house, a whole slew of relatives had arrived, and they had brought along lots of food.

I was surprised that most of the dinner conversation was cheerful. I knew that some of the guests didn't really know Granddaddy but were distant relatives who had attended the funeral only out of respect. But the others - they couldn't forget Granddaddy that fast. I would always remember

Granddaddy. I would still feel sad, even after I turned fifty. Why did people forget, laugh in the face of loss? Was that the only way most people could get by? Was death something too terrible for them to accept?

I slept that night, knowing that the morning sun would not look as bright as before. I had five days left before school started the day after Labor Day. Each day would begin with breakfast, and each day I would stare at an empty chair. I would feed and water Cricket, play with him or take him for a walk. Later I might pick a pear from the tree and eat it, wander in the field, walk to The Thicket, swing on the tree swing, explore paths in the back yard bushes, or sit in my favorite spot between field and drive. But nothing felt the same. The little things that used to give me pleasure did nothing now. At times I wished I could forget Granddaddy too, but then I would feel so guilty I'd double over with pain from crying. In my entire life I pushed aside pain, pretended it wasn't real. I tried to hide from my parents' deaths, from Fuzzy dying, from all death and decay. *Change* was a cuss word. Now the ultimate change had twisted my life into a knot, and I didn't know how to untie it.

When school started, I tried to lose myself in the routine. I had a few friends, but preferred to focus on classwork. Without Granddaddy to take me to school, I was riding the school bus. Billy and Dan Conwell also rode that bus and picked on me, although Billy did tell me he was sorry about my granddaddy dying. I liked the rooms in the rock school, old steam pipes providing heat in cool weather. I thought Mrs. Clarkson was a good teacher. It was good to see a familiar face each day, a face I would also see at church every Sunday.

Bruce McAdams was back in my class. We would sometimes spend the entire play period pretending to be astronauts. We rarely played with the other children, but one really good friend was enough for me. My fulfillment was making A's in all my classes and winning the class spelling bee every week. Some classmates were jealous. Others accused me of being a teacher's pet. Most left me alone, and that was fine with me.

I tried hard to be good to Granny and stay out of trouble. If R.J. came over, I went out of my way to avoid fighting, especially if it involved sticks. Granny loosened up on her restrictions on our riding bikes and allowed us to ride on Randallsville Highway to Farris Road and as far as the country store. We also went the other direction on Farris Road to Mr. Parker's store, which was closer. Granny would give me money to buy a Coke or a Popsicle.

R.J. and I would also bicycle around after school or on Saturday to Uncle Frank's place. We would sometimes play HORSE or basketball with Buddy Conway.

I was also reading more library books than ever, especially books about the planets or other subjects in science. Books took me into different worlds, worlds that seemed better than this one.

I gathered an ample supply of watermelons until mid-September. I wanted to eat as many as I could as a reminder of the goodness of Granddaddy's garden. One day, in late September, I couldn't find another watermelon. I searched the patch, already overgrown with weeds that were half my height. I got down on my knees, grass scratching my legs until they were full of red marks. That was okay as long as I could find another watermelon. Finally, I found a little one barely bigger than my hand. I rushed to the hose and washed it off. Then I went to the kitchen, found one of Granny's peeling knives and tried to cut the melon. The rind was tough, and the fruit inside was light pink, not red. I tried it. It was barely sweet enough to eat. I ate all of it that I could stand then took the remains to the watermelon patch and set them down in the same spot that I found them.

I searched again, every inch I had not searched before. I found nothing. It was a second death. I sat on a bed of weeds and wept.

I sat a long time. When I stood up and walked around the garden again, I discovered that all the cantaloupes and cucumbers had also died, their brown vines left to rot. Uncle Lawton had already dug all the potatoes, and I knew there were some in the house. At least they would last a while longer.

I walked over to the rows of lima beans and peas. The plants had begun to turn brown, but they were still producing. I found a bucket in the garage and picked as many beans and black-eyed peas as I could. Many of the pods had dried, but Granny could still cook them or put in them jars. They would keep for a year or two.

I walked past the tomatoes to the corn. All the stalks were long dead. A few stray corn cobs hung like lonely lights with their brown husks. I plucked a few, pulled off the husks. The ends had been worm-eaten. I broke off the ends and kept the rest. The corn was hard and bone dry, but I knew what to do with it. I would brush the silk off the corn, rub my thumb over the grains to loosen them from the cob. Then I would add oil and salt, put the mix in a pan. After an hour in the oven - parched corn. It was not as good as popcorn, but it wasn't bad. And Granddaddy had grown it.

Finally I backtracked to the tomatoes—I had set them on top of the crops already in the bucket. Although the ends of some of the vines had begun to brown, the rest of the plants were green and would produce for a few more weeks. I found ten ripe ones. I went inside, washed the tomatoes, brushed and shelled the corn, and sat on a glider to shell the peas and beans. For a second or two I saw a man in blue and red checkered shirt beside me, but when I turned my head, no one was there.

Another month passed. Life went on. Fourth grade continued, and I had begun to feel at home at the new school. I liked moving from grammar to reading to math to science to social studies. I enjoyed the social studies unit on the American Indians. I was fascinated by the Navaho, living on the desert plateau, and I relished the story of the Plains Indians hunting buffalo. Most play periods I kept talking with my friend Bruce about astronauts. I heard that there would be a flight around the moon in December, and looked forward to watching it on TV.

At school I could sometimes forget my grief for a while, but at home reminders were in every bush and in every blade of grass. In late October, not long before Halloween, I visited the garden again. Everything was dead. If Granddaddy had been alive, he would have set out turnips. I loathed turnips. And turnip greens were nearly as bad. Even pepper sauce, made of vinegar poured over hot peppers, could not hide the bitter taste. But now I would have given almost anything to see them growing in the garden, to watch Granddaddy hoe and harvest them.

Church was hard for me. I still enjoyed seeing Aunt Jennie and Uncle Lawton and enjoyed the feel of the cushioned pew. I still liked to smell the grape juice as it passed by and the shine on the quarter that Aunt Jenny gave me to put in the collection basket.

When Brother Andrews walked to the front to lead the singing of a hymn, my heart filled with too many feelings at once. I wanted him to choose songs that Granddaddy liked, and I didn't want him to choose them. When I heard Brother Andrews say, "Please open your song books and turn to number one-hundred fifty-four," my heart felt like a heavy rock. I couldn't stop myself from crying when the congregation began to sing *Sweet Bye and Bye.* I was glad when it was over, and I hated that it was over.

I could not bring myself to listen to the sermons. My anger at God had grown over the months. I would never forgive God for taking Granddaddy, not the way He did it, so fast. I thought God resented anyone being happy and would do anything to destroy that happiness. I had stopped saying my bedtime prayers after Granddaddy died. I vowed never to pray again unless it was to say something mean to God.

Sunday dinners were lonely, even on days in which everyone from the usual crowd came. I sat in a glider with the men after dinner. I could not understand how I could feel so lonely in a crowd of people I knew and loved.

One day in late October, I went fishing with Grandpa Conley. The lake water sparkled. The cool breeze was slightly chilly, and I was glad that I wore a jacket. Grandpa Conley caught two largemouth bass, and I caught a rock fish. Grandpa Conley told me stories about my daddy. "When he was a boy, 'bout four years old, he took a likin' to eatin' worms. We caught him one time pullin' earthworms out the ground and eatin' them. Ruined perfectly good fishin' bait. We took him to the doctor, said they wouldn't do him no harm. We took him home, spanked him and told him not to eat worms. Next time we looked outside, there he was, eatin' those worms again. It must have took us two weeks to break him from that."

I laughed, and that felt good. Overall, it was a good day, although I remembered that Grandpa Conley had once invited Granddaddy to go fishing with him. Granddaddy would have laughed at such stories, and he would have caught some big bass, too.

At home, Cricket helped me as much as anyone. I came out of the house to feed Cricket every morning, early, even before breakfast. Cricket always said hello to me with licks before eating. Then he galloped toward me - I made sure I was lying on the ground. I had learned before that Cricket had grown big enough to knock me down. He whimpered with joy as he licked my face again. It made my face feel sticky and yucky, but that was okay. I was teaching Cricket to fetch a ball, the same old baseball I had used with Fuzzy. Cricket would take the ball, sit down, and chew on it without returning it to me, even when I called him back. "Come on Cricket! Give me the ball! Stop! You're chewing it apart!"

Cricket wasn't a very smart dog. I was glad that he was on his chain most of the time, since he tried to get to every car that came by. Maybe Fuzzy's spirit had somehow gotten into him. I wanted to keep him safe, difficult as it was. Cricket would run off when I took him for a walk in the field. If there was a choice between Cricket chasing a rabbit and chasing a butterfly, he would go for the butterfly.

Granny did her best to be kind to me. She didn't talk much, except to remind me to shake the spiders out of my shoes every morning and to stop slamming the screen door. But she spent hours fixing Sunday dinner and worked hard to fix good meals for us. She made sure I wore enough clothes when it was cold and nursed me when I had the flu. I felt loved.

Granny watched the local news every night at six and the Red Skelton Show on Tuesday nights at 7:30. But her favorite show was the one Granddaddy had also liked - Lawrence Welk. They watched it every Saturday night at 7:30. Old people liked that show. For me, it was a good time to go to my bedroom and read or get a snack in the kitchen.

Another month passed. I didn't cry as often about Granddaddy. Aunt Jenny and Uncle Lawton had cleaned out Granddaddy's dresser and drawers. Granny said I could have Granddaddy's records and could play them whenever I wanted. I moved the record player to my bedroom. Uncle Lawton took Granddaddy's bed apart and stored it upstairs in the attic. The tools were divided between the great uncles. Aunt Jenny took most of Granddaddy's clothes to the thrift store in Randallsville. The hats she took upstairs and stored in a box.

I looked over the bedroom where Granddaddy once slept, where Granny's bed sat on one side. There was a strange open space where Granddaddy's bed had been. The calendar above the bed was tacked onto a wall near the back entrance of the house. I wondered if

Granddaddy's spirit was blowing away into nothingness, with fewer and fewer signs that he had ever lived.

November was cold and wet. Days passed with highs in the forties and drizzle that was just hard enough to keep me inside after school. That didn't help my mood. I often thought of those summertime trips to the square, the bike ride, every moment I had shared with Granddaddy before that first heart attack.

When Thanksgiving arrived, I was thankful for the break from school. Relatives came for dinner, and we had the traditional turkey. Uncle Lawton gave the blessing, "Father, we thank Thee for this day set aside to remember the many blessings Thou hast bestowed on us. Help us to be always thankful. At this time, we thank Thee for this food. Please bless it for the nourishment of our bodies. In Jesus' name. A-men."

I added silently, *And I thank Thee for stealing my Granddaddy and my summer. Because you don't even exist. In Jesus' name, A-men.*

I took a nap after Thanksgiving dinner, while the men sat in the living room watching the Detroit Lions play some other football team. Granddaddy's absence at the table was more noticeable on a holiday.

CHAPTER 26

Thirty years later, I raised my head from my hands. I didn't know how long I had been crying. Light rain turned into sleet. I knew the time had come to walk into The Thicket, although my legs felt as if they were sinking into quicksand. Foot in front, in front, I forced my feet forward. I passed a patch of brush and remembered the day I had stepped hard around it to get the rabbits to run. I hoped, once and for all, to find Granddaddy again. The only untouched place where my memories might yet live was The Thicket. The best day of my life had been spent there, a day I thought could not be better. It was the day I had faith that the world would stay the same for me, that my life with Granddaddy would continue until I was an adult. It was the day I believed everything and everyone that mattered in my life would survive forever.

I contemplated the years of my life since

Granddaddy's death. Staying with Granny through junior high and high school. Uncle Lawton's death. College and graduate school. Marriage. My Ph.D. My teaching position, professional success, publications. By any reasonable standard my life had been a success.

But I continued to obsess over Death. Granddaddy's death remained a black hole in my life, and every subsequent death had served only to deepen it. When Uncle Lawton died, I cried for an hour after everyone else but Aunt Jenny had left. We buried Uncle Lawton in the plot next to Granddaddy's grave - and now Granny was gone. I also had gone - back to my childhood memories - for what? I prayed The Thicket would tell.

The Thicket's border loomed dark and bare in the drizzle and sleet. It no longer appeared to be a place of hope, but I had to find out. The ground was getting saturated. Mud caked my boots halfway up. Every nerve of my body was on edge. I felt numb all over, as if some force was tingling the hairs on my skin. Every step I took toward The Thicket made my heart pound harder, and I wondered if I would live to reach it. I knew something would happen there - but for good or ill?

I breached the outer border of The Thicket. Tall, bare trees towered above me. I walked through fallen leaves to the fence bordering Mr. Blake's farm. The ground was bare, and I didn't see any cows. I supposed they were cold and staying in the barn.

I found the old pear tree, although a storm had broken off a greater portion of the trunk, and I leaned against what was left, found it could still support my weight, and looked out at the woods over the fence. They seemed to go on without limit. I wondered if I started to walk in those woods where I would end up. Maybe California.

Then I found a looped vine. It seemed to grow from the same place where I had swung that June with Granddaddy. It could not possibly be the same vine, but God, it sure looked like it. In a moment that seemed beyond time, my heart grew full to the point of bursting. I hung on the vine, half sitting, supporting some of my weight with my feet so as not to break it. I began to swing.

At some point, Granddaddy came. He energized the vine, and I felt as if I could swing to the stars, land on airless planets, and live without a space suit. I knew it was Granddaddy. There was no need to see a checkered shirt or horn-rimmed glasses or a Fedora hat. But I knew without a doubt that he was there and that he was happy and wanted me to be happy. If he was happy, he had to have come from heaven, not hell. But if he went to heaven, God must not be heartless after all. God was good. He had forgiven Granddaddy for being mean to Granny.

It was then that I realized I had been all wrong after Granddaddy died. Uncle Frank had been wrong. God *did* exist. And Brother Noland had been wrong in his belief that God was vengeful, hateful, demonic. The all-seeing eye was not looking for ways to roast people in hell. For the first time since Granddaddy was sick, the world seemed right, the way it was supposed to be. People would die and things would change. Granny, my great aunts and uncles, and Aunt Jenny would one day pass away. Someone would tear the log house down, or it would burn to the ground. One day, I would die too. But it was okay. My insides felt warm, even as the cold wet wind hit my face. I would see Granddaddy and Granny again, my parents, Uncle Lawton, my great-aunts and great-uncles, the house, The Thicket, the garden. Everything that mattered would be preserved, but this time they would never change, never pass away. The summer that began in June would last for eternity. It didn't matter that the time it took an eagle's wings to wear down a steel earth and sun was only a fraction of eternity. Eternity would be good and all that is bad would be banished forever.

I glanced at the barbed wire fence separating The Thicket from the larger woods. The fence bobbed up and down with each swing, and I felt exhilarated, as if I were riding a roller coaster. Suddenly, a rabbit streaked by and disappeared into a brush pile. I remembered the rabbit heart, but now everything had changed. I imagined the rabbit's strong heart racing, full of life. I realized I had had it all wrong - my fascination with the heart was not about death - it was all about *life*.

But if the heart was about life, how could it be wrong for me to have a fetish for a woman's heartbeat? Love, sex and life, all bound together - it all made sense now. What I had told my wife had been true - how could it not deepen my physical union with a woman to hear the source of her being? I decided then not to worry about the fetish—I would accept it, accept myself, and move on.

As for Asperger's Syndrome, after my journey through childhood memory, I recognized the signs were there when I was a child - my preference for being around adults, my obsession with particular subjects such as death and the heart, my love for repetitive motions such as swinging and, I thought, the heartbeat, my distrust of change. But I figured that was okay - without the Asperger's, I would not have had the curiosity that led me to study religion, to be the first person in my family to attend college, to receive the Ph.D., to become a college teacher. My condition was a gift, not a curse.

Even though my legs and back ached and my hands were sore, I kept swinging. I felt as if I had been sitting on the vine for hours. Finally I sensed it was time to go, and I checked my watch. Only an hour had passed since I parked my truck in the ditch and started to walk.

I made my way to the place where I once slept after drinking a Coke. A soft bed of leaves was still there. I didn't sit on the wet leaves, but looked, listened, feeling Granddaddy move to that spot. Just then, there was a break in the clouds, and a beam of sunlight penetrated the leafless trees. It illuminated with an orange light that shimmered like a flame—but not like the flames of hell. It was more like the orange flames from the wood stove that warmed my cold body in winter.

The light faded, and I knew Granddaddy's spirit was on the move. I walked to the border of The Thicket, took two steps into the field. Far away, a cow lowed. Down the row of trees bordering the field I heard a dog's bark that faded into the sky, but that I knew for certain came from Fuzzy. The clouds parted for good, and the sun illuminated the entire field. It was as if a match had been struck, new fire flooding the ground with light.

ACKNOWLEDGMENTS

The work of many people contributed to the writing of this book. Mike Parker of WordCrafts Press gave me valuable advice on how to improve the manuscript. I would like to thank my editor at Wordcrafts Press, Anna Owen, for her hard work and good suggestions. I also wish to thank Charlotte Rains Dixon of the Writers Loft at Middle Tennessee State University, who worked with me on editing the novel. Professor Michael Colonnese, my colleague at Methodist University in Fayetteville, North Carolina, also worked through the manuscript. Another colleague, Robin Greene, has been a constant source of encouragement and advice. I thank two fine writing programs from which I graduated: The Writers Loft and The Odyssey Writing Workshop at St. Anselm's College in Manchester, New Hampshire. I am grateful to the Weymouth Center in Southern Pines, North Carolina, for allowing me to stay and write for ten days in that beautiful setting. Most of all, I thank my wife, Karen, for being patient with my long absences as I worked on the novel.

Made in the USA
Columbia, SC
21 May 2018